A PASSIONATE PEOPLE—
DRIVEN FROM THEIR LAND

"Judah, do you hear something?" Virginia asked, listening intently. "It sounds like drums. Perhaps the Legion is drilling."

The instant Judah Bascomb recognized the sound of cannon booming in the distance, he snapped erect and went to the window.

"Virginia," he said, trying to keep his voice calm, "the militiamen said they were going to destroy Nauvoo if all the Mormons didn't leave. That's their cannon you're hearing—they're attacking the city from the north. We have to get out of here. Right now!"

He saw the terror in Virginia's eyes as she stood there stiffly, staring at him, shaking her head as if she were trying to deny the truth of his words.

Outside, Judah saw the dense pall of gray smoke begin to rise above the city to the north.

They're trying to burn us out! he thought angrily.

He turned back to Virginia. "Let's load the wagon," he said. "We're leaving."

"No! I'm afraid!" she screamed shrilly, the terror deepening in her eyes.

"We have to go, Virginia. You know what they'll do if they catch us. And they won't leave Nauvoo until every last Mormon has been murdered . . ."

The Making of America Series

THE PROPHET'S PEOPLE

Lee Davis Willoughby

A DELL/EMERALD RELEASE
FROM
JAMES A. BRYANS BOOKS

Published by
Dell Publishing Co., Inc.
1 Dag Hammarskjold Plaza
New York, New York 10017

Dell TM 681510, Dell Publishing Co., Inc.

ISBN: 0-440-06858-4

Printed in the United States of America

First printing—June 1983

PROLOGUE
HIRAM, OHIO. 1832

THE house was located far from its neighbors. Washed in the light of the bright moon which was riding high in the March sky, it sat silent beneath the tall trees which loomed behind it. Frost glistened on its shingled roof. Shadows spilled from its eaves.

The trees, which formed an effective windbreak, were as unmoving as the house itself. None of their branches swayed in the windless and chilly night. From somewhere in the distance came the mournful hooting of a night owl, the sound drifting through the otherwise quiet darkness to

1

haunt it briefly before fading away. A frightened field mouse, its dark pelt temporarily turned to silver by the moonlight falling upon it, darted across the grassless ground and ducked into its burrow.

Through the cracks of the house's closed wooden shutters, lamplight leaked out into the night. The slivers of yellow light severed some of the shadows lurking near the stone chimney. One of them partially illuminated the tin washtub that sat on a wooden bench just below one of the blind windows.

The escaping lamplight proved that life was being lived inside the house. The closed shutters seemed to suggest that life outside the sheltering walls of the house had been shut out. Kept at bay.

Inside the house, Emma Smith was bending down before the fireplace and using a broken-handled hoe to shove ashes over a section of the blazing fire in order to dampen it down for the long night ahead.

Behind her, at a rude wooden table, her husband, Joseph, sat poring over the printed pages of a thick book. The lamp on the table flickered. Smith blinked and went on reading, his finger tracing the lines on the page before him, a faint smile on his face, a smile of pure joy.

The lamp flickered again and then went out, drowning the room in a darkness which was broken only by the faintly glowing embers of what now remained of the fire.

Emma straightened and turned around. "Joseph, you've let the lamp go out." She stood there a moment, smiling fondly at her husband who, to her amusement, continued to try in vain to read the book that was lying on the table in front of him.

"Emma—the light—" Smith looked up at her.

Emma turned up the wick of the coal oil lamp, removed

its chimney, and then, using a thin wax paper, lit the wick. "It's late, Joseph," she said.

"But tomorrow is the Sabbath," he reminded her, his eyes on her face, his right hand, palm down, on the book before him. "Tomorrow we may rest."

Emma sat down at the table and folded her hands on it. "The Lord's day," she said softly. "Joseph, I do think that is a misnomer."

"I'm afraid I don't quite understand, Emma."

She looked up at him, her expression sober. "Every day is the Lord's day."

Smith reached across the table and took her hand in his. "My dear one, you have a way of seeing the world as the world should be. I wish, oh, most truly do I wish, that I—and others—had your gift. We—and the world itself—would be far better off were we able to share your wisdom."

"Wisdom, Joseph?" Emma shook her head. "I'm not wise. Would that I were. I am just a woman with a head too often full of fancies—and a heart full of love for you."

Smith tightened his grip on Emma's hand. "And we are, you and I, so fortunate, aren't we? We are young—I'm only twenty-six and you're not yet that and we're strong and we have a lifetime ahead of us in which to live for the Lord and walk in His ways."

Emma frowned. She withdrew her hand.

Smith closed the book. On its cover were the words: Book of Mormon. "What is it, Emma?" he asked, concern in his voice.

She brushed back a strand of hair which had fallen over her forehead, the gesture seeming to dismiss Smith's question.

But he repeated it and she answered it with evident reluctance. "I am . . . sometimes . . . afraid, Joseph."

He knew without asking what it was that she was afraid

of. He said, "We must remain steadfast. The Lord lets those whom He loves be chastised."

"Chastised, yes. But martyred?"

"The Gentiles have killed none of us."

"But they have hurt some of us. Maimed some of us. Driven us from our homes. Destroyed our crops."

"It is not wrong to be afraid, Emma," Smith said patiently. "But it is wrong not to trust the Lord and it is wrong not to believe what He has chosen to reveal to me."

"I sometimes wish—forgive me for saying this, Joseph—but I do sometimes wish that He had not chosen you to be his Prophet."

"But he has done so and, though it is a heavy burden for me to bear at times, I will bear it. It is also a privilege I don't deserve but one which I shall try my best to be worthy of." The smile of barely contained joy was back on Smith's face as he gazed fondly at his wife.

"Thy will be done," Emma murmured. She got up from the table and went to the trundle bed that stood against the far wall of the room. She drew back the patchwork quilt and then went to the door to make sure the latch was firmly in place. When she had satisfied herself that it was, she began to undress.

Later, wearing her floor-length cotton nightgown which was tied at her throat, she slipped beneath the quilt and drew it up to her chin. She lay without moving in the bed, her fingers clutching the thick quilt, her eyes on the ceiling where shadows, prodded by the lamplight and the faintly flickering flames of the nearly dead fire, scurried and danced.

Smith opened the Book of Mormon again. His index finger ran along the lines of black print:

And the lord of the vineyard caused that it should be dug about, and pruned, and nourished, saying

*to his servant, 'It grieves me that I should lose
this tree; wherefore, that perhaps they perish
not, that I might preserve them to myself, I have
done this thing.*

He closed his eyes. *Preserve me, Lord, that I
may live in peace among the Gentiles as your
faithful servant. Prune me, Lord, but preserve
my roots. Let them not perish so that I may
continue to do Thy work.*

Emma glanced at her husband. "Joseph?"

He opened his eyes. "I'm coming, my dear." He closed
the book and rose. He turned down the wick, extinguish-
ing the lamp, and went to the bed where he undressed and
put on his flannel nightshirt and nightcap.

Once in the bed beside Emma, he reached out and
embraced her. Then he kissed her cheek lightly. "I won't
let anything happen to you, Emma. Don't be afraid."

She moved closer to him. But she said nothing.

Smith took her hand in his. "We mean no harm to the
Gentiles," he whispered. "They have no reason to fear us
or our Church of Jesus Christ of Latter-day Saints."

"The Gentiles do not fear us. They hate us."

"It is the same thing. That is to say, hate is the spawn
of fear. What a man fears, he quickly learns to hate. In
that way, I think, he hides his fear from himself. And,
Emma, there is hope!" Smith's hand tightened on hers.
"We have welcomed many converts to the Church. And
more are joining us every day!"

"I suppose that is a reason to be hopeful."

"Of course it is! Think, Emma. These men and women
who have become Mormons were once Gentiles—outsiders.
Some of them have freely confessed, as you know, to
hating us and our religion before their conversions. But we

talked to them. We explained. We exhorted. And they saw
the truth and have put away their hatred and joined hands
with us.''

Emma closed her eyes. She withdrew her hand and
murmured, ''Good night, Joseph.''

''Good night, my dear.''

Smith lay in the bed, the words he had read in the Book
of Mormon racing through his mind, as he tried to quiet
the rapid beating of his heart by lying perfectly still. But
joy continued to course through him, driving sleep away.

Nearly an hour passed before he wearily closed his eyes
and let sleep descend upon him.

He did not know how long he had slept before being
awakened by Emma's outcry.

''What is it?'' he asked, his mind slowed by sleep. Fire,
he thought. But the fire was out.

''Someone knocked on the door,'' Emma said. ''I woke
up and—''

Someone began to pound on the door.

Smith started to get out of the bed but Emma put out a
hand and restrained him.

''No!'' she whispered. ''Joseph, don't!''

''Someone may be in trouble,'' he said, gently setting
aside her trembling hand.

The pounding continued as Smith got out of bed and
groped his way across the dark room toward the door. His
hip struck the edge of the table and he pressed his lips
together, trying to ignore the pain he was feeling.

''Joseph!'' Emma called out to him. ''Don't open the
door!''

Smith hesitated. He stood in the darkness, listening to
the pounding that was now being made, he guessed, not by
fists as had been the case earlier but by some sort of

battering ram. He took a step backward—and bumped into the table again.

The door splintered. The latch ripped free. Fragments of wood fell to the floor. Moonlight flooded into the room, giving it and the furniture it contained an unreal and ghostly look.

"Smith!" a man's voice yelled.

"Come on out of there, Smith!" another man's voice called out.

Emma sprang from the bed and ran to her husband. "The window in the back!" she whispered breathlessly. "You can climb through it—get away. Joseph, *quickly!*"

Smith half-turned as if he intended to head for the window Emma had mentioned, but then several men burst into the room, their faces daubed with lampblack to hide their identities.

"Grab him!" one of them shouted.

"No!" Emma cried, stepping in front of her husband. "Get out of my house!"

A man shoved her aside and she fell back against the table, knocking the Book of Mormon to the floor.

"Got him!" a man yelled as he seized Smith's right arm.

Smith struggled to free himself from the man and, in the process, stepped on the foot of one of the other men in the angry mob.

"Clumsy fool!" the man whose foot Smith had stepped on snapped. He swung a clenched fist which struck Smith on the side of the head.

Someone grabbed Smith's left arm.

The two men holding him half-carried and half-dragged him out of the house. Someone tore the nightcap from his head and threw it to the ground. Someone else grabbed his flannel nightshirt and ripped it from his body.

"Joseph!" Emma screamed from the doorway of the house, her hands clasped together and held out before her, her eyes wild, her body shaking as if she were suffering a convulsion. "Let him be! Please! I beg you! Please let my husband be! He hasn't hurt any of you. Don't hurt him!" She began to cry, her body racked with wrenching sobs.

"Get inside the house, woman!" one of the men shouted at her. "Be glad we're not going to take you too!"

"Maybe we should take her," somebody suggested. "Might be fun, come to think on it."

Smith struggled. But strong hands were gripping his shoulders and both of his arms.

Someone's hands suddenly circled his throat.

He gagged as the fingers tightened their grip.

The moon in the sky began to whirl as Smith, his head thrown back, clawed at the anonymous fingers that were choking the life from him.

The moon bounced in the sky. Disappeared.

And then someone was shouting, something about "not yet," and Smith, recovering now that the fingers were gone from his throat, gasped, sucking in the air, his lungs burning within him and his chest heaving.

A moment later, he was barely able to ask, "What is it you want with me?"

"We want to teach you a lesson—you and the rest of your kind who have the nerve to go around calling yourselves Saints."

"You don't understand," Smith muttered, still sucking in the cold night air. "We—"

A fist cracked against his ribs and he doubled over, unable to continue speaking.

Someone grabbed a fistful of his hair and yanked his head up. "You see this, Saint Smith?" the man asked, grinning.

Smith stared at the long-bladed knife in the man's hand. He tried to back away from it but someone behind him pushed him forward—toward the knife which gleamed in the moonlight.

"You're—you're going to kill me?" he managed to ask.

"No!" declared the man holding the knife, his grin widening. "Got us a better idea. We're going to—"

"Not here!" someone said. "We'll—"

Smith didn't catch the man's last words because Emma's anguished scream drowned them out. He turned his head.

Emma had fainted and was lying on the threshold of the house.

Smith felt himself being picked up bodily and thrown over the shoulder of a burly man as if he were nothing more than a sack of grain. He flailed with his fists at the man's broad back. The man merely laughed, an ugly sound in the night. Around him, men moved, taunting him, jabbing him with their fingers, switching him with branches.

Smith gritted his teeth and struck out wildly at his tormentors.

They danced, laughing, out of his reach.

A branch landed with a cruel *splat* on his bare buttocks.

He kept his teeth clenched tightly together.

"Here we are!" someone announced gleefully. "You got the knife?"

The man who was holding it raised it toward the sky.

To Smith, it looked as if the man had impaled the moon. He shuddered with fear and from the chill of the night on his naked body.

The man who had been carrying him suddenly threw him down. Smith grunted as he hit the frozen ground and tried to get to his feet.

A man kicked him and he fell back. "Stay put!" the man ordered. "Now, let's do it!"

The man holding the knife hesitated a moment and then offered the knife to the man who had just spoken.

The man shook his head. "It was your idea to castrate him," he told the man with the knife in his hand. "So you do it."

"Who wants the privilege of making sure Smith here don't sire any more little Saints?" the man with the knife asked, glancing around at the men in the mob surrounding Smith.

No one spoke. No one stepped forward to take the knife from the man who was holding it out at arm's length in front of him as if he were suddenly afraid of what he held in his hand.

"*Damnation!*" someone snarled. "If none of us is going to geld him, let's get on with the rest of what we planned. I hope we got us enough guts to go through with that much at least."

Sudden movement. The mob fragmenting.

A fire being kindled.

Then Smith saw the iron kettle that was suspended above the fire, saw the man with the long wooden paddle stirring the contents of the kettle, smelled the pungent but not unpleasant odor of heated tar.

He glanced to the left and then to the right. There was an opening to his right. And some distance beyond the break in the line of men surrounding him were trees. Though leafless, Smith thought he might have a chance of hiding among them. The moonlight was not as bright there as it was in the open where he crouched shivering.

He drew a deep breath and scrambled to his feet. He dashed past the men whose eyes were on the bubbling tar in the kettle, heading for the trees.

"Get him!" someone bellowed. "He's gone and made a run for it!"

Smith ran, his heart pounding, through the cold night.

Behind him, booted feet pounded the hard ground as the mob pursued him.

They caught him before he reached the shelter of the trees. Rough hands, some gloved against the cold, seized him and carried him, struggling vainly to break free, back to the kettle and its contents.

"It's ready," the man stirring the tar announced moments later.

And then he removed the paddle from the kettle and advanced toward Smith, holding the paddle out in front of him. Tar dripped from it and steamed in the frosty air.

"Throw him down on the ground," the paddle-wielder ordered. "Spread-eagle him."

When the men had spread-eagled Smith on the ground, and were holding him there, the man with the paddle moved toward him.

Smith stared up at the man and then his eyes dropped to the dripping paddle the man held in his hands. As the man daubed his genitals with tar, Smith began to pray without moving his lips or uttering a sound.

The hot tar seared his skin as the paddle was drawn down his chest, across his stomach, and then thrust between his legs again before being brutally shoved into his mouth.

He spat but he could not rid his mouth of the hot sticky tar.

The paddle touched his body again and again, seeming to caress it obscenely.

"Turn him over!"

The men turned Smith over, spread-eagled him again, and the paddle was savagely thrust between his buttocks.

Then there was a moment of respite as the paddle-wielder went back to the kettle for more tar. He returned and the process was repeated until Smith's body was blacker than the ground on which he had been thrown.

"Get out of Hiram!" a man shouted at him.

"Get the hell all the way out of Ohio!" another man shouted.

The paddle whacked Smith's buttocks, a hard blow, and came away with a sucking sound. His wrists were freed and then his ankles. As his captors' hard hands released him, Smith jumped to his feet and fled through the night, tar dripping from his naked body. He used his fingers to tear lumps of tar from his mouth which were threatening to choke him.

He didn't know how long he ran or in which direction. He was driven by only one thought—one all-consuming thought: to escape, to survive. To live!

Light.

Just ahead and off to the left.

He ran toward the light and then slowed his pace. What if the house in which the light glowed like a welcoming beacon belonged to a Gentile, someone who was not a Mormon? Someone who had been in the mob?

But then Smith recognized the house. It belonged to John Johnson. He almost fainted with relief as he ran toward it. Johnson, a recent convert, would not turn him away. Johnson would help him. And he desperately needed help.

Because the mob might decide to come after him. What if they decided to use the knife on him after all? Perhaps one of them had by now gained the courage to wield it, to cut—

As Smith reached the house, he fell against the door and knocked weakly on it.

It opened.

"What—"

Smith met the startled eyes of John Johnson. "Help me, Brother Johnson."

As Johnson stepped back from the door to admit him, Smith saw Emma standing just beyond the threshold, her eyes stark with horror as she stared at him.

"Your missus," Johnson said, "came here to ask if I'd seen you."

Smith nodded.

"Come into the kitchen. You can lie down on the table there. We have knives—"

Smith grimaced.

"—which we'll use to scrape off the tar."

Smith let Johnson and Emma lead him into the kitchen.

As he lay down on the table, Emma wordlessly took the knife Johnson handed her, tears in her eyes. Johnson chose a knife he used for hog butchering. The two of them began to scrape away the viscous tar, unable to avoid damaging the outer layer of Smith's skin in the process.

He winced but did not speak or cry out.

As Emma continued to work at the task of cleansing the body of her husband, she began to sing the words of a psalm:

> By the rivers of Babylon, there we sat down, yea, we wept, when we remembered Zion.

Zion, Smith thought. We will build it. Somewhere. Someday.

> For there they that carried us away captive required of us a song; and they that wasted us required of us mirth, saying, Sing us one of the songs of Zion.

Zion—the Heavenly City, Smith thought. Pain wracked his body as Emma scraped it and Johnson murmured words meant to be soothing.

"How shall we sing the Lord's song in a strange land?" Emma sang and then fell silent.

The question echoed in Smith's mind, bringing a kind of pain to him that was far worse than the pain he felt in his burned and battered body because he did not know how to answer it.

PART ONE: BABYLON

ONE

SEVENTEEN-YEAR-OLD Virginia Delano gripped the back of the wing chair which stood in front of her dressing table. She braced herself for the ordeal facing her as her white-capped maid began to lace the stays of her demi-corset.

"Tighter, Selena!" she demanded. "Else I'll look like a sow!"

"Hush, Miss Virginia," the plump and middle-aged Selena said. "You've a fine figure and you'd look right well even without stays. And I daresay you know it, Missy.

"Tighter!" Virginia repeated, her fingers gripping the back of the chair. *"Ooohhh!"* she moaned as Selena again tightened the laces and then fastened them in place. "I can still breathe—but just barely," she sighed.

Selena opened a drawer of the highboy that had been skillfully painted to resemble intricately grained wood and removed Virginia's camisole and embroidered pantalettes.

As Virginia took them from her and slipped them on, she said, "Father says that he may be a very dangerous man." She began to don the first of her three petticoats which she had earlier ordered Selena to dampen so that they would cling and reveal the shapeliness of her legs. "I can hardly wait to meet him!"

"You shouldn't have run away from Elm Academy," Selena chided. "Then you wouldn't have the chance to meet men—dangerous or otherwise."

"But it was frightful there. Lessons all the time. And a nightly curfew. That awful school was operated as if we were living in eighteen *twenty*-four, not eighteen *forty*-four!"

Virginia pouted. And then brightened. "Father says he's a man with a mission and such men are always dangerous, no matter what their cause. I think Father's probably right. We studied all about Jean Paul Marat at the Academy and he was certainly a man with a mission during the French Revolution." She giggled. "But he was assassinated by Charlotte Corday who didn't at all agree with him although she was actually on his side at the beginning."

Selena harumphed. "Somebody or other just might do in Mr. Joseph Smith if a body's to believe the tales being told about him. They say him and his people do awful things together."

"Awful things? What sort of awful things have you heard about him?"

"You're much too young to hear such things, Missy."

"Tell me!"

"Well, I've heard it said that he and his followers—those Saints of his, as they call themselves—have secret ceremonies in which they drink the blood of wee infants they've sacrificed and then they pay their respects to the Devil."

Virginia's blue eyes widened. "Surely you don't believe such tall tales? You couldn't." She laughed lightly "But I'll admit that I have heard that Mr. Smith is never able to remain in one place for very long because people always drive him out so perhaps—"

"It's true," Selena said, interrupting. "Him and his people were driven out of Missouri years ago. They had a settlement near Independence where I was working at the time. Now I hear tell they're hiding out somewhere in Illinois."

"Hiding out? Maybe Mr. Smith truly is a Satanist. But, if he is, I wonder why Father would dare to invite him here. I must say, though, that I'm awfully glad he did because I just dote on dangerous men."

Selena pursed her lips and clucked her tongue.

Virginia turned to the mirror and wagged a finger at Selena's reflection. "I don't care a fig if you do disapprove of me, Selena. The plain fact of the matter is that dangerous men are the only ones truly worth a woman's attention. They help to make her life—oh, exciting." With a sly smile at Selena's reflection, she added, "And, perhaps, eventful."

"He's married," Selena snapped sourly as she handed a green silk dress to Virginia.

Virginia slipped the dress over her head. It bared her shoulders and she made certain that its bodice bared nearly an inch of her cleavage. The dress reached to a point just above her ankles. It had a tucked swag around the neckline, was sharply pointed in front, and its bodice had several stiffly boned seams. Its short sleeves ended in ruffles of creamy lace which matched the lacy flounce on its skirt.

"I don't care if he is married," Virginia declared haughtily. Then, with a trace of a smile, "Married men and dangerous men—they're actually interchangeable categories, don't you agree, Selena?"

"Married more than once, some say," Selena commented, catching Virginia's eye in the mirror and winking conspiratorially.

"Now whatever do you mean by that, Selena?"

"They say he's got more than one wife. Some say a lot more than just one."

"At the same time? He's married to them all at once? How perfectly fascinating!" Virginia leaned toward the mirror and rubbed at a spot on her nose where the powder she had applied earlier had caked. When she was satisfied that her skin was clear, she asked, "Do you suppose he'll bring them all to dinner tonight?"

With a stern expression and speaking in a gruff voice meant to sound male, Virginia declared, "I'm pleased to introduce to you my wife, Mrs. Smith Number One. And this is Mrs. Smith Number Two. And to my right, Mrs. Smith Number—" She collapsed in the wing chair beside her dressing table, doubled over with laughter.

"Mr. Joseph Smith," said Selena, "*claims* to have but one wife."

"Then perhaps he's not dangerous after all," Virginia said, sounding disappointed, as she raised her feet and held them out to Selena.

Selena bent down and placed flat-heeled patent leather slippers on her feet after which Virginia rose and faced the mirror to appraise herself.

She was slender, but neither slight nor thin. Her provocative hips and ample breasts proclaimed her femininity to which her slenderness lent a certain grace. She was tall but she refused to slump the way some tall women did, as if they felt that their height was something for them to be ashamed of or, perhaps, strictly characteristic of the male sex and therefore embarrassing to them.

Her large blue eyes were thickly lashed, lively, never still. They missed nothing and were surprised by very little that they saw. Her forehead was broad above her sloping, slightly upturned nose. Her lips were full and painted a faint pink. Even in repose, they seemed to smile because their corners were slightly lifted.

Sometimes she wore it straight, but tonight her thick blonde hair fell to her bare white shoulders in a bouncy bundle of slender sausage curls.

She turned blithely away from the mirror and, with her arms flung out at right angles to her body, she twirled, rustling her skirt as she did so. "How do I look, Selena?"

"As pretty as a picture. But then you always do and you know it, Missy."

"Do you think the Prophet will agree with you?"

"The Prophet?"

"That according to Father, is what Mr. Smith has taken to calling himself. Or is it that his followers call him the Prophet?" Virginia frowned. "I'm really not at all sure, now that I come to think about it. But no matter."

She picked up a small bottle from her dressing table and placed a drop of the lotion it contained in each of her eyes in order to make them sparkle. Then, after slipping on elbow-length white gloves which were delicately trimmed with swansdown, she quickly crossed the room and opened the door.

"Do enjoy yourself this evening, Miss Virginia," Selena called out to her.

"Oh, I'm quite sure I shall. Especially if Mr. Smith will be kind enough to let me join his harem."

Selena's pudgy hand flew up to cover her mouth, a shocked expression on her face.

Virginia gaily blew her a kiss and went through the door, moving gracefully along the upstairs gallery toward the stairs.

When she reached them, she halted and carefully adjusted her skirt and bodice. Then, as if she were in no hurry at all to get to the sitting room below, from which male voices now drifted up to her, she slowly began to descend the stairs.

She paused in the foyer at the foot of the stairs. Her father was in the sitting room, standing with his back to her beside the blazing fireplace, a cigar in his right hand which he was waving about as he addressed the two men who shared the room with him. The older of the two men, Stanley Asher, sat rather stiffly in a writing-arm Windsor chair. Standing beside him in front of the tall case clock was a younger, blond man who had his hands clasped behind his back.

Asher had been a friend of the Delano family since Virginia was a child and now she recalled how he had often let her ride him piggy-back, enjoying the experience as much, if not more, than she herself had.

The younger man, Simon Grant, shifted his stance and, as he did so, he caught sight of Virginia and his eyes brightened.

Just then, the knocker on the front door sounded.

"I'll see to it, Father," Virginia called out and turned to open the door.

"Good evening," said the older of the two men standing outside in the moonlit mid-March evening. "My name is Joseph Smith and I've come to call on Mr. Arthur Delano. He is, I believe, expecting me.''

Virginia hardly heard the words Smith had spoken. Her eyes were fastened on the younger man who stood on Smith's left.

She tried to look away from him and found that she couldn't. His gaze transfixed, almost hypnotized, her. She sensed his strength, his physical power, which seemed to emanate from him in invisible waves that threatened to overwhelm her. She nervously touched her curls. And as nervously smoothed her skirt.

He was taller than she was by several inches. His shoulders were broad, his hips narrow. He wasn't just staring at her. He seemed, she thought, to be glaring at her as if she were his enemy. She felt her face flush and again tried to look away from him, but again her eyes remained on his rugged face with its prominent cheekbones and the thin lips which formed a faintly grim line beneath his strong nose.

He's young, Virginia thought. Not much older than I am. He's no more than twenty, she finally decided. But there were wrinkles at the corners of his dark brown eyes and his forehead was deeply creased. The skin of his face, she noted, had been darkened by the sun, and now, in the shadow cast upon it by the brim of his army cap, he looked faintly foreign.

And decidedly handsome, Virginia found herself thinking, fighting the odd and rather disturbing impulse to reach out to touch that brawny body, that stern face with the almost ominous expression on it.

His hair was thick, uncombed and unkempt, and as brown as his eyes. It covered the collar of his drop-shouldered white cotton shirt over which he wore an open sheepskin-lined canvas jacket. A single suspender supported his tight denim trousers. His sideburns were also thick and they reached almost to the corners of his unsmiling eyes.

At last, by an exercise of sheer willpower, Virginia lowered her eyes, noting as she did so the man's black, canvas-lined leather boots, their tops turned down to just below his knees.

Arthur Delano appeared at her side. "You mustn't let our guest stand on the threshold, my dear," he boomed in his genial baritone. "Come in, Mr. Smith, do."

Virginia drew back and Smith stepped into the foyer, took Delano's outstretched hand and shook it.

The younger man remained standing on the doorstep, his eyes on Virginia's face. Then he turned his head slightly and squinted into the dim interior of the foyer.

"We thought you might not be coming after all, Mr. Smith," Delano was saying as he led his guest into the sitting room. "We thought that perhaps other pressing business here in Saint Louis might have demanded your attention."

"No, no," Smith said. "I've completed my business in Saint Louis. But, on our way here, the surrey we rented threw a wheel and Judah, although an accomplished wheelwright, had some small difficulty repairing it. I'm sorry that we're late."

Judah.

So that was his name, Virginia thought. As he stood on the doorstep, his eyes moved from her face, traveling down her body and then back up again.

"Won't you come in, Mr.—" she asked, suddenly angry at his insolent and undisguised appraisal of her.

"Bascomb."

"Judah!" Smith called. "Come along."

Judah Bascomb stepped into the foyer and Virginia closed the door behind him.

Without removing his cap, he strode across the foyer and into the sitting room, his walk rangy, almost cat-like.

Virginia hurried into the sitting room where Simon Grant was holding out a hand to welcome her.

"Good evening, everyone!" she said brightly, taking Grant's outstretched hand and curtseying to her father's guests.

"This is my daughter, Mr. Smith," Delano said, his eyes glowing with pride. "Virginia has just returned to us. She has been attending Elm Academy in Kentucky."

"An educated woman," Smith intoned, glancing in Virginia's direction, "is a jewel and an ornament any man would be proud to call his own."

Virginia gave him a dazzling smile, wondering whether such a mild-mannered man might really have several wives.

Smith was, she thought as the conversation of the men swirled around her, quite attractive. But not in the same way that Judah Bascomb was. Smith lacked the ruggedness that characterized Judah's face and body. He was more refined in appearance and his dark eyes were mild, unlike Judah's which she found fierce. Smith's hair, darker than Judah's, was oiled and neatly parted on the right side, while Judah's was somewhat unkempt.

Smith surrendered his beaver hat and frock coat to the manservant, Nelson, who had entered the sitting room, revealing his ruffled white shirt which he wore under a plain gray vest. He wore a high white stock with turned-down points and an equally white neckcloth. His trousers were black and strapped beneath his patent leather evening pumps.

Nelson turned to Judah, who handed over his jacket and cap.

"You look absolutely ravishing this evening," Grant whispered to Virginia.

"How sweet of you to say so, Simon," she whispered, but her eyes were on Judah, who was moving about the room as if he were searching for something.

"Sir," Delano said, addressing Judah, "may I be of some service?"

Judah ingored the question as he felt behind the drawn velvet drapes bordering the window. He opened the ornately molded doors that led to the dining room and peered into the room before closing them again.

"I'm sure everything is all right, Judah," Smith said to him. "I doubt that an assassin is hiding behind the drapes or lurking beneath the sideboard."

"You want them searched?" Judah asked Smith, pointing to Delano, Grant and Asher.

"I say, sir!" Delano said angrily. "Search us? What is the meaning of this, Smith?"

"I should have explained earlier," Smith said. "Brother Bascomb is my personal bodyguard. I'm truly sorry to have to employ one but I have had to do so because of certain recent unpleasantnesses. I do apologize if we've offended you."

Delano was apparently mollified. "I suppose you have your reasons for such precautions, Mr. Smith," he said. "Anyway, no offense taken."

Delano introduced Smith to Stanley Asher, and the two men shook hands. "Stanley is an old friend of the family," Delano explained. "He's in the fur trade—has been for more years than I can remember. He runs an office here in Saint Louis for the American Fur Company."

"Ah, yes," Smith said. "That would be Mr. John Jacob Astor's company, would it not?"

"It is, sir," Asher said stiffly.

"And this young gentleman standing so possessively next to my daughter," Delano said with a flourish of his right hand, "is Mr. Simon Grant who has the honor—and I use the word unabashedly—to have won my daughter's heart and hand. They are to be married in a fortnight."

Virginia was shocked to realize that she had totally forgotten her impending marriage while she had been studying Judah Bascomb. Guiltily, she gave Grant a smile and squeezed his hand.

"It is not only an honor," Grant said, running a hand through his blond hair, "but a privilege to make such a charming and beautiful young woman my wife." He returned Virginia's smile and bowed to her.

"Simon's also with American Fur," Delano said. "He's been transferred here from Astor's New York offices. When he came out here to Saint Louis last month, he met Virginia. It was what I think they call a 'whirlwind courtship.' They plan to make their home here in the city once they are married, but until then, Simon is staying with us."

"My congratulations to both of you," Smith said, nodding to Virginia as he vigorously shook Grant's hand.

Grant's patrician features—slender nose, full lips, finely chiseled chin—seemed to glow as he accepted Smith's congratulations.

"May I offer you gentlemen something to drink?" Virginia inquired. "Some port? Perhaps a little claret?"

There were murmurs of assent and Virginia went to an elaborately inlaid table which was flanked by lush potted palms. On it rested several decanters and a number of crystal wine glasses. She poured her father's favorite claret and handed him the glass after which she poured port for Asher and Grant. When Smith refused any wine, she turned to Judah.

He was lounging against one of the built-in shelves which were tightly packed with books, one booted foot propped up on a stencilled Hitchcock chair.

"Did you say you would take port, Mr. Bascomb?" Virginia asked him.

"Nope."

"Then you prefer claret, I take it."

"Whiskey," Judah said in his richly resonant voice.

Smith shot a disapproving glance in his direction.

Judah noticed it and said, "Brother Joseph, maybe I'm just not altogether fully converted yet. I still got me a taste for forbidden pleasures."

Smith smiled wanly and then shrugged.

Virginia pulled the bell rope and, when Nelson appeared, directed that whiskey be brought.

When the servant returned with a cut glass decanter, Virginia poured some whiskey into a glass and carried it to Judah, who accepted it from her with a curt nod.

He downed the whiskey and held the glass out to her.

She wasn't sure whether he was simply returning it to her or whether he was, in his crude way, asking her to refill it. She turned on her heel and refilled the glass. After handing it to him, she asked, "Do you Mormons have other forbidden pleasures? I mean besides drinking spirits?"

"We Mormons," he replied, "are forbidden to be liars or fornicators." He raised his glass to Virginia and then emptied it.

"I'm so sorry to hear that," she said sweetly as Judah handed her his empty glass again. "You Mormons must lead terribly dull lives."

"Not all of us Mormons are as strongly rooted in our faith as Brother Joseph is," Judah countered with evident amusement. "So I've not found my life to be what you could call dull."

Virginia found him infuriating. Was the obviously unlettered lout mocking her? Was he teasing her? Well, if he was, two could play that game. She said, "Do I understand, Mr. Bascomb, that you are admitting to being a liar?"

"That too."

Virginia couldn't help herself. She blushed, ruefully admitting to herself that he had won the game. She turned quickly and went over to where her father was engaged in conversation with Smith. She hooked her arm through her father's and said, "Don't let me interrupt. I just want to listen. I'm most interested in new ideas—especially philosophical ones." She would not, she vowed, turn to see what Judah Bascomb was doing.

"Mormonism," Smith said, "is not a philosophy, Miss Virginia, but a revealed religion."

Delano said, "Do tell us about it, Mr. Smith. As you know, that's why I invited you here to supper and to stay the night with us—in the hope of learning what is fact and what is fiction where your new religion is concerned. Rumors about you Mormons are rife in the land, as you no doubt know."

Smith shook his head sadly. "I know. Unfortunately, the Saints have many enemies."

"Since my wife died five years ago," Delano said, "I have been—how shall I put it—adrift in a spiritual sense. She was a rock, was my Elizabeth." His eyes misted. "Now I have only my lovely Virginia left, and I am soon to lose her as well."

Asher spoke up then. "You referred, Mr. Smith, to Mormonism as a 'revealed religion.' What, pray tell, did you mean by that?"

"Our Lord Jesus Christ and God, the Father, both appeared to me when I was but a boy—only fourteen years old. Later, the angel Moroni also appeared to me and told me where to find the golden plates on which was inscribed the Book of Mormon which had been written by Moroni's father, Mormon.''

"You actually saw angels?" Virginia asked sceptically.

"Yes, my dear, I did," Smith answered. "Moroni directed me to the place where the plates lay hidden in the earth and permitted me to excavate and eventually transcribe them.''

"You'll pardon me, sir," Asher said, "but I have heard it said that you were a mere money-digger.''

"Untrue, Mr. Asher," Smith responded without anger. "It is true that, as a young man, I was employed by Mr. Josiah Stoal to search for a silver mine in Susquehanna County in Pennsylvania. I believe that is the source of the money-digging charge that has been leveled against me.''

"And you have received divine revelations?" Asher asked tartly.

"It was Divine Revelation that led me to the plates which contained the history of the vanished race which once inhabited the Americas. Moroni was, in life, that race's last prophet.''

Virginia listened with rapt attention as Smith went on to recount how he had received another divine visitation, this time from John, the Baptist, who conferred, by laying his hands on the heads of Smith and the other men with him at the time, the priesthood of Aaron. She could not help marveling as Smith described a still later visitation involving the apostles Peter, James, and John who conferred the higher, or Melchizedek, priesthood which allowed Smith and his followers to establish their church.

She continued to listen as her father closely questioned Smith about the new religion and she felt a twinge of pity at his apparent desperation to find a new faith to replace the one he had lost when her mother died and left him desolate.

There was no mistaking, she realized, Smith's conviction in his faith nor his passionate zeal as he spoke of his goal of building what he referred to as 'God's Kingdom here on Earth.' She found the man compelling, and what he had to say equally so.

Her father said, "then your Book of Mormon—it replaces the Bible?"

Smith shook his head. "Mormons accept the Bible—where it has been properly translated. The Book of Mormon supplements the Bible. Our Church of Jesus Christ of Latter-day Saints—"

Delano interrupted. "What do you mean by Latter-day?"

"We view ourselves as the spiritual descendants of the early Christian Saints. The true Church of Christ, Mr. Delano, was taken from the early Christians as a direct result of their apostasy and corruption but we have now reclaimed it."

"Most interesting," Delano mused, stroking his chin whiskers. "I must say that the organized religions of our day don't seem to have anything of import to say to me. I find them not only hypocritical but more interested in things of this world than in those of the next."

"I agree with you on that score, Mr. Delano," Smith said heartily. "But we have restored the true Church, redeemed it from the hands of the corrupt and restored its spiritual authority. We have turned it back toward the true teachings of our Lord Jesus Christ where it once was."

"I've had enough—entirely too much—of the things of this world," Delano announced vehemently. "I'm rich as Croesus and getting richer by the minute. For years I've been shipping goods on the Missouri to Independence Landing, Saint Joseph, Fort Leavenworth—all the jumping

off places for settlers heading west. And I've been successful at selling those goods at a sizeable profit in all those
river towns. But I feel, somehow, that at this point in my
life my business has it's lost its meaning. As my life has.''

"I have a copy of the Book of Mormon in my surrey,"
Smith said. "Perhaps you would like to read it, Mr.
Delano.''

Delano had bent his head as he spoke. Now he looked
up and said, "How very kind of you! I would very much
like to read the book.''

"Do you not find it presumptuous," Asher asked Smith,
"to claim that our Lord visited you in person?''

"I do not," Smith replied. "It happened and I accepted
the fact of the matter with as much humility as I could
manage to muster in light of the admittedly miraculous
event.''

"Why did God choose *you* to visit?" Asher persisted.

Smith looked down at the floor and didn't answer.

"You consider yourself the Prophet of your new
religion?" Simon Grant asked Smith.

"Yes, I do. Like Moses, who was born an Israelite but
who was raised in the house of the pharaoh, and who fled
into the wilderness crying out against the degradation of
his people under the Egyptians—only to return and lead
the Israelites back to their identity as an independent
nation—I preach the truth of the Book of Mormon to those
who will listen in the hope that I might lead them, bathed
in glory, into the Kingdom of God.''

"You've been having a bit of trouble building your
heavenly city," Asher commented crisply.

"We have tried four times," Smith admitted. "Three
times the Gentiles have driven us out.''

"Gentiles?" Asher looked puzzled.

"We refer to non-Mormons as Gentiles," Smith explained. "This time," he continued, "we shall succeed in building our New Jerusalem with the help of our Lord."

"I understand that you've started a Community of the Faithful in Illinois," Delano said.

"Yes, North of Quincy, Illinois. We call our city Nauvoo, which is the Hebrew word for 'beautiful plantation.' It is there that we hope to accomplish the Gathering of Zion."

"Why do you suppose your neighbors have frequently driven you from their midst?" Asher asked.

"They find us—some of our ways—strange, I suppose."

"You mean your custom of multiple marriage?" Asher asked, scorn evident in his tone.

"Many false charges have been leveled against us," Smith said with equanimity, meeting Asher's rather angry gaze.

"Then you deny the charges of polygamy that have been made against you?"

"We cannot control what people say about us, Mr. Asher."

"Stanley, Stanley," Delano said, reaching out and laying a hand on his friend's shoulder. "Don't bait the man." He turned to Smith. "Stanley worries about me. He thinks I might do something foolish with my life—and my money."

"To become a Mormon, I humbly submit," Smith said, "is not to do something foolish. On the contrary."

"Stanley," Delano said, "has appointed himself guardian of my best interests."

Asher said, "I am merely playing devil's advocate, Arthur. You can't have forgotten that fiasco last year with Madam Franchette."

Delano grimaced. "Mr. Smith, I thought that Madam Franchette—a good but, I am now convinced, a misguided woman—I thought her astrological advice would . . . well, the past is dead and best left buried."

"Mr. Smith," Virginia said. "I take it that your church promises salvation to its true believers?"

"Only God can promise salvation, my dear. We, by obeying God's laws, hope to be saved."

The wooden door of the dining room opened. The man-servant reappeared and announced, "Supper is served, Mr. Delano."

Delano took Smith by the elbow and led him toward the dining room. "We must continue our conversation during supper, Smith. I find what you have to say intriguing, to say the very least."

Grant took Virginia's hand as Asher and Judah went toward the dining room.

"You are my salvation," he whispered, drawing her close to him. "Or you will be soon, at any rate."

"What a worldly man you are, Simon."

Grant kissed her lips and then let his right hand come to rest on her left breast.

Virginia pushed his hand away and then drew away from him. "Not only are you worldly, Simon, but you are also positively sinful!"

"I can't help myself, Virginia. Because I love you. I love you so very much. I'm sorry."

Virginia was also sorry, but not because of Grant's lingering kiss or his brief caress. She was sorry because, as he kissed and caressed her, she had found herself wishing that the lips pressed upon hers, and the hand which had warmly cupped her breast, were not Grant's— but those of Judah Bascomb.

TWO

JUDAH, as he entered the dining room, barely suppressed the exclamation he had been about to utter. The dining room was even more impressive than the sitting room had been. It looked to him like a room in which ceremonies should be conducted, not simply a room in which to eat a meal.

The room was large and rectangular in shape. At its far end, facing Judah, the red and yellow panes of two tall glass windows gleamed. Between him and the windows, in the center of the huge room, stood a round pedestal table.

It was covered with a linen cloth. On it were crystal goblets and bone china plates. In the center of the table was a silver candelabrum supporting lighted candles.

Against one wall stood a press in which china dishes and ceramic figurines were displayed behind glass doors. Opposite the press was a carved sideboard, and covering the floor to within a few inches of the room's four walls was an Axminster carpet.

Two large tapestries hung on opposite walls. One depicted a medieval hunting scene featuring a dead boar; the other showed a rustic harvest scene with pink-cheeked and, it appeared to Judah, decidedly drunken peasants making merry in the tall corn. A stag's head mounted on a walnut base also adorned one wall.

Above the table hung a crystal chandelier which held four lamps, all of them lighted, each of them helping to brighten the intricately inlaid marble ceiling.

Judah went over to the table, pulled out a heavy chair, and sat down. He looked down at the array of silverware, and the two glasses at the right of his plate.

He suddenly became aware of the fact that the conversation of the other people in the room had died. He looked up.

Delano was standing behind one of the chairs. Next to him stood Smith. On his other side, Asher.

Judah turned his head as Virginia and Grant entered the room.

Grant drew back the chair next to Judah's and eased it under Virginia as she seated herself at the table.

The other men then drew back their chairs and sat down.

Conversation resumed. No one spoke to Judah. Delano and Smith continued their discussion of the origins and tenets of Mormonism. Asher, a sour expression on his face, unfolded his napkin and placed it across his lap.

Judah, watching Asher, did the same with his napkin. Just then, a neatly uniformed serving woman appeared bearing a large silver tureen, which she placed on the sideboard. A moment later, she set a bowl of soup in front of Virginia and then proceeded to serve the others.

When a bowl of soup was placed in front of Judah, he stared at the spoons of several sizes resting beside his plate for a moment. He chose the largest of them, which he promptly plunged into his bowl.

As he placed the first spoonful of soup in his mouth, surprise showed on his face. Turning to Virginia, he said, "This soup's cold."

"Of course it is."

"How can you eat cold soup?" he asked her.

"It's vichysoisse," she said and giggled, almost spilling some soup as she did so.

Her answer had told Judah nothing. He put down his spoon and reached for a basket the serving woman had placed on the table. He rummaged about under the basket's covering napkin and came up with a warm roll. He speared a round ball of butter from a cut glass dish and spread it on his roll. He shoved the roll into his mouth and began to chew.

Virginia lifted her glass, which the serving woman had filled with a Rhine wine, and sipped from it.

Judah, ignoring the cold vichysoisse, took another roll, buttered it, and ate it.

"Have you been in the body guarding business long, Mr. Bascomb?" Virginia asked.

Swallowing most but not all of his roll, Judah answered, "Some months now."

"And what did you do before that?"

"Worked as a ranch hand mostly. Down in Texas. Drifted north after a time. Met Brother Joseph. And here I am."

"What exactly does a ranch hand do?" Virginia inquired, emptying her wine glass as the serving woman began to remove the soup bowls.

"Most everything a man can name that needs doing. Running cattle. Riding the rough off mustangs. Fixing broke wagons. Like that."

"Simon, did you hear? Virginia's tone was gay. "Mr. Bascomb fixes broke wagons."

"Chuck wagons," Judah said, as a plate of squab was set before him, along with a small side dish of broccoli. "Spring wagons. Buckboards. Flatbeds." He glanced at Virginia but she had leaned back in her chair and he saw instead Grant's smiling face. "Something funny, Grant?"

"I've never learned how to fix a broke wagon," Grant answered.

Virginia giggled again and picked up her wine glass, which the serving woman had just refilled.

Judah wondered what had amused her and Grant. He watched her as she drank her wine, and then he picked up a knife and fork and proceeded to dismember the fowl on his plate, forking pieces of meat into his mouth as fast as he could sever the roasted flesh from the bones. He placed a stalk of broccoli in his mouth, grimaced, and spat it into his napkin.

Virginia's arm accidentally touched his and he noticed that she had removed the gloves she had been wearing. Her touch, though slight, was enough to arouse him. He glanced at her and his eyes dropped to her breasts. His grip tightened on his knife and fork. She was beautiful, no doubt about it. He couldn't recall ever having seen a woman quite so beautiful. So desirable. In his experience, he had found that women usually needed a few years of living before they blossomed. But this one—this young girl—had evidently blossomed early. Was it because of Grant, he wondered. Had Grant awakened the woman within her?

Probably, he decided. It took a man to bring a woman to ripeness. Just as it took sun and rain to ripen wheat, and get it ready for the reaping.

Virginia Delano, he thought, looked ready for reaping. Had Grant . . .

Judah decided that Grant might very well have harvested Virginia Delano, although Grant didn't strike him as a very aggressive sort. But that wasn't the point. The point was Virginia herself. He had seen the way she had looked at him as he stood on the doorstep upon arriving at the house. He'd seen that look in women's eyes before. That hungry look. She had tried hard to hide it but it was there just as plain as the sky above them. He had felt himself begin to stiffen then as they stared at one another—just as his hot thoughts were causing him to stiffen now.

He envied Grant. Damn the man's eyes, he thought. The lucky bastard. Even if Grant hadn't had Virginia yet, he soon would. The old man had said his daughter was to marry Grant in a fortnight, whatever that was.

Judah devoured the last of his squab as conversation swirled around the table. There was a parlor house on Vine Street, he remembered. He'd visited it a year ago when he'd been drifting and had passed through Saint Louis. He wanted to get up from the table and head for that house now. There had been a woman there last year—he had forgotten her name but not what she had done to him, nor what he had done to her, to their mutual delight. It hadn't mattered to either of them that their coming together in that small stuffy room on the second floor of the parlor house was purely a business transaction. Judah, when he had money, bought what he wanted—or needed. And that night he had needed the small but voluptuous woman and he had had money in his pocket, a rare event. So he had paid and he had received what he considered to be more than his money's worth.

He discovered that the plate containing the remains of his squab was gone. In its place was a long-stemmed glass dish. In it was something that looked a little bit like ice cream.

"Don't you just adore sherbert?" Virginia asked him.

It took Judah a moment to realize that she was speaking to him about the orange mound in the dish before him. "Can't rightly say," he told her. "Never did taste such as this before."

He spooned some of the sherbert into his mouth. "It's good. But it's not something that I could adore."

"I suppose it's only your Mormon God that you could adore," Virginia remarked, drinking the last of the wine in her glass. The others were deep in their own conversations.

"Him, sure, I guess. Along with a woman or two that I've met in my time."

"But you never married?" Virginia inquired archly. Then, leaning close to Judah, she whispered, "Or do you have a harem of your own, as Mr. Smith is rumored to have?"

Judah could only stare for a moment at her mounded breasts rising slightly above the swag of her dress. "I never married. Might some day."

"How many wives?"

"One'd do—if she's amenable."

"Oh, I'm sure she would be, Mr. Bascomb. After all, you're a very attractive man—or you could be if you wore the right clothes and visited a barber."

Judah felt fury rise up within him, but he kept his face impassive. "Those things might help a man like the citified one you've picked out for yourself—probably they already have helped him. But me, now I seem to attract the kind of women who're out to get right down to basics without too much tarrying or worrying about when I last had my hair trimmed."

Virginia abruptly turned her attention to her sherbert, which was beginning to melt, and Judah, watching her, smiled for the first time that night.

"Gentlemen," Delano said, glancing around the table, "shall we take our coffee and brandy in the sitting room?"

Virginia said, "I hope you'll all excuse me. I'm afraid I have a terrible headache."

Grant reached out and took Virginia's arm. "I'm sorry, dear."

"It's nothing really. But I would like to lie down. Perhaps I shall feel quite fit soon and then I'll be able to return and join you gentlemen once again."

The men rose as she did, all except Judah who remained seated, spooning the last of his melting sherbert into his mouth.

Later, in the sitting room, he sat on an Empire chair, his legs spread out in front of him and his hands clasped over his stomach as he listened to Delano and Smith discuss the city of Nauvoo and the Temple that was being erected there. Asher, he noted, took little part in the conversation, apparently having decided to let his friend Delano chart his own course through Smith's spiritual waters.

Judah tilted his chair back against the wall, crossed his booted feet, and closed his eyes. He had refused Delano's offer of both coffee and brandy and now, almost dozing, he let his mind wander.

He lazily recalled his years in Texas during which he

had been rootless, drifting whichever way, it seemed, the wind blew him. Stopping to work at a ranch for a time and then moving on again. Always moving on, unable to remain very long in one place, however much he might be wanted or needed there. He hadn't known it at the time, but he had been searching for something—something he could not have named even if he had known he had been in pursuit of it. It was something he had once possessed but lost.

As his thoughts roamed, Judah found himself recalling his boyhood in the hills of Tennessee where his father had taught him to hunt.

He had downed many deer. He had learned to trap and build deadfalls. He owed his skill with both rifle and pistol to his father, that well-remembered figure who had loomed so large in his life before a falling tree had crushed him to death.

After that tree had fallen and destroyed his mother's world, her decline had been slow—almost imperceptible— but steady. She had liked to laugh, Judah remembered. But her laughter had also been killed by that falling tree. After the accident that had killed his father, his mother seldom even smiled.

He was not surprised when she came down with a fever not long afterward, nor was he surprised when she died of what the doctor called "complications" four days after taking to her bed.

Then everything seemed to happen so fast, he recalled. Distant neighbors appeared as if a barn were to be raised or a dance to be held. He attended the funeral, aware that a new part of his life was beginning because his mother's life had so suddenly ended. He had been eleven years old at the time.

When neighbors told him that his older sister, Naomi,

was going to live with them, and that his younger brother, Isaac, was going to live with a family whose name he didn't even recognize, he protested. He told the people surrounding him that the three of them would stay together as a family.

The well-meaning neighbors said that it was not possible. Too young, they said. Such young children could not make do for themselves, they said sadly. Not alone. He had insisted that they would do just fine, the three of them. He could hunt. Naomi knew how to bake bread and cook. Isaac could sow.

Naomi was hustled into a cabriolet and driven away. He ran after the carriage, shouting her name over and over again for more than a mile. When he returned to the gravesite, few people remained. Isaac had disappeared.

A man named Morrison seized Judah and carried him, struggling and screaming, to a wagon where he held him tightly as his wife drove the team toward a future Judah knew he would not—could not—accept.

During the night of the day he had arrived at the Morrison farm, he ran away and went back to the home which was no longer a real home for him. Loneliness came to live with him. It listened but did not care as he vowed out loud, in his anger at his father for having let himself be killed and at his mother for dying and also leaving him, never to trust anybody again. Never.

He plowed and he planted, yearning for what had once been and would be no more as he walked behind the plow. As the great bulk of the draft horse pulled the plow down countless furrows, the sweat streamed down his face and body, although the blood that ran in his veins was frigid. It frosted his heart.

A week later, he reached a decision.

But when he went to the neighbors who had taken

Naomi from him, he found their home deserted and, after questioning other people who lived in the hills, he at last learned that his sister's new family had gone "away." No one knew precisely where. He never saw Naomi again.

When he finally found the family who had taken Isaac to live with them, he was told that his brother had died of whooping cough.

He returned to the homeplace and kept it going—but he was a boy and the work was meant for a man. The house began to fall into disrepair. The fields gradually became overrun with weeds and tall grass. Fences rotted, fell, and were not rebuilt. He struggled long and hard, but was finally forced to admit defeat.

When he was thirteen, he walked away from the homeplace and didn't look back at it. He went westering. He wanted to see the world, he told himself at the time. He wanted to learn how to live in it like a man. He left a vanished sister and a dead brother behind him. And his dead parents.

He did not know that he was looking for something to replace his lost family, nor did he know that he was hoping to find a way to heal the still raw wound deep within himself that had been caused by the losses of those he had, in his own almost secretive fashion, loved so very much.

His healing began soon after he met Joseph Smith. He was welcomed into the homes of the Saints in Nauvoo and, although he would not at first trust them completely, he found himself slowly beginning to share their hopes and occasional despair. Imperceptibly, the tightness within him began to loosen. He gradually stopped holding himself apart from other people. He began to realize that he had found a new family—the Mormons of Nauvoo—to replace the one he had lost. And he had found something else as well—the ability to trust other people again. He began to know the peace that is born in a man once he has discovered who he truly is and where he really belongs. He had once again found love and the joy of sharing it.

His thoughts scattered as he heard his name spoken. He opened his eyes and found Delano standing in front of him.

"We thought you were asleep, Mr. Bascomb," Delano boomed. "You've reminded us that it's time for bed."

"You got yourself good locks on all your doors, have you, Delano?"

"Yes."

"How about the windows?"

"They have latches. And the shutters can be closed and latched if you deem such precautions necessary."

"I'll see to the windows. You look to the doors, Delano." Judah rose and went to the nearest window, which he opened. He drew the shutters, latched them, and then latched the window itself.

Delano walked with Asher to the door and, when the manservant had brought Asher's cloak, the two men bade each other goodnight. When Asher had gone, Delano locked the front door.

Judah, after finishing latching all the ground floor windows, went to the front door and opened it.

"Where are you going?" Smith asked him.

"Going to take me a look around outside before turning in," he replied.

"Mr. Bascomb," Delano said, "Your room is the first one off the gallery at the head of the stairs. I'll leave the door ajar for you. Please put out the lamps when you return."

Judah nodded and went outside. He circled the house, poking one booted foot into some shrubbery that grew beneath the stained glass windows of the dining room and then, when he was satisfied that no prowler lurked near the house, he went back inside and locked the front door. He went from room to room, putting out the lamps—all but one, which he picked up and carried with him as he mounted the stairs.

Once inside his room, he put the lamp down on a bedside table and began to undress. The coverlet on his bed had been turned down and the bed's two pillows propped up against the oak headboard. Judah tossed one of the pillows into a chair and then climbed into bed, the linen sheets cool against his naked body.

Should have kept my longjohns on, he thought. Anything happens in the middle of the night, I'll make some sight running around in the altogether.

His thought brought another one in its wake. A thought of Virginia lying in bed in one of the bedrooms of the house. Naked? He grinned and then closed his eyes, locking his hands behind his head. Moments later, he unclasped them and turned on his side, the image of Virginia a bright fire in his mind.

He turned over onto his other side, punched his pillow, and drew his legs up.

Minutes passed. And then more minutes.

Cursing, he threw off the coverlet and got out of bed. He lit a lamp with a taper and then pulled on his trousers and boots. Since he couldn't sleep, he might as well read something. Maybe, among the many books on the sitting room shelves, there would be something not too exciting, a book which would bore him and therefore encourage sleep. Carrying the lamp, he left his room and made his way down the stairs and into the sitting room.

He set the lamp on a table and ran an index finger along a row of leather bound books. He didn't want to read about somebody named Marcus Aurelius. Or about The Gentle Art of Horticulture.

His finger stopped on a gilt name. Charles Dickens. He had heard of the writer. An Englishman, as he recalled. The equally gilt title—Oliver Twist—didn't sound exciting to him, so he took the book down from the shelf. As he did so, he dislodged the book next to it, which fell from the shelf, hit the table on which he had placed the lamp, and knocked a humidor full of cigars to the floor.

Judah picked up the cigars and stuffed them back into the humidor, which he then placed back on the table. He opened the book. It had been, he noted, published in England. He riffled its pages. Leaning down toward the lamp, he read a passage selected at random from the middle of the book.

Then, as he snapped the book shut and picked up the lamp, he saw Virginia standing in the entrance to the sitting room.

"Mr. Bascomb, I gather you couldn't sleep either."

Judah stared at her in genuine surprise. She was carrying a lighted lamp and wearing a soft white nightgown. A blue ribbon ran through eyelets at the gown's high neck and its ends were tied at the base of her throat. The gown's hem was embroidered with blue daisies.

She crossed the room and took the book from Judah's hand. She glanced at the spine and said, "Trash."

"I didn't mean to make any noise but a book fell off the shelf and it hit—"

Virginia extinguished her lamp and set it down next to Judah's. She turned down the wick of his lamp until it gave off only the faintest light. "I was awake and I heard the noise. I decided to investigate."

Judah, when he spoke, lowered his voice to match

Virginia's low tone which was almost a whisper. "How's your headache?"

"I never had one. That is a lady's polite way of saying she is bored with the company or the conversation—or both."

A faint smile appeared on Judah's face. "Now what would Grant say if you went and told him that?"

Virginia shrugged. "I suppose I had better go back to bed."

"Might be best."

Virginia didn't move. "You have a very hairy chest, Mr. Bascomb."

"And you have a very bold tongue, not to mention brazen manner, Miss Delano."

Virginia laughed and then quickly covered her mouth with her hand. Recovering herself, she said, "I think I shall take that as a compliment."

"Wasn't meant to be one, though." Judah's smile widened. "Did they teach you at that Elm Academy to prowl around in the night with a half-naked man?"

"They taught me simply everything but that. So I ran away to broaden my education on my own as I'm doing at this very moment."

"What're you learning at this very moment?"

· That I should have run away years ago." Virginia put the book down on the table. "How badly do you want to kiss me, Mr. Bascomb?"

"Miss Delano, you are a wonder."

"That isn't answering my question, you know." Virginia placed both of her hands on Judah's bare shoulders and kissed him on the lips.

He was surprised when, a moment later, she parted her lips. He thrust his tongue into her mouth and she moaned faintly as she began to suck on it.

Suddenly, she shuddered and drew away from him.

"Miss Delano, you'd best be getting yourself back to bed."

"I don't always do what is considered the best thing."

"That's plain to see."

"Young ladies," Virginia said, staring into Judah's eyes, "are not supposed to give their favors lightly but I expect you know that. Young ladies are supposed to deny themselves such pleasures in order to entice men into marriage. It is, I know, the accepted way, and approved by society at large. Personally, I think such an idea is utter nonsense."

"You do, do you?"

Virginia reached up and drew Judah's head down. She kissed him again and then said, "society would not only not approve of what I'm doing, it would also consider it outrageous that I am doing it with a man who is so clearly beneath my station in life."

"There's some things, I happen to think, that are more important than a person's station in life."

"You are perfectly correct, Mr. Bascomb, although I daresay there are many in my social circle who would not agree with you. I should be ostracized from polite society were it to become known that I, a woman engaged to be married to a perfectly respectable young man, chose to soil my reputation by throwing myself into the arms of a—of a *cowboy*."

"So why'd you go and do it?"

"Isn't it obvious? You excite me, Judah Bascomb. And I love excitement. You're crude and you're rude—and I've never met a man like you before."

"There's lots of men like me."

"But you're here and this is now and I want you to kiss me again—quickly!"

"You're the one that did the kissing. You're making a

bad mistake. You said as much yourself. I'm not a fit man
for you to be fooling with, couldn't ever be. Like I said
before, you'd best go on back to bed and forget—"

Virginia threw her arms around him and kissed him a
third time and, although he gently tried to free himself
from her embrace, she refused to release him.

"Virginia!"

She spun around.

Judah stared steadily at Grant, who was standing with a
lighted lamp in his hand at the entrance to the sitting room.

Grant, anger twisting his features, said, "You are a cad,
sir!"

Before Judah could respond, Virginia quickly crossed
the room to face Grant. "Simon, it wasn't Mr. Bascomb's
fault. You see, he came down here to get a book and I
heard him and, thinking that perhaps someone might have
entered the house surreptitiously, I also came down. Mr.
Bascomb and I were talking and then—Simon, please
don't look at me in that awful way!"

"I'm shocked, Virginia," Grant exclaimed, his voice
strained. "I would never have expected—never have thought
you capable of such rash behavior."

"Oh, Simon, please don't be foolish. You know me
well enough not to say such an absurd thing."

Judah wondered what she meant by her last remark.

"Go to your room at once, Virginia," Grant said.

She drew back from him and placed her hands on her
hips. "You dare to order me about in my own home?"

"I want you out of this man's sight. You are not
modestly dressed and this man is a stranger to you. It is
not fitting for you to appear even before me dressed as you
are."

"I warn you, Simon. Don't lecture me. Do not order me

about. I will not be lectured, nor will I have you or anyone else tell me what I should do or when I should do it!''

"Grant," Judah said. "I owe you an apology. I guess I went and lost my head. Miss Delano told you the truth about what happened except for the part about—well, the part you saw. I forced myself on her. You got yourself a quarrel, you got it with me, Grant.''

Grant, speaking to Virginia and ignoring Judah, said, "If you are capable of such scandalous behavior with this—" he gestured angrily in Judah's direction, "—this *boor*, what will you not be capable of in the future? Shall I be forced to post guards in our house once we are married to make certain that you don't scurry down the backstairs and run off into the bushes with the gardener or the groom?''

Virginia slapped Grant's face.

His hand rose slowly to his cheek. "I am," he said somewhat haughtily, "a man of some substance and position. I do not need a wife who will bring shame to me or my house.''

"And you think I will shame you, is that it?'' Virginia snapped.

"I know what I saw just now,'' Grant retorted, his hand still on his cheek.

"You may consider yourself a very fortunate man, Simon,'' Virginia told him calmly.

"Fortunate?'' Grant's hand dropped to his side.

"Fortunate insofar as you have found out in time that I am not to be trusted, nor am I to be left unchaperoned when there is a handsome young man about.'' She turned swiftly and crossed to Judah, slipping her arm through his. "Don't you think we make an interesting pair, Simon? A bully-boy and his doxy?''

"Virginia!" Grant cried, shock registering on his suddenly pale face.

"I will not marry you, Simon," Virginia announced matter-of-factly as if she were telling him the time of day. "I wouldn't want to risk disgracing you."

"Now see here, Virginia. We're both tired. In the morning—we can talk about this in the morning."

"There is absolutely nothing to talk about. I have made up my mind. There will be no marriage." Virginia ran across the room and out into the foyer.

Judah heard her slippered feet padding up the stairs. And then silence.

"Bascomb," Grant snarled, "I will see to it that you suffer for what you have had the gall to do here tonight."

"I told you, Grant, that I apologize. Now you seem to like to think of yourself as a gentleman. Seems to me that a gentleman such as yourself ought to be content with my apology."

"I am not content!"

"Simmer down some, Grant. Miss Delano, she's young. Young as she is, she most likely doesn't always think before she acts. Young women like her don't concern themselves all that much with consequences. They want to do something, they often just up and do it. Don't mean much most of the time. What happened here tonight, it don't count for so much as a cat's whiskers."

"You have dishonored your host, Bascomb, as well as Miss Delano and myself. I intend to see to it that you pay for having done so."

"If you've got fighting on your mind, Grant, why, let's just take ourselves outside and have at it."

"I am not a man who indulges in fisticuffs—certainly not with a ruffian such as yourself."

"Then what have you got in mind in the line of getting even with me?"

"You will discover that in due course."

"You're bluffing, Grant. Instead of trying to humble me, you ought to be thinking on how you can make Miss Delano change her mind about not marrying you."

Grant's eyes flickered. "She'll marry me. I'll see to it that she marries me."

"Well, I sure do wish you luck. But Miss Delano, now she strikes me as a woman who'll go her own way and neither hell nor high water'll stop her or alter her course once she's on her way."

Grant turned quickly and left the room.

When his footsteps on the stairs had faded, Judah picked up his lamp and book and made his way out of the sitting room and up the stairs to his bedroom, grinning all the way.

THREE

"DAMN him!" Virginia exclaimed the next morning as Selena was helping her dress.

"Miss Virginia! Such language!" Selena frowned and then slyly asked, "Who are you wishing into perdition?"

The question dismayed Virginia because she had been about to answer, "Simon Grant." But then an image of Judah had flashed through her mind. Had she really been damning Grant? Or Judah Bascomb? Both of them, she swiftly decided, but for different reasons. Grant for having been such a prig. Judah for not having embraced her last night. For not so much as laying a hand on her. For forcing her to make the first move and every other move after that.

"Miss Virginia?" Selena prompted.

"Oh, do hush, Selena. I'll wear my plaid dress. Get it, please."

As Virginia dressed, her anger began to dissipate. A plan began to take shape in her mind. Soon she was smiling and, a moment later, laughing out loud. She clapped her hands together in delight.

"Whatever is the matter with you this morning?" Selena asked anxiously.

Virginia hugged her puzzled maid. "There is absolutely nothing the matter with me!" she declared happily. "Everything is just fine, Selena! Everything is working out just beautifully."

When Virginia freed her, Selena frowned. "You're up to something. I just know you are. Don't deny it. When you get that look on your face . . . Well, I hope whatever it is doesn't have anything to do with me. I know you, Missy, and I have to say I don't always like what I know."

"Have you seen Mr. Smith this morning?"

"He was breakfasting as I came up here. With your father."

"Mr. Grant?"

"I didn't see him about."

"What about Mr. Smith's bodyguard?"

"Who? Oh, you must mean that handsome young gentleman."

"He's no gentleman!"

"He left the house to bring Mr. Smith's surrey around," Selena said, ignoring Virginia's outburst.

Virginia suddenly fled the room, leaving Selena to stare after her in astonishment.

Downstairs in the dining room, she kissed her father on the cheek and said that she wasn't hungry. "I would very much like to have a word with Mr. Smith," she said. "When you're quite finished with your breakfast, sir," she added demurely.

"I've just finished my second cup of chocolate," Smith said. "Shall we talk now, Miss Virginia, before I'm tempted to accept a third?"

He rose and Virginia took his arm. "We'll be but a minute or two, Father. Do excuse us, please."

Half an hour later, as Nelson, the Delano's manservant, admitted him to the house, Judah heard someone shouting in the dining room. He recognized Delano's voice. He made his way to the room and paused in its entrance.

Delano was standing and pounding the table with a clenched fist. "No!" he shouted. "I absolutely forbid it!"

Virginia sat quietly at the table across from her father. She was sipping a cup of coffee, her eyes cast down.

"Why, the very idea is preposterous!" Delano bellowed. "You'll stay right here in this house where you belong!"

Judah glanced at Smith, who stood beside Virginia's chair, his hands clasped nervously in front of him.

"Mr. Delano," Smith said, "please don't condemn me in this matter. It was your daughter's idea, not mine. I merely agreed to her request—I had no idea it would upset you so."

"Well, sir, it does upset me!" Delano thundered. "And it smacks of collusion between the two of you, which I consider to be grossly unfair to me."

Smith looked pained.

Virginia looked up at her father and calmly said, "Really,

you mustn't fuss so, Father. It will only be for a little while. After all, you have always said that you wanted me to be a woman of the world."

"I never said any such thing!" Delano roared hotly. "I said I wanted you to have a good education. But it seems that you decided otherwise. You ran away from Elm Academy and you—" He sighed deeply and threw up his hands.

Virginia said, "I found what Mr. Smith had to say last night about his religion and then privately to me this morning most intriguing. So I simply asked him if I might visit Nauvoo, to learn more about it—and to study the Mormon way of daily life. Surely there is nothing unreasonable about that?"

Judah heard footsteps behind him and a moment later Grant shouldered him aside as he strode into the dining room.

"Don't talk nonsense, Virginia!" Grant said as he sat down at the table. "I overheard what you were saying just now. There is no point in your going to Nauvoo or anywhere else for that matter. We have our wedding to think about and our plans for the future to make."

"Oh, that reminds me, Father" Virginia said sweetly, without looking at Grant. "I forgot to tell you. I have decided not to marry Mr. Grant."

Delano began to splutter. Finally, he found his voice. "You have decided *what?*"

"I have decided not to marry Mr. Grant," Virginia repeated.

"*Mr.* Grant!" Delano cried in exasperation. "Since when have you taken to calling your future husband Mr. Grant?"

Virginia took a sip of coffee. "Mr. Grant will not become my husband."

"But it's all been settled!" Delano exclaimed, his face reddening. "It's all been arranged!" He glanced helplessly at Grant.

"We had a slight misunderstanding last night," Grant volunteered. "But I'll have a talk with Virginia this morning. I'm sure it can all be easily straightened out." He glared at Virginia who seemed to be finding the coffee in her cup of extraordinary interest.

"Virginia!" Delano said.

She looked up at him, her eyes innocent. "Yes, Father?"

"It is much too early in the morning for you to be talking such utter nonsense. Marriage is a solemn matter and it should not be treated with levity."

"I am not going to marry Mr. Grant, Father."

Delano threw up his hands.

Virginia put down her cup and got to her feet. She circled the table and threw her arms around her father's neck. "You really mustn't worry about me, you dear old thing. I shall be perfectly all right, I assure you." She shot a glance at Judah over her father's shoulder and added, "I'm sure that Mr. Bascomb will be able to guard my body as well as he does Mr. Smith's. You will be able to do that, won't you, Mr. Bascomb?"

Judah, taken totally by surprise, could only nod dumbly.

Virginia gaily kissed her father's cheek again and then ran from the room, calling back, "I'll tell Selena what to pack for me. I won't be but a few minutes!"

Delano slumped down in his chair. "What am I to make of all this?" he asked no one in particular. "Last night—Grant what happened between you two last night?"

Grant, his eyes glittering coldly, glanced at Judah before answering. "Nothing important. As I said earlier, a slight misunderstanding, nothing more. You mustn't worry, Arthur."

Delano groaned. "I *am* worried. Who wouldn't be with a daughter like Virginia? I never could control that child. I pampered her too much, that seems clear now. She has always managed to have her way with me—as she did with her mother when she was alive. Neither of us ever knew quite what to do with Virginia. Headstrong and willful, that's what she is and what she has always been."

Judah caught Grant's eye and grinned.

Delano continued, "I thought at last—now that she was to be married—everything would be different. I hoped she would at last settle down. Be more patient and, well, a bit more docile.

"I confess that I do not know what to do with her. My fortune—all of it—will go to her one day. And what do you suppose she will do with it?" he asked rhetorically. "I hate to think about that. But there is no one else for me to leave it to. Virginia was an only child. *That's* probably the root of the trouble! If she had had brothers and sisters—then she would have swiftly learned that she is not the center of the universe. If she had had siblings, she would quickly have learned to give as well as to take."

"I'll talk to her," Grant said.

"I've seen her like this too many times," Delano declared wearily. "I doubt that anything you might say to her at this point would go very far in changing her mind."

"I love her, Arthur," Grant said warmly. "I must try to talk to her. I don't want to lose her."

Delano looked up at Smith. "If she does indeed go with you to visit Nauvoo, Smith, promise me that you will look after her."

"All of us will, Mr. Delano," Smith assured him. "Won't we, Judah?"

Still stunned by the sudden turn of events, Judah could

only nod again. Grant, he realized, was glaring at him. He couldn't help himself. He gave the man another big grin.

A week after his return to Nauvoo, Judah sat his horse on the parade ground south of the city and listened to the rousing music being played by Captain Pitt's brass band. He hooked his left leg over his saddle horn and watched the fourteen companies of the Nauvoo Legion, resplendent in their blue coats, white trousers, tall gleaming boots, and feathered hats, as they drilled under the leadership of General Joseph Smith, who sat astride his splendid white gelding.

The music spilled out over the parade ground and down into the city, which was nestled on a peninsula jutting out into the Mississippi River from the Illinois side.

The men of the Legion, which was officially a part of the Illinois state militia, shouldered their bayonet-tipped rifles with obvious pride and stiff military precision.

Smith's gelding pranced as if in time to the music, which was occasionally abetted by the whistles of boats moving up and down the river beneath their rolling clouds of white steam.

Four thousand men, Judah thought as he watched the drill. Enough? He doubted it. His hand went to the folded newspaper he had earlier thrust into his pocket.

As the formation wheeled and marched toward the river, he pulled the copy of the *Warsaw Signal* from his pocket, unfolded it, and read again the editorial written by the paper's editor, Thomas Sharp. The few paragraphs were clearly designed to rouse the Gentiles' fears of and hatred for the Mormons.

When he finished reading, he looked up at Smith in the distance and something not unlike fear swept over him. He had heard the ominous talk among the Gentiles. He had tried to dismiss their ugly words and occasional threats from his mind as merely the emotional outbursts of bigots. But he could not, although he tried to, forget them. They echoed in his mind at times, and now, as he watched Smith astride his gelding, his body grew cold and he felt his heartbeat quicken.

Thomas Sharp, he knew, had been intensifying his editorial attacks on Mormons in general and on Smith in particular. There was no mistaking Sharp's intent. He had made it clear in several recent editorials. He wanted nothing less than to have Illinois' Governor Thomas Smith revoke the city charter of Nauvoo, disband the Legion, and order all Mormons to leave the state immediately.

The music stopped.

Smith gave an order and then, as the militiamen disbanded, he rode over to Judah and greeted him warmly.

"Have you seen this?" Judah asked him, handing Smith the newspaper he was holding.

Smith took it and glanced at the editorial. "These are dangerous words, Brother Judah. But there remains the rule of law and we shall persevere under it. Justice shall be ours."

"John Bennett's stirring up trouble too," Judah remarked, referring to the man who had gathered about him dissenting Mormons and formed a counter-organization in Nauvoo that was vehemently opposed to Smith and some of his policies.

"Brother Bennett will come to his senses," Smith said. "I'm sure he will."

"He's telling anybody who'll listen that you have dozens of wives."

Smith turned to watch the militiamen who were walking in groups from the parade ground. "As I've said, Brother

Bennett will soon come to his senses and return to the Church.''

''What Bennett's been saying about you, about you getting sealed in celestial marriage more than once—it's not true?''

Smith sighed. ''I must ask you not to repeat what I am about to tell you, Judah. Will you promise me that you will not?''

Judah nodded.

Smith hesitated briefly and then said, ''I have had another divine revelation—had it, as a matter of fact, some time ago. The Lord revealed to me that we Mormon men must practice plural marriage. I have made my revelation known to the members of the Council and to the Twelve Apostles. Some of them, like myself, have secretly followed the commandment given to me in the revelation. We have taken more than one wife as did the prophets of the Old Testament.''

''Then Bennett's been telling the truth. Him and Sharp.''

''Truth, Judah, is a strange thing. It can be made to seem unclean when it is told through unsympathetic lips like those of Brother Bennett and that scribbler, Sharp.''

Judah didn't know what to say. If the command to marry more than once had come to Smith, as the Prophet had just claimed it had, in a Divine Revelation, then there was the stamp of Divine Guidance upon it. The mark of holiness. Judah knew Smith well and he knew the man was not a liar but now, as he met the Prophet's gaze, he found that his thoughts were in a turmoil.

''I understand that this comes as something of a shock to you,'' Smith said to him. ''It did to me, too. Many of the others in the church hierarchy also find it difficult to accept even now. Brother Brigham Young, for example, has confessed to me that he spent many hours in searching his soul and in prayer before sealing himself in celestial marriage to other women.''

"Brother Brigham has . . .'' Judah couldn't find the words to finish his sentence.

Smith nodded. ''Remember, Judah, you are sworn to secrecy in this matter. I shall personally make known the revelation I have received to the rest of the faithful when the time is propitious.''

''Might be a good idea to tell them right now. That way, you'd have a chance of cutting the ground out from under men like Bennett and Sharp.''

Smith shook his head. ''I shall not need your services for the rest of the day, Judah.''

As Smith rode away toward Nauvoo, Judah sat on his horse and stared after him. It's no wonder, he thought, that the rumors are flying about secret rites practiced by the Mormon leadership. The charges of riotous orgies, he now realized, had their roots in the fact of Smith's—and others'—ractice of polygamy. He wondered if he were being blasphemous because he had just found himself wishing that Smith had not received any revelation directing him and other faithful Mormon men to take more than one wife.

He swung his left leg over his horse's neck and thrust his booted foot into its stirrup. When, heeling his horse's flanks, he rode south, thinking as he rode that polygamy might have its advantages. If you grew tired of one woman and had married several—well, you'd likely be bound to have at least one ready and maybe even eager to welcome you into her bed and body. He couldn't help smiling as he mentally pursued the many possibilities that polygamous marriage had to offer a man as lusty as he knew himself to be.

*   *   *

As he reached the log cabin he had built for himself on a plot of fertile ground south of Nauvoo, on the eastern bank of the river, the ghost of a smile was still on his face; It quickly faded when he saw that the front door of his cabin was open.

He halted his horse, his eyes on the open door, his ears listening for any sound that might be coming from the cabin. When he heard none, he dismounted and, leading his horse, cautiously approached the cabin. When he reached it, he dropped his horse's reins and flattened himself against the cabin's outer wall near the open door.

Now he could hear someone moving about inside.

The sounds that the person inside the cabin was making were muted. Stealthy sounds, he thought with some apprehension. He moved quickly through the door and into the center of the room, his hands fisted and ready for a fight or a friendly greeting, depending upon who it was who had entered his unlocked home while he had been on the parade ground.

"Good afternoon, Judah," Virginia said from where she stood in a corner of the cabin's single large room. "I must say I'm disappointed in you."

"What are you doing here?" he asked gruffly, not sure whether he was glad to see Virginia or not. But he was definitely sure that she was just as beautiful as ever.

"I thought you would have had the good grace to come calling on me. Apparently I expected too much of you. So I decided to remedy the awkward social situation by coming here to call on you."

"You don't belong here. You belong where Brother Joseph placed you—with the Denton family."

"They are lovely people," Virginia said sincerely. "But I quickly grew tired of attending ward meetings and meetings of the Nauvoo Relief Society."

"You said you came to Nauvoo to learn about how we live."

"And I've been learning. I must say I admire the way you Mormons look out for the poor and distressed among you. But if I ever have to make out even one more list of items to be distributed to needy families I swear I shall just refuse to do so. Donated: one chicken by Mrs. Soames. Two pounds of butter by Miss Avery. Four comforters by Mrs. Tremayne." Virginia scowled.

"It's good work the Relief Society women do. It's necessary work."

"But boring."

"For a society lady like yourself, I guess it might get to be."

Virginia looked around the room. "You are not a very tidy man. And not a very well-organized one either. I've swept the floor—as well as a dirt floor can be swept. I've made your bed. You really should wash your dishes, Judah. I would have washed them, but there doesn't seem to be a pump. Or a well outside."

Judah laughed heartily. "Have to haul my water from the river on account of this place doesn't have much in the way of modern conveniences. But it suits me fine."

"I don't doubt that for a minute. It's a crude structure. But strong. Not altogether unattractive—in a primitive sort of way. Like its tenant."

"How'd you get out here?"

"The oldest Denton boy drove me in their cutdown."

"Why'd you come?"

"To see you."

"You've seen me."

Virginia crossed the room and stopped in front of Judah. She reached up and put her arms around his neck. "Are you glad I came?"

Judah knew now that he was, aware that he had several times wanted, on one pretext or another, to stop at the Denton house in Nauvoo in the hope of seeing her.

"I've got to see to my horse," he said, as he removed Virginia's arms from around his neck.

She followed him outside and then over to the small log building he had built in the rear of the cabin, which served him as both barn and storage shed. She stood just inside the door, watching him as he removed the bridle and saddle from his horse.

He eased the animal into a stall and filled the wooden trough at its end with a mixture of barley and oats. As the horse ate, he used a clean piece of muslin to wipe the animal down. He went outside and filled a bucket in the rain barrel. Then he brought the bucket back inside the shed, and placed it inside the stall beside his horse.

"It smells of sweat in here," Virginia commented, wrinkling her nose.

"Mine and his," Judah said, jerking a thumb in the direction of the horse.

"And leather."

"That, too."

"You're very considerate of your horse."

Judah looked at her in mild surprise. "A man depends on his horse out here, and he's got to take care of it."

"Then it's not a matter of tenderness on your part? Or of concern for a fellow creature?"

"It's more a matter of common sense."

"I feel as if I'm living in another world," Virginia commented. "The people here are so—well, plain. No one seems to have very much money. The houses are so ordinary and so plainly furnished. I went to call on a family in the fifth ward with Emma Smith the other day, and they had such a small house and so little furniture. Yet they seemed so happy."

"Probably they were. Big houses and fancy furniture don't give a man a guarantee of happiness."

"What does? What could guarantee you happiness, Judah?" Virginia moved toward him as he came out of the stall.

"A good meal and not too long before the next one. Some sound sleep from time to time. The sight of the sun coming up all brand new each morning and the same old shiny stars in the sky every night. It doesn't take too much to make me happy."

"You're a sensualist, that's what you are."

"I've had me a woman or two in my time, if that's what you're getting at."

Virginia giggled.

"You think I'm a funny man, do you?"

"I think you're a very desirable man." She took his hands and placed them, palms down, on the small of her back. "I think you're unlike any other man I've ever known. You smell of the earth and of animals. You have eyes that seem to see straight into a person's secrets. In a way—at times—you frighten me."

"Don't mean to."

"I like to be frightened—a little. I like a man who just might be a little bit dangerous."

"I'm not dangerous. At least, not to the likes of you, I'm not."

"I think you're wrong, Judah Bascomb. I think you could be a very real danger to me. I have a terrible feeling that I shouldn't have come to Nauvoo. I almost wish you hadn't ever come to Saint Louis—that I'd never met you."

"All that doesn't make much sense to me. You come out here to see me and you wrap my arms around you, and then you go and say you wish you'd never met me. Nope. Don't make any kind of sense to me.''

"I'll tell you the truth." Virginia rested her cheek against Judah's chest. "I had to come to Nauvoo because it was where you were going. It was a dangerous thing for me to have done. Now do you see what I mean?''

"Can't say as I do."

"I want you, Judah."

"Well, looks like you got me at the moment."

"Not just this way. You know very well what I mean."

"Reckon I do, Miss Delano."

Virginia drew back and looked up into his eyes. "Miss Delano? My name is Virginia."

"Didn't want to seem too abrupt with you, and I might have seemed so had I started using your up-front name too quick.''

"Say it."

"Virginia."

She returned her cheek to his chest. "One day soon I shall have to leave Nauvoo."

Judah found himself wanting her and wanting her almost desperately. But he said, "Now's the time you should go away. Right now. Before—"

"You don't want me then, is that it? You don't find me attractive?''

Judah released her. "You're too headstrong for your own good and that's a true fact. You don't think first before you act. You just up and do whatever it is you want to do. What about your intended?''

"Simon? You heard me tell my father that I will not marry him."

"I don't as a rule try to tell people what they should or shouldn't do. But I feel I got to tell you that you'd best get out of here—and out of Nauvoo—now. Go home where you belong, where it's safe and—"

"*Safe!*" Virginia seemed to spit the word at Judah. Then she laughed. "I don't want to live in a place that is merely safe! I want to live an exciting life. I want—" She smiled coquettishly. "I think you know what I want."

"Reckon I do."

"Then take me, Judah. Or must I beg?"

Judah felt his heartbeat quicken. Why was he holding himself back from her, he wondered, when he yearned for her, yearned to touch her and hold her close to him. Was it from some sense of honor? But he owed Simon Grant nothing. And the woman standing in front of him was able to make up her own mind about the way she lived her life. So why did he hesitate?

"I'll go," Virginia said. "You're probably right. I shouldn't have come here. Please forget everything I said."

As she started to move toward the door of the shed, Judah couldn't help himself. He stepped in front of her.

She looked up at him.

"Don't go," he said, his voice low. "I don't want you to go."

"What do you want me to do?"

Instead of answering her question, he took her in his arms and kissed her.

At first, she didn't respond. She remained standing with her arms at her side as his tongue touched her teeth. But then, slowly, her arms rose and encircled his body.

Judah, breathless, said, "Not here."

"We'll go to your cabin." Virginia took him by the hand and led him from the shed.

They walked beneath the setting sun toward the cabin and, once inside it, Judah closed its door as Virginia went to the low rope-slung bed that stood against one wall and sat down upon it's straw-filled pallet.

As she kicked off her pumps, Judah went to the cabin's single window and closed its wooden shutters to darken the room.

He pulled his shirt over his head and tossed it to the floor. Then, sitting down on a three-legged stool he had carved from a tree stump, he pulled off his boots. He dropped his trousers, stepped out of them, and then stripped off his longjohns.

Virginia, when she was completely naked, pulled the rough woolen blanket from the pallet on the bed and wrapped it around her, holding it tightly as she stared at Judah who was moving toward her, a dim figure in the shadowy room.

He sat down beside her and kissed her cheek. His right hand rose and unlocked her fingers which were clutching the blanket she held up to her throat. "You won't need that," he said softly as he draped it over the bed. He eased her down on the bed and then shifted position so that he was facing her as he sat on the edge of the bed. "The rest of you is just as beautiful as your face. I knew it would be."

"Will it hurt?"

Judah's eyes narrowed as he looked down at her.

Her arms were lying stiffly at her sides. Her eyes were wary.

"You don't mean to tell me that this is going to be your first time?"

She nodded.

Judah shook his head and said, "Well, I'll be damned! The way you talked—so saucy—the way you acted just now and at your house the night we met." He cupped her right breast in his left hand. "You sure you want to go through with this?"

"I'm not sure, but—I asked you will it hurt?"

"Some. But it's over quick enough and then you'll most likely enjoy what follows."

He bent his head and his tongue touched the nipple of her right breast. When it hardened, he moved to the left breast, letting his right hand slide along the curve of her belly, down along her thigh, and then back up again to rest between her legs. He continued to touch one nipple and then the other with the tip of his tongue, thinking that he'd best go slow, best take care not to turn her skittish, marveling that she was a virgin, half-disbelieving it. She'd teased and taunted him so openly that he found it hard to believe now that this was to be her first time. Had she lied to deceive him, to make him think she was something she was not—a virgin? He doubted it. There had been real trepidation in her voice, if not fear, when she had asked him if it would hurt.

He gently massaged her, using his index finger to lightly probe but not enter her.

Her hands came to rest upon his shoulders but, as they did so, she closed her eyes.

He had stiffened quickly and, as he felt the driving urge to take her immediately, he restrained himself. He reminded himself that this was no experienced whore he had brought to his bed who would be ready for anything, and able to handle any man, no matter what his tastes might be or where his lust might lead him.

"Judah?"

"What, honey?"

"What am I supposed to do? I don't know what I'm supposed to do."

Her innocence served only to inflame him further. "You

do whatever you feel like doing,'' he answered hoarsely.
"Mostly, things come natural at a time like this."

He felt the moistness of her and, as he lay down beside
her, his hardness pressed against her hip and he thought
she flinched. Quickly, he kissed her lips. While their kiss
lasted, he fondled her breasts, letting himself press heavily
against her warm flesh.

He rolled over on top of her and then adjusted his
position so that his erection throbbed between her legs,
which he had gently parted. He felt her thighs tighten on it
and he kissed her again, inserting his tongue into her
mouth and moving it about until she began to suck tentatively on it. He chose that moment to insert a portion of
himself into her, keeping his back arched and his hips
suspended above her pelvis. When she moaned faintly, he
eased deeper into her.

She pulled her head away from him and gave a sharp,
breathless cry of pain.

"It's over," he whispered. "The worst of it's over
now. Just lie still now. Both of us, we'll lie real still for
awhile."

They did.

Judah felt the urge to buck rioting through him but he
fought it and remained motionless within her.

Her arms went around his body as she said, "I'm—it's
all right now, I think."

He began to move, slowly, rhythmically, reveling in her
while at the same time holding himself back, wanting to
reassure her, wanting to make sure that she experienced as
much pleasure as he did.

Almost a minute passed before she began to move beneath him to match his rhythm. And then, suddenly, she
was reacting wildly to him, her hands clutching his back,

her fingernails tearing at his flesh. Her knees rose as she clasped him tightly in her arms. Her teeth nipped his neck.

Slowly, he withdrew from her—almost completely—and looked down at her.

"*Judah!*" she cried and her hands slid down his back to grasp his buttocks and force him back inside her again.

Moments later, he felt her body lurch violently beneath him and then shudder spasmodically. He increased the speed of his eager thrusting, letting himself surrender completely now to the passion that tore like a whirlwind through him. And then he exploded within her. But his body continued to thrust and he remained stiff, breathing heavily. Gradually, he quieted and came to rest. He felt her hands release his buttocks and move up along his back until they came to rest on both sides of his face.

She stared at him wordlessly for a moment and he started to withdraw from her.

Her hands quickly left his face and seized his buttocks again. "Don't!" she said almost fiercely. "Not yet."

He reentered her and lay there, feeling the heat of her body and that of his own blending with it.

"Judah Bascomb," she whispered, as if she were tasting his name in the deepening darkness in which they lay locked together. "It's odd," she added.

"What is?" he asked, nuzzling her neck.

"The fact that you told me earlier that I should go home where I belong and now I feel so strongly that I am home and that I belong here with you. And the fact that I feel now that I never want to leave you."

"You don't have to leave me," he murmured. "Not if you don't want to."

FOUR

BY mid-April, Simon Grant could stand it no longer. He had been certain that Virginia would "come to her senses," as he had put it to himself, and return to her home—and to him.

But, as April was about to end, he put aside his wounded pride and made it a point to talk to Arthur Delano. During their conversation, he expressed deep concern about Virginia's well-being and Delano confessed that he had received only one letter from her and, although she had written in it that she was happy and well, he was nevertheless very worried about her. Grant volunteered to go to Nauvoo and bring Virginia home. Delano had been delighted to accept his offer.

And so Grant had journeyed to Nauvoo, determined to bring Virginia back to Saint Louis. He wouldn't even consider the possibility that she might refuse to return with him. He couldn't let himself consider that possibility because it was vital to his plans for the future to have her return with him. For him, there was too much at stake and so he dared not—and would not, he promised himself— fail in the mission he had embarked upon.

In Nauvoo, as he walked through the city after registering at its only hotel, he marveled at the clean wide streets and neat frame houses lining them. The city was spotless.

He stopped in front of the limestone Temple and stood there, impressed at the industry of the men working on the structure. One man whistled as he worked. Other workers called out to one another from time to time—friendly comments, occasional joking remarks.

Grant stopped a man who was carrying a heavy piece of timber on his shoulder and asked directions to the home of Mr. Joseph Smith, which the lumber-carrying man promptly and cheerfully gave.

Later, as Grant stood in front of Smith's house, he fixed a careful smile on his face. He would have to be cautious, he warned himself. He would have to determine just what Virginia was doing in Nauvoo and, most of all, he would have to be careful not to arouse any hostility on the part of Smith or any of his followers as he went about putting his plan into action.

But he would, he vowed, see to it that Virginia returned to Saint Louis with him, because he intended to marry her.

His smile widened. He intended, he thought, not only to marry her, but also to share with her at some future date the Delano fortune, which she would inherit when her father died. The day of Delano's death danced gaily in Grant's mind—a day greatly to be desired, a wonderful day of days.

The old man, Grant knew, had frequently of late complained of chest pains. Delano thought they were caused by indigestion. Perhaps they had been. But Grant hoped they signaled the failure of the old fool's heart.

Still smiling, Grant climbed the steps to the porch and used the brass knocker to announce his presence to whoever might be inside the house.

When the door opened, he found himself facing a woman with a decidedly sour expression on her face.

"Excuse me," he said to her. "I've come to speak to Mr. Joseph Smith, if I may."

"And you are?"

"My name is Simon Grant. I met Mr. Smith last month in Saint Louis at the home of Mr. Arthur Delano. Is Mr. Smith at home?"

"Out back," the woman said bluntly. "Chopping firewood." She shut the door.

Grant left the porch and went around the house. He found Smith in his shirtsleeves, chopping wood and carrying on an animated conversation with another man.

When Smith noticed Grant, he stopped working and, leaning on the long handle of his axe, asked, "Sir, what may I do for you?"

Grant, with outstretched hand, went up to Smith. "You may not remember me, Mr. Smith. I'm Simon Grant. We met at Mr. Delano's home in Saint Louis last month."

"Of course!" Smith shook hands with Grant. "I knew your face was familiar but I couldn't place you for the moment. What, may I ask, brings you to Nauvoo, Mr. Grant?"

"I've come to see Miss Virginia Delano, for one thing. She has sent word to her father that she finds Mormon life of great interest and I thought I should see something of it for myself. I hope you don't mind, sir."

"Mind?" Smith smiled broadly. "Not at all, Mr. Grant. We are always glad to satisfy the curiosity of Gentiles. We have found that some of them, once their curiosity has been satisfied, have converted to our faith. So you see it often benefits us to indulge the interest of outsiders in our religion. Is that not so, Brother Brigham?"

The man standing near Smith nodded solemnly, his blue eyes on Grant.

"This gentleman, Mr. Grant," said Smith, "is Brother Brigham Young. Brother Brigham, I have the pleasure to present to you Mr. Simon Grant of the American Fur Company in Saint Louis."

Grant shook Young's hand. He found that the man had a firm grip. Young's light hair was long, nearly shoulder-length. He was stockily built, with a broad forehead above his keen blue eyes. His nose was also broad and his thin lips seemed permanently pursed above his square chin.

"I'm pleased to make your acquaintance, Mr. Young," Grant said.

"A pleasure, sir," Young responded.

Smith said. "We have a fine hotel in town, Mr. Grant. I suppose you'll be staying there?"

"I've already registered. And may I say that you have quite a bustling little city here. It's most attractively sited. The river view is quite marvelous."

"You'll want to see Miss Delano as soon as possible, I imagine," Smith said, cutting through the pleasantries. "I hope you don't mind my saying so, but I hope she has relented and is willing to resume her relationship with you. I'm not being too personal?"

Grant beamed at Smith. "I appreciate your kind thought," he said. "I'm sure everything will turn out all right. Miss Delano, as you have undoubtedly noticed, is a very impulsive young woman."

Smith turned to Young. "I met Mr. Grant in Saint Louis." He proceeded to describe the meeting, concluding with an account of Virginia's decision to visit Nauvoo, making no further reference to the rift that had developed between her and Grant.

"We hope," Young said, "that you will look kindly upon us, Mr. Grant. We'll do all we can to make your stay among us a pleasant one. Please feel free to call upon us if we may be of service to you."

"How very kind of you," Grant said enthusiastically. "I shall do that, I promise you. May I add that if I can be of any service to you, I shall be available at any time. I have read newspaper accounts of your recent difficulties with the authorities here in Illinois and I must say, quite candidly, that I think you and your people have been treated outrageously."

"Lies and slander," Smith said heatedly. "That's what they're spreading about us. They say and print the most terrible things—that I, for example, am a threat to American democracy—that our way of life, which is one of sharing among ourselves all that we collectively own, is undemocratic. Sometimes I come close to despair, Mr. Grant. I freely confess it. But the Lord lifts up my heart again and then all is once again well. We go on."

"I did read something about your having declared yourself king of your people," Grant said. "I suppose that is not so either."

"That, sir, is one more example of how the newspapers—deliberately, I do believe—distort what we Mormons do and say."

"What the Prophet means, Mr. Grant," Young said, smiling, "is that last month—on the eleventh of last month, to be exact about it—the Council of Fifty crowned him king. That much is true. But not king of the temporal world. Quite the contrary. He was crowned King of the Kingdom of God which we intend to establish in the heavenly city of Zion here on earth."

"I see," Grant said, mildly amused by the notion of this perspiring woodcutter who was standing in front of him being the king of any domain. It seemed to him both unlikely and not a little bit ridiculous. He kept his facial expression sober, almost somber, as Smith spoke again.

"Sometimes I have the desire to destroy these newspapers that malign us so awfully."

"Mr. Smith, I have friends in Saint Louis. Friends who have influence in both political and financial circles. One or more of them must be prevailed upon to say a word here, a word there. Certain people might be—shall we say, encouraged—to mute their criticism of you. Perhaps recant where their calumnies are concerned."

"How very good of you to suggest such a thing!" Smith exclaimed. "Brother Brigham, I know the Lord has sent us a very good friend in Mr. Grant. Do you not feel it?"

"Mr. Grant is most generous in his sentiments," Young commented, his smile gone. "But perhaps overly optimistic."

Grant, noticing the absence of Young's smile, became wary. Smith, he decided, was one thing. The man was not only an obvious visionary but also rather childlike in his enthusiasms and willingness to take people at face value. But Brigham Young, he felt, was another matter altogether. Young seemed shrewd. Cautious. And he was apparently far more sceptical than Smith.

"I understand," Grant said, "that there have been attacks upon your people by some of the—what was the word you used? Ah, yes, I remember now. By the 'Gentiles' both in Nauvoo itself and from the surrounding areas."

"That's correct," Young said, his eyes narrowing as he studied Grant. "The mobs of Gentile vigilantes—we refer to them as wolf packs."

"I think it was right of your young men to retaliate," Grant said firmly. "The Sons of Dan, I read, are not to be underestimated as vigilantes themselves."

"What you have read about the Sons of Dan is largely untrue," Young declared. "There have been no so-called holy murders."

Grant caught the sharpness in Young's tone and warned himself to tread lightly. "I'm sure that's so, Mr. Young. I only wanted to say that I sympathize with any—uh, counter measures the members of your faith take, in light of the recent attacks on them."

"We have the Nauvoo Legion to protect us," Smith said. "There are some of our young men who—" he winked at Young, "—accompany state and federal officials about Nauvoo during their often annoying visits, whittling all the while."

"The whittling deacons as the papers have been calling them?" Grant inquired with a smile.

Smith winked at him this time. "So we feel quite safe actually in the face of threats of violence."

"I must go, Brother Joseph," Young said suddenly.

"I wish you godspeed, Brother Brigham. I trust the Lord will guide you in your important work."

Young shook hands with Grant again and then with Smith.

As he made his way across the lawn, Smith stood staring after him until he had disappeared around the side of the house. "Brother Brigham is going to our Eastern

Mission to oversee our work there. We have made a number of converts in the East. Some of them have come here to Nauvoo already and more are expected. The Heavenly City is growing, Mr. Grant, I can assure you. With every new soul that enters Zion, we grow in power and shall, before very long, be recognized as the bearers of the truth that shall light the way of the whole world.''

King of the Kingdom of God, Grant thought cynically. And then, not so cynically, he found himself wondering if this self-proclaimed prophet might indeed one day rule— but rule what? Perhaps the world, he thought. Or one of his own making. The thought alarmed him as he watched the faintly manic light in Smith's eyes smolder and then go out.

"I wonder, sir," he said, "if you can direct me to Miss Delano."

Smith, lost in his own thoughts, failed to answer.

Grant repeated his question and this time Smith replied, "Why, of course, Mr. Grant. She is staying with a fine Mormon family here in Nauvoo. Their name is Denton."

Grant listened carefully as Smith gave him directions to the Denton home and then he politely took his leave of Joseph Smith.

Judah lounged against the wall of his cabin, watching Virginia ride his horse back and forth in front of him.

"Don't turn him so sharp!" he yelled to her. "Ease up some on the reins or the bit'll cut his tongue to ribbons!"

The sun glinted on Virginia's blonde hair, which bounced brightly as she urged the horse from a trot to a gallop. Her eyes glowed and there was a smile on her face. She was wearing a pair of Judah's jeans and one of his shirts. On her feet was a pair of stout shoes.

She's a beauty, Judah thought. No question about it.

"Use your knees!" he yelled to her. "Hold onto him with them so's you don't bounce!"

He folded his arms, squinting into the sunlight as he watched her ride, thinking that he was a very fortunate man. She had stayed with him since that first visit and every one of their nights after that—and some of their days as well—had been spent delighting in the joy that their coupling brought to each of them.

But there was more.

Virginia, as the days passed, seemed to gradually shed the traces of her previous life in Saint Louis. She had changed, Judah thought, in small ways. He could see the changes in the clothes she now wore, clothes which paid no obeisance to fashion, but which, in fact, defied it. He liked the way she now wore her hair—loose and abandoned to the caress of the sun and the fingers of the wind.

She had taken to helping him in his fields without him having asked her to do so. She had hoed and weeded right beside him. She had bought calico in Nauvoo and sewed—not very skillfully, even he had discerned—a pair of curtains for his cabin's single window. At first, he had cooked the plain meals they shared, but then one day she had tried her hand at cooking. He recalled how the two of them had laughed together over the hardened yolks of the eggs she had fried, and the gummy rice she had boiled too long.

She had insisted then that he show her how to cook, and he had done so willingly.

She had learned all that he could teach her about cooking amid their shared laughter and his teasing—his swearing that he was losing weight and was slimming down to the size of a sapling.

But he had no illusions. It wouldn't last. He knew it wouldn't. It was just a new and very fine time in his life that would one day come to an end. He sometimes hoped that it wouldn't end, but he forced himself to see the situation he found himself in realistically. She was playing a new game. Learning a new way of life. But soon she would tire of the game, he knew, and she would remember Saint Louis and her luxurious home, parties, fine clothes, the attentions of men who would swarm around her once they learned that she was no longer pledged to Simon Grant.

One day soon he knew he would see shadows in her eyes, the ghosts of the thing she had left behind her. The shadows would deepen while he waited for the day when she would speak his name and tell him that it was over, when she would tell him that the game she had been playing had begun to bore her, and that she was going home where she belonged.

But until that day . . .

Judah smiled to himself. He was enjoying her presence and her eagerness to make love to him. He accepted her as little more than an opportunity not to be missed and never mind the fact that the opportunity would someday slip away from him. Until then he would take what she was willing to give and exult in the taking. It was, their being together like this, as much a game for him as it was for her, he realized.

We're like two children, he thought. We try to pretend that the sun won't set on us and let darkness come to end our game and send us scampering away to the separate lives we have to live.

Virginia turned the horse and headed toward Judah at a gallop. Just before she reached him, she reined in the big animal and stopped. She sat in the saddle, smiling down at him. "Did I do well?" she asked eagerly. "I think I did quite well, don't you?"

Judah gripped the horse's bridle and said, "You did

passable but you've still got a lot to learn about how to sit a horse. Oftentimes you looked like a sack of beans bouncing about up there in the saddle.''

Virginia pretended to pout. ''You just won't give me credit where credit is due. After all, I had never ridden a horse until I came here.''

''There's also one or two other things you never did till you came here,'' he said, grinning up at her.

She dropped the reins and clapped her hands. ''Oh, you're right! And isn't it wonderful that you were kind enough to teach me how to fry eggs and boil rice!''

''That wasn't exactly what I meant.''

She blew him a kiss. ''I know that, because I know now what you think about—and would *do* if you could—twenty-four-hours of each and every day.''

''With a fine figure of a woman like you about, how can you blame me?''

''Oh, Judah, I'm not blaming you!'' she cried happily. ''I'm not in the least. These past few weeks—they've been the happiest of my entire life!''

Judah thought of the fact that she had been a virgin that first time. It wasn't him, he believed, who had made her happy. It could have been any man who happened to have the good fortune to be able to introduce her to the pleasures of the flesh. No, he had no illusions about himself in relation to Virginia and the past few weeks they had spent together. The most he could hope for, the most he could reasonably expect, was that his luck would hold a little while longer before she grew restless and tired of him and the kind of hard life he led.

''. . . coming.''

''What? I didn't catch what you were saying.''

Virginia pointed in the direction of Nauvoo and said, ''Someone is coming. There—in that surrey.''

Judah stared at the approaching carriage. It was rare that he received visitors but it might be someone sent by the Prophet to summon him.

A man was driving the carriage and, Judah noted with annoyance, that he was using a whip to spur on the horse that was pulling the carriage.

"I don't believe it!" Virginia cried, still seated on Judah's horse. "I simply do not believe what I am seeing!"

It was at that moment that Judah recognized Simon Grant, who was whipping the horse mercilessly as the surrey came careening up to the cabin.

Grant reined in the horse and flung his whip aside. His hands, white-knuckled, remained on the reins. The horse snorted, saliva dripping from its lips and sweat covering its overheated body.

No one spoke.

It was Virginia who finally broke the silence by saying, "Well, Mr. Grant, what brings you here?"

Grant drew a deep breath, his eyes on her face. "I should think that the answer to your question, Virginia, would be perfectly obvious."

"A vacation?" she asked, and Judah almost grinned.

"Your father is very worried about you, Virginia."

"Father is such a dear. He will fret over me. He has done so ever since I can remember. Whatever is a woman to do with such a worrier?"

"The best thing to do," Grant said, "under the circumstances, it would seem to me, is for you to lay his worries to rest. You can do that by coming home with me, Virginia."

"Yes, I suppose that would put Father's mind at ease."

Judah felt himself tensing. Was this the moment that he had been expecting? Was this the day he would lose her?

Virginia said, "But I suppose a letter would accomplish the purpose just as well, don't you think so, Mr. Grant?"

"Please stop calling me 'Mr. Grant,' Virginia. My name is Simon."

"Would you carry a letter back to Father for me—Simon?"

"It is not a letter he wants. It's you."

"Father sent you to fetch me?"

Grant hesitated briefly before answering, "Yes."

Virginia laughed. To Judah, she said, "Let me give you fair warning. When two people get to know one another very well, each of them soon learns the peculiar habits of the other. The habits that sometimes betray one. So take care, Judah.

"Now Simon—when he is about to fib—he always hesitates first. Sometimes, I've noticed, he also swallows hard. Did you see Simon hesitate a moment just now before he said that Father had sent him to bring me home?"

Judah remained silent.

"Virginia," Grant said solemnly, "you have placed yourself in an untenable position. I spoke to Mr. Smith earlier today and he directed me to the Denton home, where, he informed me, you were staying. But, when I went there, Mrs. Denton told me that you had come here weeks ago, ostensibly on a visit, and that when her oldest boy returned to take you back to Nauvoo, you refused to go with him."

"That is all quite true, Simon."

"Mrs. Denton also told me that you had her son bring your personal belongings back here from the Denton house."

"That is also true."

"And now I come here and what do I find? I find you dressed like a man, your face dirty, your hair quite undone, and sitting astride a horse in a most unladylike fashion."

"You were always so observant, Simon."

"I should mention that Mrs. Denton asked me to tell you that you would not be welcome under her roof were you to leave here and try to return to her home. She told me that people in Nauvoo are talking about you and that she has always kept a respectable house so she would not be able to offer you lodging in the future."

"I am quite content here," Virginia declared. She dismounted and went to stand beside Judah. Taking his hand in hers, she said, "The two of us have been managing rather well. Judah is teaching me to ride and I have learned to plant corn and cultivate it. He has even had the patience to teach me to cook. Can you believe it, Simon? Me? A cook? Why, I never so much as brewed a cup of tea until I came here to visit Judah."

"*Visit!*" Grant roared, his face pale. "Visits generally do not last for a matter of weeks!"

"This one of mine has, as you now know."

"Please get into the surrey, Virginia. I'll send someone back later for your clothes."

"Simon, I am so glad that I decided not to marry you. I have never been at all good about taking orders. Especially when they are practically shouted at me. It would not have worked out, Simon. Surely you can see that now?"

"I see only that you have allowed yourself to be degraded by this—this roughneck." He did not look at Judah.

This time Judah did grin.

His grin widened as Virginia slipped her arm around his waist.

And then it faded. "Virginia," he said softly, "maybe you ought to go on back to see your father. Maybe—"

"You see, Virginia!" Grant said, having heard Judah's words. "Even this debaser of young women is not totally without good sense. Virginia, I'm *waiting!*"

Judah strode over to the surrey, reached up, seized a fistful of Grant's shirt, and hauled him down from the carriage.

"You got yourself a nasty mouth, mister," he muttered, backing Grant up against the surrey. "You go around calling other men bad names, well, you'd best be prepared to deal with them should they take it into their heads to rear up on their hind legs and take offense at your name-calling like I happen to be doing right this very minute."

"Release me. Release me at once!"

Judah shook Grant as if he were a disobedient puppy and Grant's head bobbed wildly back and forth. The chimney pot hat he had been wearing fell to the ground.

"Virginia!" Judah said. "You intend going away with Grant?"

"Of course not," she answered from behind him.

"You heard her, Grant. She's not going off with you so it's high time, I figure, for you to git!"

Grant reached behind him, seized the leather whip he had dropped earlier, and brought it slashing down across Judah's face.

A thin red welt appeared on Judah's cheek where the whip had struck him.

Grant took advantage of Judah's shock, throwing a fumbling fist which glanced harmlessly off Bascomb's jaw.

Without loosening his grip on Grant's shirt, Judah muttered, "I've been hit harder by hailstones." Then he abruptly released Grant and, at the same time, delivered a right uppercut that landed on Grant's chin, snapping his head backward. He followed it up with a left jab which plunged into Grant's mid-section, doubling the man over.

Grant gagged, dropped his whip, and clutched his stomach with both hands.

"Your turn, mister," Judah said to him.

Grant slowly straightened up. Blinking at Judah, he said, "I don't know what you've done to her but—"

"Haven't done anything to hold her here by force, if that happens to be what you're getting at. She's free to leave whenever she wants to go."

"Virginia!" Grant called out weakly. "Surely you can't prefer—"

Virginia hurried up to stand facing Grant. "Go home, Simon. Judah's hurt you and I'm sorry about that. I'm sorry too that you came here. I know it must be hard for you to accept things the way they are. Especially after you and I—after we thought we were so happy together."

"We were happy! *I* was!"

"And I thought I was. But things have changed radically, as you can clearly see. *I've* changed radically. I'm not sure whether it is for the better or the worse but there is no point in denying that it has happened. I would ask you to forgive me, Simon, but I honestly don't feel that there is anything to forgive. Please try to understand, and please don't think too harshly of me."

"Get up there and get going!" Judah ordered Grant, pointing to the surrey.

Grant backed away from him, one hand rubbing his chin where Judah's fist had landed. He climbed up onto the surrey's seat and picked up the reins.

"You've made a mistake, Virginia," he told her bitterly. "It's not too late to rectify it. I will ask you just once more. Please come with me."

Virginia shook her head.

"You," Grant said to Judah, "have also made a mistake. One *I* will rectify!"

As he drove away, leaving his hat and whip behind him, Virginia sighed and said, "Poor Simon."

"To hell with him!"

"Judah!" she exclaimed, pretending to be shocked. And then, after a moment, "I do feel sorry for him. I suppose I've wronged him." She paused and then, without looking at Judah, said, "Shall I tell you a secret?"

"You want to, tell it."

"You sound so disgruntled. I'd better not."

"Suit yourself."

Virginia caught Judah's arm as he was about to walk away from her. "That night—when Simon happened upon us in the sitting room. He infuriated me—his whole righteous attitude did. I determined then and there to teach him a lesson. I made up my mind to say that I wouldn't marry him. Then, next morning, I decided I would come to Nauvoo, knowing he would think it was because of you. Well, it wasn't."

"It wasn't? You real sure about that?"

"All right. Yes, it was partly because of you."

"Figured as much. The way you eyed me when you opened your front door that night—well, I figured you were a bit taken with me."

"How dare you!"

"It's the truth, isn't it?"

"Yes, it's the truth, but you needn't act so smug about it."

Judah hugged her.

She continued, "I wanted to make Simon jealous. In time, I intended to return and marry him. When I was sure he had been chastened by my actions and had learned his lesson."

"What's this secret you were going to tell me?"

"Why, I've just told it to you!"

"Hell, honey, what you just told me, that was no secret. I had you figured out on that score right from the start."

"You didn't!"

"Did."

"Judah Bascomb, you are an insufferable and insolent man!"

"I'm more a matter-of-fact kind of man, the way I see it."

"You let me make a fool of myself!"

"Did you feel like a fool our first night together?"

"No, but—"

"You've felt like a fool since?"

"No, but—"

"A man like me and a woman like you—well, when two such as us get together, things are just about bound and determined to change for each of us."

"Have things changed for you since I came here?"

"They started changing when I first set eyes on you."

"How have they changed?"

"I was pretty much my own man up till then. But since then—" He was silent for a moment. "I'm not so sure I could make do with just myself to look after now."

It was Virginia's turn to hug Judah. "I feel exactly the way you do. I never needed anyone before either, not really. "That's what you were trying to say, wasn't it?"

"Reckon it was."

"But I need someone now, Judah. I need you."

"I'm real glad things have worked out like they did."

"In fact," Virginia said thoughtfully, as they stood with their arms around one another, "I think I'm learning to love you, Judah Bascomb."

Judah, looking into her eyes and, feeling her so close to him, knew that the time had come for him to say what he had never before said to any woman. "I learned weeks ago how to love you, Virginia, only I wouldn't let on to myself on account of I figured you'd be leaving here—me—one of these days. I thought I'd best keep my mouth shut tight

and not say anything that might make you think I was
trying to tie you to me.''

"I do believe I've been tied to you since the first
moment I saw you. Certainly since our first night together
in the cabin.''

"I'm real glad about that,'' Judah said sincerely.

"So am I,'' Virginia said as sincerely.

FIVE

AFTER returning from his visit to Virginia and Judah, Simon Grant sat in his hotel room and fumed.

He had failed in his mission.

No, he corrected himself, not failed. He had merely lost one battle in what he swore to himself would be a continuing war with Judah Bascomb. The victor in that war would win Virginia. Grant made up his mind to be the ultimate victor. Meanwhile, he would bide his time until the right moment for revenge was at hand.

He was not a poor man but he was a man who wanted to

be more than just not poor. He wanted to be rich. Very rich. Virginia—and the Delano fortune that would one day be hers—would make him very rich.

He considered strategies and made plans.

He would not return to Saint Louis. He had to remain here in Nauvoo. He would undoubtedly lose his job with Astor's American Fur Company as a result but that was only a short-term loss, a sacrifice he had to make in the hope of winning a far greater gain over the long term.

He wrote to the company and resigned.

Then, as he walked the streets of Nauvoo, he pondered his next move. He considered telling Smith about the illicit relationship which existed between Judah and Virginia. But he rejected that plan—for the present. He would tell Smith in time—when the time was right. He suspected that Smith might already know about what was going on between the two, but he decided that he would, at some future date, force Smith to act against them in the interest of stamping out sin.

He chuckled to himself. Sin? If the rumors that were rampant about Smith and other authorities of the Latter-day Saints were true, and Grant suspected they were, then Smith was little more, in his opinion, than a rogue. He was masking his concupiscence under the guise of "celestial marriage." Grant doubted that the marriages Smith was rumored to have made were entirely spiritual, as the Prophet was said to have claimed on more than one occasion.

Grant spent days talking to both Mormons and Gentiles in Nauvoo, listening carefully, learning as much as he could, probing, gathering information about the church, about Smith, and about those who were growing increasingly opposed to the Prophet and his often autocratic actions.

He learned much, and a great deal of what he learned

would be, he knew, helpful to him as he plotted to destroy the relationship that now existed between Judah and Virginia.

Less than a week after arriving in Nauvoo, he paid a second visit to Smith and was met at the door by the same sour-faced woman he had met on his first visit. She was, he learned that day, Smith's wife, Emma. It wasn't long before Grant guessed correctly that Emma's sour expression came from her attitude toward her husband's many secret marriages with which she was familiar. They were, Grant learned, a thorn in the woman's side, although she had tried to convince herself that they had resulted from her husband's having received a Divine Order to establish the practice of polygamy among the Saints.

"I hear you've been having trouble with the work force building the Temple and Nauvoo House," Grant said to Smith as the two men sat sipping tea in the dim parlor of Smith's house.

"It's because of Bill Law and Bob Foster," Smith said, nodding. "They've been rafting lumber down the river from Wisconsin and they've set themselves up as private contractors. They're luring my workers away."

"You could get them back easily enough. Instead of paying them in redeemable scrip and supplies as you have been doing, you could pay them wages as Law and Foster are doing."

"I won't do it. It is not our way."

"Your refusal means, as you must know, that the Temple will not be built on schedule. Nor will Nauvoo House."

Smith looked glum but resolute.

"I'll see if I can help to change the situation, if that's all right with you," Grant said.

"Why would you want to do that, Mr. Grant?"

"Because of my sympathy toward your goals and aspirations," Grant answered. "I hate to see them thwarted, and I thought I might be of some help to you in the matter.''

When Grant left Smith's house with the Prophet's enthusiastically expressed gratitude echoing in his ears, he went directly to the waterfront where, he had learned, many less than respectable activities took place. Counterfeiting was one of those activities he had been told of by one of the sympathizers of the dissident Morman John Bennett.

In a saloon, Grant ordered whiskey and spoke to the bartender about the weather.

The bartender listlessly agreed that it had been an unusually hot spring.

"Things are heating up in Nauvoo," Grant commented, "and it's not just because of the weather."

"Trouble's brewing," the bartender agreed. "The Prophet's going to have both of his hands full of it before long. He's made enemies not just among us non-Mormons but among a lot of his own people too. Mark my words. He's asked for trouble and he's going to get it."

"Well, I for one am going to give him all I can," Grant said vehemently, downing his drink.

"He's caused you grief, has he?" the bartender asked as he refilled Grant's empty glass.

Grant began to tell the bartender the lie he had rehearsed in his mind. "One of his Mormons has been trying to convert my sister. He proposed marriage to her. A man named William Law who happens to be married already."

The bartender laughed jovially. "Sorry, I didn't mean to mock your trouble. But the Prophet did the same thing with Bill Law's wife, Jane."

"I heard something about that. Law's been excommunicated from the Church, hasn't he?"

"Him and his wife both. That was Smith's doing."

"I wish there was some way I could get revenge on Law," Grant muttered.

"Why don't you join some of the boys on their next raid? Might be you could lead them to Law."

Grant's eyes brightened and he leaned over the bar toward the bartender. "I would—I want to—but I don't know any of the men who have been raiding the Mormon's homes and businesses. Listen, will you help me? Will you tell me how I can get to know them? I want to avenge the insult Law gave my wife—and me."

The bartender hesitated, studying Grant. "I don't know you from Adam, mister."

Grant let his shoulders slump. "I hoped you could help me."

The bartender stroked his chin for a second before saying, "I guess it wouldn't do you any harm to talk to Ralph Kane."

"Where can I find him?"

"That's him sitting over there. On the bench next to the door."

Grant thanked the bartender profusely and went over to where Kane was sitting. "Excuse me," he said. "The bartender told me your name. May I sit down, Mr. Kane?"

Kane was unshaven and wore the clothes of a riverman. His eyes were faintly bloodshot and his nose looked as if it had been broken at some time in the past. His fat lips parted and he said, "This here's a public place."

Grant sat down beside him and told him the same story he had just told the bartender. When he had finished, he added, "I'd pay you well to hire men who could do damage to Law."

"What kind of damage?"

"Law's getting rich in Nauvoo as a private contractor. If he couldn't get lumber, he wouldn't be so rich. He'd be out of business fast. Maybe then he wouldn't have the wherewithal to go around proposing to young women like my sister.''

Grant went on to tell Kane about the lumber Law was rafting down from Wisconsin to Nauvoo. ''If that lumber of his were to be destroyed—'' He watched Kane's face. The man's expression remained impassive. ''I'd pay fifty dollars to have Law's lumber burned and his scows scuttled.''

He took out his wallet and counted out fifty dollars which he placed on the bench between himself and Kane.

Kane's eyes were drawn to the money. ''How do you know you can trust me?'' he asked. ''I might just take this money and you might never see me again.''

''Yes, you might do that. But it would not be wise for you to do so.''

''No?'' Kane's eyes glinted. ''Why not?''

''Because then you would not receive the other fifty dollars I intend to give you when you complete the job I just mentioned.''

''Another fifty dollars?''

''That's right, Mr. Kane. Another fifty dollars. And another hundred after that for another task I have in mind and which you may want to execute for me. There is a man named Judah Bascomb I want eliminated.''

Kane picked up the money and pocketed it. Without another word to Grant, he rose and left the saloon.

A month later, Judah left Smith's house, rage seething within him, and leaped astride his horse which had been tethered to a fence post outside. He dug his heels into the animal's flanks and galloped down the street, across the parade ground, and along the bank of the river.

He was still in a rage when he reached his cabin. He

dismounted and, leaving the reins trailing to keep his horse from wandering off, he stormed into the cabin.

Virginia, who was bent over a kettle that was suspended in the fireplace, straightened up. "What's wrong?" she asked when she saw the expression on his face.

Instead of answering her, he tore his hat from his head and flung it across the room. It hit the wall and fell to the floor.

Virginia placed her hands on her hips after dropping the dish cloth she had been holding and said, "Judah, tell me what's wrong."

He sat down at the table and slammed a fist down upon it. "The Prophet no longer has any use 'for my services,' as he put it. He's hired himself a new bodyguard. A man named Kane. And Kane isn't even one of us—he's a Gentile."

"So am I," Virginia said as she sat down at the table opposite Judah.

He ignored her comment. "It's Grant. Grant's behind this."

"He's still in Nauvoo?"

"Yes, and he's been a very busy man during the past month, Simon Grant has."

"What do you mean?"

"I told you how he got Brother Joseph to baptize him. That was the first step. I don't know how he did it, but the fact is he did do it. Brother Joseph will take any convert to the faith he can get these days, I guess. Anyway, after he got himself baptized, Grant started hanging around Brother Joseph. I tell you, it's got so he can twist the Prophet around his little finger as easy as if he were a piece of twine!

"Next thing I knew, Grant was a member of the Aaronite priesthood. That didn't much surprise me seeing as how

Honey, _____ the Church.
Belonging to it's just about the most important thing in my life outside of you. It really is." Judah's fists dissolved and he clasped Virginia's hands. "I was next to nothing til I joined the Church. I believe in it. It's what keeps getting up in the mornings and going on day after day. given me a place to belong and a people to belong to. I want to go back to living the way I did before I it. It was a lonely way to live. A man needs g that matters a whole lot to him. He really does

most every grown Mormon man is a member. But what did surprise me is how Brother Joseph went and took him into the Melchizedek priesthood just as if he'd been a devout Mormon for a whole lot of years.''

"Judah, are you jealous of Simon?"

"*No*," of course I'm not!"

"You have no reason to be jealous of him, you know. At least, not where I'm concerned, you don't."

"There's talk in town. There's folks who say Grant hangs out with a bad crowd—some of the river rats that're to be found down in the saloons along the waterfront. They're saying he got some of his new friends to burn Bill Law's lumber yard and sink the boats he was using to raft his lumber downriver."

"Who is Bill Law?"

Judah told her. "There's been bad blood between Law and Brother Joseph for some time now. Law claims the Prophet's been siphoning off some of the tithing money that's supposed to go for building the Temple and Nauvoo House. They say he used the money to finance his own personal land speculations."

"Did he?"

"I don't know. But what I do know is that Brother Joseph seems mighty pleased that Law and his partner, Foster, are on the verge of failing in their contracting business. Now, they were doing just fine even with Brother Joseph trying to get control of all construction going on in Nauvoo—both public and private. Well, he's got control of most of it now, since somebody's just about put Law and Foster out of business."

"And you think Simon has something to do with it?"

"I told you there's talk in town. I wouldn't put it past Grant. I can't think of anybody else who'd want to fire that lumberyard or chop holes in those boats."

did for him.

"I have an idea!" Virginia cried. "We'll Saint Louis!"

Judah, who had been staring at the looked up at her and frowned. "Wh do there?"

"Why—why, we would—.''

"You see? We couldn't liv way we live here in mine."

"Perhaps he could find you a po

"I can't believe Simon would do such a thing. You said yourself that he and Brother Joseph are very close. Which would mean that—"

"Kane."

Virginia looked puzzled.

"Kane was fired from one steamboat after another on account of drunkenness and brawling. Now Grant brings him in to take my place as the Prophet's bodyguard and Brother Joseph goes right along with the idea. I wouldn't put it past Kane to have done the dirty business against Law and Foster. I'd bet Grant paid him to do it so's he could get in real good with Brother Joseph."

"But Brother Joseph would never allow such a thing to happen!"

"He wouldn't if he knew about it. Maybe he didn't. I'll tell you something else. Brother Joseph told me that Grant's temporarily taking Brother Brigham Young's place in the quorum of the Twelve Apostles while Brother Brigham's off doing missionary work. I don't like it one bit. I think Grant will bear watching. He's as slick as spring ice."

Virginia reached across the table and placed her hands over Judah's clenched fists. "You can find another job."

"Maybe. Fact is, I got to. I don't have any money saved. Brother Joseph always paid me in scrip for what I his business. I know he could! He's always in need of good deckhands for his steamboats.''

"You'd live at home while I went traveling back and forth along the Missouri river, is that it?''

Virginia looked up and said, "Well, we have to do something, don't we?''

"We do, thanks to your Mr. Grant.''

"He is not *my* Mr. Grant.''

"Something else happened in Nauvoo.''

"What happened?''

"Brother Joseph told me I ought to stop living in sin. He said the way we're living here together, it adds fuel to the fire that men like Bennett are setting in the newspapers to discredit us Mormons. He told me either I put you out or he might have to excommunicate me.''

"What does that mean?''

"Cut me off from the Church.''

"Oh, Judah!''

"He said Grant told him you and me were a disgrace to every decent Mormon.''

Virginia's eyes flashed. "Oh, he did, did he? Well, I think I will just go into town and have a talk with Simon Grant. I will not let him tell me how to live—or you either!''

"Honey, I don't want to be thrown out of the Church

if he's not to die a little bit every day, if he's not to die inch by awful inch.''

"I understand," Virginia said quietly. "Judah, do you want me to leave you?"

"God, no!" he cried, squeezing his eyes shut as if he were in pain. "Once—back when I was sure you were going to go off just about any minute—I was braced for it the way a man braces himself for a fall off a bucking bronc. But then—when you said the things you did to me—and when I let myself admit what I wanted—what I needed so bad—I mean you, Virginia, well, I confess I just don't know what a man's supposed to do in a spot like I've gone and got myself into.''

"If you're right in your theory about Simon—in believing that he has caused Brother Joseph to order us to separate—Judah, things may not be nearly as bad as they look at the moment.''

"What do you mean? I don't want you to leave me and I don't want to go to Saint Louis with you and I don't want to be excommunicated and—''

Virginia placed a finger on his lips. "We could be married.''

"Married!''

"Men and women do, upon occasion, marry one another.''

"But—''

"But what?''

"You'd—you would really be sealed with *me*?''

"Of course I would. Gladly!''

"Your father—''

"My father has nothing to do with this. I am capable of making up my own mind and of living my own life in whatever fashion I happen to choose, as you well know.''

Judah rose and began to pace the room, his hands thrust

into his pockets, his head lowered. "I have to say that I'm real proud to hear you say you'd marry me. I mean I'm humbled, as a matter of plain fact. But I always thought I'd marry a woman of my faith and you—what religion do you belong to, honey?"

"None. Oh, we went to one church or another most of my life. But I was never really committed to a single one of them. I'll become a Saint, that's what I'll do!" Virginia giggled, a hand flying up to cover her mouth the moment she did so. "Won't that surprise Simon and Brother Joseph? I'll be baptized and turn from sinner to Saint during my total immersion."

"Don't mock."

"I'm not mocking anyone or anything," she said seriously. "But I do have a sense of humor, Judah. Can't you see the funny side of all this and of the way it's working out?"

He grinned. "Well, I guess I can at that." He paused thoughtfully. "But that won't solve the problem of me not having a job to support the two of us."

"The three of us."

"What do you mean, the three of us? There's only— Honey? You're not—are you—"

"I think so. Yes, I think I'm pregnant."

"Great day of glory!" Judah whooped. He slapped his thighs and whooped again. He threw back his head and let out a happy howl.

"Stop it, Judah! You'll bring the Nauvoo Legion down on us! They'll think we're the victims of one of those terrible wolf packs because of all the noise you're making."

"Your people, too—real soon." Judah pulled her to her feet and embraced her. Then he let his right hand slide down her body and come to rest on her flat stomach. "A baby," he whispered, awe in his tone. "*Our* baby."

"I didn't intend to tell you so soon, but with the way things have so suddenly changed and because of what we've decided to do, I thought it best to tell you now. But first, Judah, I wanted to be sure you didn't want me to simply leave you. I wouldn't have tried to hold you because of the baby. I'd go away and have it somewhere—there are homes where women can go until their babies are born—and then I'd take up my life again."

Judah drew back and looked down into her eyes. "I never had much schooling. I know you know that words don't come easy to me but I wish I could tell you that you're wonderful and about how much I love you and how I like the touch of you, and the way your eyes—"

"Judah."

"What?"

"You've just told me."

"Damn, if I haven't at that!" he yelped and then, releasing Virginia, he let out a whoop of pure delight, throwing his hands high into the air as if he were reaching for the moon, his heart leaping wildly within him.

The following day in his home in Nauvoo, Smith celebrated a victory with Simon Grant by falling to his knees and crying out his gratitude to the Lord.

Grant, kneeling in the parlor beside Smith with his head bowed, murmured "amen" when Smith had finally finished his almost festive praying.

As both men got to their feet, Grant held out a hand and, as Smith clasped it firmly, said, "Congratulations, Brother Smith. I knew your candidacy would be successful and now that the nominating convention has chosen you to run for the Presidency of the United States, I see only big things ahead for you."

"I owe much of my success to you, Brother Simon.

You wrote my campaign speeches. You were absolutely tireless in your efforts on my behalf—speaking engagements, arranging for the printing of the posters, seeing to it that our voters came out in goodly numbers—I am deeply indebted to you.''

''I did it not only for you personally, Brother Smith,'' Grant said piously, ''but for the greater glory of God as well. It is time that this country was governed as a theocracy. You have amply demonstrated your ability to govern in your position as Mayor of Nauvoo. As President, you will be able to turn this country away from evil and toward truth and goodness.''

''I hope to have the opportunity to try, certainly. But you know that there are those violently opposed to me and my platform. They talk of me as a creature of the Evil One, a man who permits holy murders by our Sons of Dan, and even worse abominations. I wonder if I dare persevere in my campaign for the Presidency. I have prayed long and often over the matter. At times, it seems to me that my course of action will serve only to bring down the wrath of the Gentiles upon the heads of our people in even more calamitous fashion that has been the case hitherto. But, as President of this country, I would have the power to do great things. For Morman and Gentile alike.''

''You must persevere, Brother Joseph. To do otherwise would be a betrayal of your divinely designaged role as Prophet and revelator.''

''Yes, that is so.''

Grant cleared his throat and then said, ''Presidential campaigns cost money, as you know. Should we not level a tax on the Saints in addition to the tithes they now pay? Most of our people, I'm certain, would be willing to pay such a tax in order to see you elected President.''

''Perhaps. But I believe we should delay the imposition

of any such tax for now. There is money currently available to us. I have been not unsuccessful in land speculation and then there are, in addition, the funds we have collected from the people to build the Temple and Nauvoo House which I think it proper to borrow on a strictly temporary basis. The money can readily be replaced later.''

Grant didn't ask how the money could be replaced. Instead, he said, ''I think we should—''

He was interrupted by the sound of the parlor door opening.

''Yes, Emma?'' Smith said to his wife who was standing grim-faced in the doorway.

''There is someone here to see you, Joseph. That woman.''

''What woman, Emma?''

''That harlot I have told you about time and time again. The one who has been corrupting Judah Bascomb.''

''She is here?''

Emma nodded, her lips twisted in distaste. ''Shall I send her away?''

''By no means, my dear. Show her in.''

''But Joseph—''

Smith held up a hand. ''Remember Magdalen, Emma. Our Lord did not scorn her nor will I scorn Miss Delano.''

''Wait!'' Grant said as Emma started to leave. Then, to Smith, he said, ''I have something to discuss with you. It is important and it concerns Miss Delano.''

''Must it be now, Brother Simon?''

''Now.''

''Close the door, Emma, and please ask Miss Delano to wait.''

When the door had been closed, Grant said, ''You yourself, Brother Joseph, have spoken of the charges leveled against you personally and the church generally. Among them, as you are well aware, are the ones denouncing the Mormons as sexual perverts.''

''But that charge is based on a misunderstanding of the revelation I received concerning multiple marriage.''

''We know that. But our detractors use the revelation to condemn us. Now that you are about to run for election to this nation's highest office, you cannot afford to have such charges continually bandied about. So, I submit to you, the flagrant behavior of Miss Delano and Bascomb should be openly denounced.''

''What would you have me do?''

''Excommunicate Bascomb immediately as we've discussed. Order Miss Delano to leave Nauvoo. As mayor of the city, you can charge her with disorderly conduct based on her scandalous relationship with Judah Bascomb. You can declare her a public nuisance. By so doing, you will have effectively countered—in part, at least—the charges being made against us.''

''I have a deep affection for Brother Bascomb,'' Smith said pensively. ''I have been sorrowing over his wayward behavior of late. Because of his sinful fornicating he will not, after the resurrection, be able to enter either the celestial or terrestial kingdoms but will be confined for eternity to the telestial kingdom. I have been hoping that he will mend his sinful ways before it is too late. As far as Miss Delano is concerned—Brother Simon, let us hear why she has come to see me and what she has to say. Perhaps she has repented. In any event, let us listen to her. Afterward, we shall decide what, if anything, is to be done about the situation.

Grant, frustrated in his effort to separate Virginia and Judah, pressed his lips together as Smith went to the door, opened it, and said, ''Miss Delano, do come in. I am sorry to have kept you waiting.''

As Virginia entered the parlor, she noticed Grant standing near the fireplace. She turned back to Smith, who was closing the door behind her.

"I didn't realize you were engaged, Mr. Smith. Mrs. Smith did not tell me that you were busy. I shall return another time."

"You know Mr. Grant, Miss Delano," Smith said smoothly. "Perhaps you also know how important he has become to me recently. Do sit down, won't you?"

Virginia cast a glance in Grant's direction and then seated herself.

"I have no secrets from Brother Simon," Smith told her. "But if you would prefer to talk to me alone—"

A faint smile ghosted across Virginia's face and then was gone. "I want to be baptized, Mr. Smith. I want to join your church."

"Well, now," Smith temporized, staring at her. "This comes as something of a surprise."

Grant said, "Brother Joseph, I trust you will remember our conversation of a moment ago."

"I remember it. But all of us are human. We stumble on the path of righteousness and sometimes we stray far from it. But, as human beings possessed of free will, we always have the opportunity to rectify our lives."

Virginia felt herself blushing and silently wished for a patience she had never possessed. "Will you take me into the Church?" she asked Smith bluntly, boldly meeting his steady gaze.

"Of course, my dear. We have been gathering converts all over the world. We will happily gather you along with the others who want to join our flock."

"Thank you," Virginia said and then added, "After I've been baptized, I want to be married—Judah calls it sealed."

"To whom, my dear?" Smith inquired.

"Why, to Judah, of course."

Smith, beaming, turned toward Grant. "The Lord has cast down His light and made smooth our path. The—uh, problem we spoke of earlier—it seems to have solved itself. Quite wonderfully too, wouldn't you agree, Brother Simon?"

"I would not!"

"Stupid of me," Smith murmured. "I had quite forgotten for the moment that you had once been planning to marry Miss Delano yourself, Brother Simon."

"No longer!" Grant exclaimed. "I would not sully my own reputation by becoming sealed to a woman who so obviously values her own reputation not at all, if one is to judge by her recent scandalous behavior."

"That will be quite enough, Brother Simon!" Smith said sharply. "We can exhort our brothers and sisters. We can point out the path of righteousness to them when they have wandered from it. We dare not take it upon ourselves to condemn the wayward. Our Lord Himself would not cast the first stone. Nor should any of us, who regrettably are also poor sinners, dare to cast it."

Virginia couldn't help herself. She jumped to her feet and threw her arms around Smith's neck. "Oh, thank you! You are very kind!" She kissed him on the cheek.

Embarrassed, Smith disengaged himself from Virginia's embrace. "You certainly are an impulsive young woman, Miss Delano."

"I'm sorry."

Smith smiled and said, "Don't be. I find impulsive young women most charming. I find you most charming, Miss Delano."

"When can I be baptized? And mar—sealed to Judah?"

"All in due course. All in the Lord's own good time."

"I want to be sealed as soon as possible," Virginia announced eagerly.

"And to be baptized as soon as possible?"

"Oh, yes—as I've said."

"Does Judah share your enthusiasm?"

"Yes, decidedly."

"Then why did he not come here with you today?"

"He didn't think it would be necessary to do so and he had work to do in the fields. But if you want to see him as well as myself, I could have him come here—we could both come here."

"First things first," Smith said, smiling. "Your baptism must come first. Then you and I and Judah can sit down and talk about your ceremony of sealing."

"Excuse me," Grant said, heading for the door. "I have matters to attend to."

"Very well," Smith said absently, his eyes on Virginia. "Miss Delano, may I explain the rite of baptism to you, so that you will fully understand the responsibilities you are assuming by joining the Church of Jesus Christ of Latter-day Saints?"

"Yes, please do," Virginia said as Grant left the room, closing the door behind him. Smith sat down in the chair by her side.

Outside, Grant found Kane lounging on the front porch. "Kane," he said, "I've got a job for you."

"What kind of job?"

"I told you the day we met that I wanted Judah Bascomb eliminated. Go out to his farm. He's there now. Take a gun with you. Bring him back here."

"Where exactly?"

"Tie him up in Beecher's warehouse on the river."

"What're you planning to do to him?"

"Teach him a lesson. One he'll not easily forget."

"Why?"

"He has what I want and the time has finally come for me to take it away from him."

SIX

JUDAH, in the forest that bordered his fields, swung his axe to cut slender branches from an aspen. As the branches began to pile up at his feet, he moved on to the next tree, hacking branches from it as well. When he decided he had cut enough of them, he bound them into a large bundle with twine he took from a pocket of his jeans and then whistled for his horse.

As the animal trotted up to him, he stepped into the saddle and rode out of the forest, dragging the bundle of branches along the ground behind him.

He halted the horse at the edge of his southernmost field, which he and Virginia had planted with peas and string beans and dismounted. Leaving the horse to idly crop the lush spring grass, he dragged the branches into the middle of the field and used them to build wide-based tripods which he lashed together where they met at each tripod's apex. After finishing each tripod, he carefully arranged the sprouting vines around the ends of the branches which rested on the ground so that the vines would be able to climb the tripods.

He knew he would lose a part of his crop. Racoons would invade the field and clumsily climb the tripods to feast. Birds—meadowlarks and crows mostly—would perch on the angled branches and fill themselves with tasty young peas and then turn their attention to the young beans.

The knowledge that his fields would soon be invaded by thieves didn't bother him. Neither did the hot May sun which was causing sweat to slide down his face and body, because he was happy and a happy man is not bothered by such trifles. Ever since Virginia had agreed to be sealed to him—and only then had told him that she would, in the months to come bear his child—nothing had bothered him. He had gone through his days whistling or singing the old songs he had learned on the Staked Plains when he had often sung cattle to sleep.

He took off his hat and wiped the sweat from his face with the back of his hand. He looked up at the sun. Late afternoon, judging by the sun's position in the sky. She'll be coming home soon, he thought, and glanced to the north. But Virginia was not yet in sight.

As he clapped his hat back on his head, he saw the rider in the distance. A neighbor? He shaded his eyes with his hand and squinted. As the rider came closer to him, skirting the edge of the forest, he recognized Ralph Kane.

He stiffened. He didn't like Kane. Not just because Kane had replaced him as the Prophet's bodyguard. There was something about Kane—the way his eyes darted, never still, always nervous. The man always seemed about to bolt, and he had always found that such men had something or someone to fear, and that made them mean both to man and beast.

Kane reined in his horse some distance from Judah. He looked out over the fields and then turned his head to peer into the dim depths of the forest. Only then did he move his horse forward again, heading slowly toward Judah, his head turning from side to side as he rode as if he were searching for something.

"You got a horse?" he barked as he neared Judah.

The question took Judah by surprise. What did it mean? What was Kane after?

"I asked you whether you got a horse."

"Miss Delano took my horse." Judah decided to provide no further information. Not until he knew exactly what Kane had on his mind.

The pistol appeared in Kane's hand as if by an act of magic. He must have had it, Judah thought as he stared at its barrel, stuck in his waistband under his vest.

"What are you pointing that gun at me for?" he asked, letting his gaze rise until he was staring directly into Kane's cold eyes.

Kane didn't bother to answer the question. He got out of the saddle and gestured with his pistol. "Get up there in that saddle," he ordered Judah. "I'll ride behind you."

"Where're you bent on taking me?"

"Never mind. Just climb aboard."

Judah decided to dispense with questions. He was sure

Kane would give him no satisfactory answers. He moved toward Kane slowly and, as he did so, Kane backed away from him and the horse.

Judah, after a quick glance over his shoulder at Kane, rammed his left boot into the saddle's stirrup. Then he suddenly seized a fistful of the horse's mane and pulled hard, causing the animal to veer in a circle. It snorted its pain and tossed its head as he succeeded in placing the horse between himself and Kane.

"Damn you, Bascomb!" Kane bellowed.

Judah ducked down behind the horse and grabbed its bridle. He pushed the horse's head and, at the same time, slapped its rump with his other hand, forcing it toward Kane.

But Kane leaped backward as the horse came toward him, side-stepping fast, and managing to get Judah in the open. "No more tricks!" he yelled. You get up there in that saddle or I'll shoot your ass off, mister! Maybe something more important than your ass. *You hear me?*"

Judah paused, then climbed into the saddle. He briefly considered making a run for it, but gave up the idea. Kane would be able to down him before he could reach the shelter of the forest.

He eased forward in the saddle as far as he could when Kane climbed up behind him. He felt the muzzle of the pistol come to rest against his ribs. He smelled the sour stench of Kane's body and the reek of the man's breath.

"Now you get yourself a good grip on the reins and you move us out, Bascomb. You try anything, you'll be deader'n a doornail."

"Where you taking me, Kane?"

"Not far. To Beecher's warehouse on the river."

"Why?"

Kane jammed the barrel of his pistol against Judah's back.

Judah clucked to Kane's horse and it moved out. He turned it and headed northwest.

They rode in silence for several minutes before Judah commented, "A man carries a gun, he ought to know he could get himself killed should he happen to meet up with another man whose also got himself a gun."

"You got no gun, Bascomb."

"Not at the moment I don't."

The silence returned to ride with them.

When the river came into sight in the distance ten minutes later, Kane said, "Keep south of the town. We don't want to be seen."

"Maybe you don't but I sure wouldn't mind being seen by somebody likely to lend me a hand."

"There's Beecher's warehouse. Cut across the parade ground and head for it."

Judah did, his eyes on the huge building which had once housed goods brought by steamboat to Nauvoo, but which now was abandoned because its owner, Stowe Beecher, had died several years ago. Now merchants used the newer warehouses which had been built farther north along the waterfront by Law's and Foster's construction firm.

Less than ten minutes later, they reached the building and, as they did, Kane slid out of the saddle and opened the big door, gesturing for Judah to ride into the interior of the building.

Judah did and Kane closed the door behind him and swung the heavy bar into place to lock it.

"Get down, Bascomb!"

Judah dismounted.

"Back yourself up against one of those uprights," Kane ordered, referring to the heavy timbers that ran in two long evenly spaced lines through the warehouse to support the roof.

When Judah had done so, Kane ordered him to place his hands behind the timber and Judah did. Kane took a coil of rope that had been tied to his saddle horn and walked around behind the upright.

"Clamp your wrists together, Bascomb. And don't move so much as a whisker or I'll shoot you down like a broken-legged dog."

Judah felt his wrists being tied together. Moments later, Kane walked around in front of him and said, "Open up your mouth."

"What for?"

Kane slammed the barrel of his pistol against the side of Judah's head. "You gonna open up now?"

As the blood began to flow from Judah's temple, he opened his mouth and Kane pulled a filthy checkered handkerchief from his pocket and rammed into into Judah's mouth, almost choking him in the process.

Then he went to his horse, unbarred the door, and went outside, closing the door behind him.

Judah strained to separate his wrists into which the rope was biting but he couldn't because the rope bound them too tightly. He tried to push the gag from his mouth with his tongue but discovered that the gag prevented him from moving his tongue at all.

He looked up at the ceiling. He could see the sky through several gaping holes in it. He glanced to the left at the huge bins and then at the vertical rows of shelves on his right.

He looked down at the dirt floor and kicked at it with his feet. It took him only moments to realize that his idea wouldn't work. The upright had been set far too deeply into the earth for him to hope to dislodge it merely by kicking away at the dirt surrounding its base.

Trapped, he thought. But why? he wondered. Why had Kane come for him? What did the man intend to do with him?

He leaned back against the upright, tilting his head to the side in order to keep the blood that was flowing freely from the wound in his temple from running into his eyes.

It was dark when Judah heard the sound of footsteps outside the warehouse.

A moment later, the door to the building swung open and Kane, a flickering lantern held high above his head, entered the warehouse. Behind him, Judah saw the figure of another man and as the pair moved toward him, he was surprised to find that the second man, revealed in the light of Kane's lantern, was Simon Grant.

"Here he is," Kane said to Grant. "All ready and waiting for you." He hung the lantern on a nail that protruded from one of the uprights.

"Bascomb," Grant said, "I had Kane bring you here so that you and I could have a little talk. Kane, remove the gag from his mouth."

When Kane had done so, Grant said, "I thought by now Miss Delano would have come to her senses, but apparently she has not done so. Nor have you, Bascomb. Surely you must realize that you should not meddle with your betters. I intend to persuade you to give up your plan to marry Miss Delano."

Judah, his mouth dry, swallowed several times in an attempt to start his saliva flowing. He tried to speak and found that he couldn't. He licked his lips and swallowed again, In a rasping voice, he managed to mutter, "Untie me, Grant. You want a fight, I'll give you one."

"A fight, Bascomb? That isn't what I want. As I've explained to you, I want you to sever your relationship with Miss Delano. Send her away. If you'll agree to do that, *then* I'll untie you and we both can go our separate ways.

"How'd you know Virginia and I are planning on being sealed?"

Grant told him how he knew and then said, "I imagine women find you attractive enough, Bascomb. You shouldn't have any trouble attracting another woman to take Miss Delano's place in your life. Will you agree to give her up—to send her away?"

"Forget it, Grant.

Grant sighed. "Make him change his mind, Kane."

Kane stepped forward, drew his pistol from his waistband, gripped it by the barrel, and slammed its butt against Judah's head.

Pain tore through Judah's skull. The stars that were visible through the rents in the roof melded into what looked to him like heat lightning.

"Well, Bascomb?" Grant asked quietly.

Judah shook his head.

Grant hit him again on the opposite side of the head.

Blood seeped from Judah's torn flesh and his skull seemed to house a wild roaring that reverberated in his brain. His vision blurred and he blinked away the blood that was running into his eyes.

"You'll be no good to your intended," Grant said, smiling, "with a fractured skull and, perhaps, a damaged brain."

When Judah said nothing, Grant nodded to Kane and said, "Use your fists on him."

Kane drew back his right arm and plunged his fist into Judah's stomach. As Judah groaned, Kane's left fist came up and caught Judah squarely on the jaw, sending his head snapping backward to slam against the upright to which he was tied.

Kane landed another body blow to Judah's ribs and followed it up with a hard right cross.

"Why don't you spare yourself this punishment and pain, Bascomb?" Grant asked with false solicitousness. "Kane is tireless. And I am a patient man. We can keep this up all night if necessary."

"It'll be necessary," Judah murmured through the red haze that was blinding him. "You'll never get her because I'll never give her up. Only way you'll get her is if you kill me. And maybe not even then. My guess is she won't want you."

Grant's expression hardened. "I'm beginning to believe we may have to kill you. Kane!"

"You want me to hit him with my pistol again? Or just my fists?"

"Throttle him," Grant snarled.

Kane's eyes widened as he stared at Grant in the light that was being shed by the lantern. "You never said nothing about murder when you said go get him. Nor after I got him neither. I'm not going to take part in no murder. You want him dead, you kill him."

"Kane," Grant said, his voice low and his eyes icy, "you'll throttle him. If you choose not to do so, I will reveal to the Nauvoo authorities that it was you who burned Law's lumber last month. You'll be jailed."

"And you right along with me 'cause I'll tell how you paid me to do it."

"I will, of course, deny the charge. Now, which one of us do you think will be believed? A wharf rat like yourself or a respectable citizen like me?"

Kane chewed his lower lip, glancing from Grant to Judah.

"Do it, Kane!" Grant commanded. "Kill him the Mormon bastard now!"

"Get out of my way!"

As Grant stepped back, Kane's fingers circled Judah's throat.

Judah let out a yell in the hope that someone might be outside in the night, someone who would hear him and come to his aid.

"Gag him, Kane!"

Kane did and then reached for Judah's throat again.

"I'd rather not watch this," Grant said. "I'll wait for you outside, Kane." He turned swiftly and made his way out of the warehouse.

When he was gone, Kane released his grip on Judah's throat. "Listen, Bascomb, I didn't ever mean for things to go this far. If I kill you, he'll have a hold on me that nothing'll ever break. You slump down on the ground. Play like you're dead. I'll tell Grant I done it and tomorrow I'll come back and let you loose. You got that?"

Judah nodded and slid to his knees, letting his head fall forward.

He heard Kane remove the lantern from the nail in the upright and make his way out of the warehouse. He heard muffled voices coming from outside as he slumped in the black interior of the building.

And then the blackness began to draw back. The voices were no longer muffled but distinct now and he realized that Grant and Kane had returned to the warehouse. He let his body hang limply, his legs twisted beneath him, his head hanging down.

"Are you certain he's dead?" Grant asked.

"He's dead," Kane answered. Look at him. He's not breathing."

As if Kane's words had been a cue, Judah held his breath. Blood from the wounds on his head dripped slowly down upon his dusty jeans.

Someone grabbed a fistful of his hair. He barely had time to close his eyes before his head was jerked up.

"You got any doubts now, Grant?" Kane asked as he held Judah's head up.

"Untie him, Kane."

"What for?" Kane let Judah's head drop. "Why'n't we just leave him lay here?"

"You heard me. Untie him."

Judah, trying to ignore the pain in his head, felt rage begin to riot through him. As Kane's fingers worked at the rope that bound his wrists together, he made himself ready for what he intended to do, pain or no pain.

"There," Kane said finally. "He's loose. Now what?"

Before Grant could reply, Judah was on his feet and lunging for Grant. Grant, taken completely by surprise, let out a strangled cry.

Judah seized him and slammed him up against one of the uprights. Holding him against the stout timber with his left hand, he hit Grant hard with his right fist. Then he hit him a second time, knocking the wind from him and causing him to sputter and spray bloody saliva from his lips, which had been split by Judah's first blow.

"I take a lot of killing, Grant," Judah muttered and flung Grant to the ground. "Now get up and see if you can take a man whose hands aren't tied."

"Kane!" Grant screeched. "*Shoot him!*"

Kane remained motionless.

Grant stumbled to his feet and, swaying, began to back away from Judah.

"Looks like it's going to be just you and me, Grant," Judah said. "You ought to know your hired hands better before you set them to doing tasks it turns out they've no taste for." He advanced on Grant, his hands fisted in front of him.

Grant's right arm shot out and pulled the pistol from Kane's waistband. He fired.

The bullet ripped into Judah's chest, spinning him around as if he had been kicked by a horse. He careened into an upright, bounced off it, and, as agony savaged his chest, he fell face down on the hard ground.

"I'm getting my ass out of here right now!" he heard Kane declare as he fought to remain conscious.

"You're not leaving, Kane. Pick him up. Take him outside and dump him into the river. If that shot didn't kill him, he'll drown."

Judah was only vaguely aware of Grant's foot turning him over and as dimly aware of some of the man's words, which seemed to reach him from a great distance.

"—over your shoulder, Kane."

He felt himself being picked up and carried out of the warehouse. He heard Kane's heavy footsteps pounding the boards of a wharf that jutted out into the river in front of the warehouse beside which a flatboat was moored.

And then, his vision blurring, focusing, blurring again, he felt himself sinking down into a dark and bottomless abyss where he drifted alone with his pain.

But he was flung headlong out of the abyss as he hit the cold water and the shock of his impact brought him back to consciousness. He felt himself sinking, and the impulse to struggle to the surface seized him as he swallowed a mouthful of river water.

But then, with brilliant clarity, all that had just happened to him flashed through his mind and he knew that he must not struggle. He knew that he must appear to be as dead as Kane and Grant believed him to be—or hoped he was. Grant, he recalled, had said something about him drowning if the bullet hadn't killed him.

He pressed his lips tightly together and let the current move him at will. He held his breath and felt himself drifting up toward the surface of the water. His instincts almost betrayed him. He battled the nearly overwhelming urge to propel himself to the surface. Every cell in his body seemed to be demanding that he fight to survive and he knew if he surrendered to their instinctive demands he would die.

He rolled over in the water, arms outstretched, legs spread. His body broke through to the surface and he lay there facing the stars, drifting with the currents, letting himself be picked up and then let down by the swell a passing steamboat left in its wake.

He spotted the warehouse in the distance upstream. Then he saw two figures emerge from its great shadow and walk out on the crumbling wharf. Grant and Kane. He was sure of it, although he could not make out their features.

As the waves rocked him, he saw the two figures leave the wharf and disappear into the night. But he made himself wait and, while waiting, remain motionless in the water.

He realized that his chest wound did not hurt now as much as it had earlier and he knew why it didn't. The cold water had numbed his body.

Not far from him, a fish broke the surface of the water and leaped into the air, a silver sliver in the night's moonlight. It fell back with a splash and then silence returned.

After turning over in the water again, Judah began to swim, using only his left arm because Grant's bullet had entered his chest just below the spot where his right arm joined his shoulder. He couldn't move his right arm. He tried kicking, but his water-logged boots were so heavy that his efforts were futile.

Swimming clumsily and drifting with the river as it flowed south to the sea, he kept his eyes on the bank, trying to make out familiar landmarks. When a cluster of cottonwoods appeared like welcome beacons in the darkness, he swam toward them, aware that his cabin lay beyond them only a mile inland.

Painfully, he dragged himself up on the muddy river bank. He got to his knees, supporting himself with his left hand and then, drawing a deep breath, he struggled to his feet. Water from his wet hair ran down his face and blurred his vision. He lost his balance and was about to fall but he put out his left hand and braced it against the trunk of one of the cottonwoods for support.

Panting, he stood there gazing out over the open land beyond the trees. He could not see his cabin from where he stood, but he knew that it was out there beyond the fields.

A wave of giddiness washed over him and he thought he was going to fall.

Could he make it to the cabin?

He intended to try.

Gritting his teeth against the searing pain in his chest, which was now returning and sending hot stabbing sensations through his upper body, he set out.

His right arm hung limply at his side. He stretched out his left hand in front of him as if he were groping for something to cling to. Step by slow step, he moved forward, the river water in his boots sloshing as he stumbled along. He had not gone more than fifty yards when his foot struck a large stone and he fell to the ground.

He lay there a moment, the grass which was damp with dew pressing against his cheek, his eyes closed, his lungs heaving.

And then, once more he got up and moved slowly through the darkness, concentrating on the simple act of putting one foot in front of the other, yearning as he shuffled along for a glimpse of his cabin.

When its lighted window came into view at last, he wanted to cry out in triumph. But he still had far to go to reach it. It would not be a difficult journey had he not been beaten and shot. But it was a terrible distance to travel for a man whose life was slowly oozing away with the blood he had already lost and was still losing.

He almost made it to the cabin.

But, while he was still some distance away from the safety its lighted window signaled, he felt the darkness swirling up around him again as it tried to suck him down into its depths. He halted, breathing hard, and kept his eyes focused on the lighted window.

Suddenly, the light in the window went out as he felt himself falling into that dead and empty darkness which unmercifully blotted out his world.

A meadowlark was trilling.

Somewhere in another faraway world.

But in the dark world where Judah still drifted, pain stalked him.

He tried to shove it away from him but it was inside him somewhere and he could not make it go away. He tried to speak but his lips wouldn't move. He tried to open his eyes but the weighty darkness, his formless enemy, pressed down upon their lids and he could see nothing.

He heard something.

What?

Not the meadowlark. Something else. Something soft. Something subdued.

Someone somewhere was weeping.

Himself?

He remembered the last time he had let himself cry.

Prince had been an old dog. His father had said, he remembered, that if Prince had been a person, the dog would have been next to ninety years old. Prince died alone in the night, and eight-year-old Judah Bascomb had stiffened when he found the cold body, just after dawn, lying in the yard outside the homeplace. His mother had come out of the house and called to him. And then she saw Prince's lifeless body and she fell silent. Judah, screaming wildly at a world too cruel to care about a boy's love and need for an aged and infirm mongrel, had run into the woods and had cried and cried where no one could see or hear him. For a long time.

Who was weeping?

His eyelids eased open and the gray light of dawn cascaded down upon his eyes.

He was in a bed. His fingers touched it. His own bed. The one he shared with—

He managed to raise his head slightly. Virginia, seated in a wooden chair beside the bed, was weeping, her hands covering her face, her shoulders shaking as she sobbed.

He tried to speak to her, couldn't. Tried again. A wordless murmur, a moan.

She heard it and raised her head. When she saw him looking at her, she dropped to her knees beside the bed and gently touched his face. "Judah!"

"Honey, I—" There was so much to say and he was too weak to say it. "How'd I—here?"

"You called my name—from outside last night. Don't you remember?"

"No."

"I had to drag you inside. Judah—the blood. There was so much of it. I washed you."

He realized he was naked beneath the coverlet.

"You've been shot. Will you be all right here alone while I ride into town for the doctor?"

"No doctor."

"But Judah—"

He feebly raised his left hand but it fell back on the bed. Virginia grasped it tightly.

He whispered, "My bowie knife."

"You want your knife?"

"Get it. You—cut out the ball."

"Judah, I could never—"

He tried hard to squeeze her hand and barely succeeded. "Boil water. Get clean cloths—my knife."

Virginia was slowly shaking her head from side to side.

He looked into her eyes, not speaking, his hand still clasped in hers.

Without taking her eyes from him, Virginia slowly rose.

When she disappeared from his sight, he closed his eyes and lay in the bed, trying not to think of what was about to happen to him, trying not to wonder whether he would be able to bear it.

He didn't know how much time had passed before Virginia reappeared, carrying a porcelain pitcher full of steaming hot water which she put down on a cracker barrel beside the bed. She went away again and returned with clean white muslin. And Judah's bowie knife.

"You got to cut into me," he told her, his voice barely audible. "My chest. Near my right shoulder. You got to find the ball. Dig it out."

Virginia placed the muslin on the cracker barrel but kept

the knife in her right hand. Her face was pale and drawn and her hand which held the knife trembled.

"A spoon," Judah said. "Get me one."

When she had gotten the spoon and handed it to him a moment later, he didn't take it from her. "Put it between my teeth."

She did. He bit down on it. Their eyes met.

Virginia bent down over him, his bowie knife in her hand.

Judah's teeth ground against the spoon as the blade of the knife pierced his chest. His eyes squeezed shut.

"Judah, please don't make me—"

His eyes opened and impaled her.

They closed again as the knife probed deeper into his flesh.

The spoon between Judah's teeth began to bend . . .

It broke and fell on the bed.

He screamed.

And heard something *plop* on the wooden floor.

Without opening his eyes, he asked, "You got it?"

No answer.

He opened his eyes. Virginia was gone. He raised his head and saw her.

She had fainted and was lying on the floor. Beside the bloody ball and the equally bloody bowie knife.

SEVEN

JUDAH leaned over the edge of the bed and reached down to Virginia. The effort sent pain howling through his chest. The blood from his gaping wound dripped down upon Virginia as she lay senseless on the floor.

He fell back on the bed. He clenched his teeth against the pain.

Then, there was a moan as Virginia slowly got to her feet, holding onto the edge of the bed for support as she did so.

"Judah," she whispered, staring in horror at his ravaged chest.

"I'm fine," he lied. "What about you?"

"I think—I'm all right." She soaked the muslin in the hot water that filled the pitcher and set about cleansing Judah's wound. When she had done all she could, she tore a long strip from a piece of muslin and bound it around his chest.

"Judah, who shot you?"

"Grant."

Shock paled Virginia's face. "Simon? But why?"

"He wants you, Virginia. He doesn't want me to have you."

"Judah, he might have killed you!"

"He meant to. Him and Kane, they threw me in the river after the shooting and figured I'd likely drown if the bullet hadn't already done for me."

Virginia sat down in a chair beside the bed, obviously aghast at what she had just heard. "We've got to get out of here, Judah. Away from Nauvoo and Simon. We'll go back to St. Louis just as soon as you can travel. Now I'm going for the doctor."

"*No!*"

"If your wound becomes infected—"

"It won't. You'll keep it clean."

"How soon do you think we'll be able to leave for Saint Louis?"

"I'm not leaving for anywhere. I'm staying right here. I've got me a score that needs settling."

"With Simon?"

Judah nodded.

"But it's not safe for you here. He might try to kill you again."

"He might. If he knows I'm alive. But he doesn't know that. I plan on staying out of sight until I'm able to go after him and even things out."

"Judah, that's an insane idea!"

"Not so insane. There's nothing insane about a man taking steps to keep himself alive."

"What are you going to do?"

"First off, I'm going to bed down out in the woods."

Virginia started to protest but Judah interrupted her. "I've slept outside about as much as I've slept under a roof in my time. That part's not new to me. But I never did kill a man before."

"You intend to kill Simon?"

"I do."

"Judah, you mustn't!"

His eyes narrowed. "You still got some feeling left for him?"

"No, it's not that. I know now that I never really loved Simon. I didn't know what love was until I met you. But I won't marry a killer and you say that's what you intend to become."

"It's a simple matter of self-defense, honey."

"It's a simple matter of murder, Judah, and you know it."

Judah brushed her remark aside and said, "There's things you got to do for me."

Guardedly, Virginia asked, "What things?"

"You're going to help me make it out to the woods. Then you're going to build me a lean-to. I'll tell you how. Then you're going to ride into town and buy some whiskey."

"Whiskey? Oh, you mean for the pain."

"No. It's to sterilize my wound with."

"But why can't you stay here in the cabin?"

"You haven't thought this whole thing through, honey, and that's no wonder. You haven't had time to do much thinking since your man showed up in the middle of the night all shot to pieces and set you to digging a ball out of his hide. But think on it now. What's Grant likely to do next now that he figures I'm dead?''

"Come here.''

"After you.''

"Judah, we've got to go away. I'm not safe here now either. Have you thought of that?''

"I have. He won't hurt you. He wants to marry you.'' Judah shifted position in the bed and then managed to sit up. "It's light now. Help me put on my pants and boots and then we'll head for the woods.''

Reluctantly, Virginia helped Judah dress and then, as he placed one arm over her shoulder, she led him, leaning heavily upon her, out of the house, across the fields, and into the woods.

It was a slow journey, and during it Judah had to pause several times when the pain threatened to overwhelm him.

But at last they were into the woods that bordered the fields and, following Judah's orders, Virginia helped him sit down at the base of an aspen, against which he braced his back.

"Get some long branches,'' he said and, later, when she had returned with some which she had broken from dead-falls she had found, he said, "Go back to the house. Bring a knife and some rope. Bring that old tarpaulin that's out in the shed.''

He remained almost motionless during the time she was gone, afraid to move and arouse the pain that lurked within him like a fierce animal held temporarily at bay. When she returned, he said, "Take that there longest branch and tie it part way up on the trunk of that tree over there. Then brace this here branch—'' he pointed to a long one, "—and tip it against the first shaft and tie it in place.

When she had followed his instructions, Judah said,

"Now lean the rest of those branches against the ridgepole and then cover them with the tarpaulin."

It took her only a few more minutes to complete the construction of the lean-to. When she had done so, Judah said, "You did a fine job. I don't know what I'd've done without you."

Virginia's lips were set in a grim line and, as she helped Judah crawl under the lean-to, she said, "You will have to learn to do without me, Judah."

"*What*?" He had hurled the word at her.

"I've had time to think while I was making this lean-to. I'm going him, Judah. In a day or two."

"Your home's here with me."

"I thought it was. But things have changed. You have been attacked and almost killed. You're not safe here and neither am I. But both of us would be safe in my father's house. He would see to it that we were. However, if you won't be reasonable and come with me in light of the present circumstances, then I have no choice but to do what I can to protect myself.

"I'll bring you food—enough for several days. I'll get the whiskey you want. However, if after a day or two you still refuse to go to Saint Louis with me—well, I'm going alone."

Judah had listened to her in total disbelief. Now, as she stood staring down at him, he had no doubts about her resolve. He knew she would do exactly as she had said she would do. Which, he realized, left him a choice. He could stay where he was and revenge himself upon Grant. Or he could run away with Virginia to Saint Louis and safety.

He was torn. He could not bring himself to run away. He wanted to wreak vengeance on Grant. But he didn't want to lose Virginia and now he knew that he might—and for good—if he did not go with her. He struggled with the choice which, for him, was almost impossible to make. And yet he knew it had to be made and made now.

His desire for vengeance triumphed over his need for Virginia. "I'm staying here," he announced firmly. And then, more softly and hopefully, he added, "Once I get Grant you can come on back."

"I could. But I'm not sure I will."

"You're going to have our baby. When your father finds that out, he'll—"

"I value the safety of our baby. The baby is the principal reason I have decided to leave. I also value my own safety as well as yours, Judah. Far more than my reputation which, I'm well aware, will be ruined because of what I've done and what has happened as a result."

"You said you loved me."

"I do love you, Judah. You know I do. And I want to marry you. You know that as well. If you do what you intend to do you will not be the man you are at this moment. I know I will not want to marry the man you will have become. I know I could never love such a man."

Judah tried to make himself change his mind. He tried as hard as he knew how to convince himself that the best thing for him to do would be to go away with Virginia. But he failed to convince himself. He considered such a course of action unmanly. Were he to take it, he believed he would always, in some secret part of himself, be ashamed of himself for having run away from danger when he should have stood his ground and revenged himself against Grant.

"If I've learned one thing in my life, Virginia," he said, "it's that a man has got to do what he thinks is right. If he don't, he won't be able to live with himself, and that's true fact. I got to go after Grant."

"I'll go and get you some food. And the whiskey you need."

Judah watched her leave and, as she began to cross the fields, he cursed himself for being the stubborn fool that he so obviously was, and he also cursed Virginia for being as stubborn in her own way as he was in his.

As she vanished from sight, he realized how dark it was in the woods where he had chosen to take shelter.

On the third day after Judah had been shot, Virginia left him and returned to Saint Louis.

Judah, when she told him she was leaving, had suggested that maybe she was doing the best thing. He had, he said, thought the matter over and decided that the safety of their unborn child was the most important thing to be considered. She had agreed with him. She had not asked him again if he intended to kill Grant. And he had not mentioned the matter either.

He remained in the woods, not wanting to return to the cabin in case Grant—someone—might see him. He had made Virginia promise not to tell anyone that he was alive and she had mentioned that there was a lot of talk in Nauvoo about his sudden and mysterious disappearance. Grant, she had reported, continued to enjoy the Prophet's favor and he was rapidly becoming a power among the Saints. Smith, she said, always asked his advice before making any important decisions. She said that Smith had attempted to reconcile her with Grant but she had announced her intention to leave Nauvoo, since she had no reason to remain with Judah gone. Playing his charade, she had asked Smith to please let her know if he or anyone else received word of Judah's whereabouts. The Prophet had promised to do so.

But Grant, she said, had importuned her every time they

met. He had offered to accompany her to Saint Louis, claiming that it was unwise for a woman to travel such a distance unaccompanied. Coldly, she had refused his offer just as she had refused to listen to any of his entreaties concerning what he had referred to as their "postponed" nuptials.

Judah found that he missed her even more than he had thought he would. On the night following her departure, he sat under his lean-to as a light spring rain fell, its sound a wet whisper in the black night. He found himself longing for her and fighting the urge to give up his plan to avenge himself on Grant and go after her, marry her, and settle down wherever she might choose to live.

As the rain spattered lightly on the tarpaulin covering the lean-to, he felt a hunger for her which was almost overpowering. It was a physical hunger that seemed to consume him, a lust of such force that it was almost painful. But his hunger for her was not merely physical. He found himself thinking of her almost constantly and his lust was fused to an even greater love for her than he had ever felt for any other woman.

He forced himself to stop thinking about her, to stop longing for her.

He thought instead of Grant. And he made his plans to settle his score with the man.

He fell asleep that night to the sound of the soft rain, his love for Virginia displaced by his hatred for Grant.

The next day, he removed the stained muslin that covered his chest wound and bathed it with the whiskey Virginia had brought him. He winced as the whiskey burned the raw flesh that was only just beginning to show signs of healing. He forced himself to douse the wound with generous amounts of whiskey in order to avoid infection. He wasn't entirely sure that the whiskey would work, but he would not go to a doctor. Even if he could swear the man to silence about his survival, it would be a risk and he wanted to add no unnecessary risks to the already risky plan he had formed for getting rid of Grant once and for all.

After clumsily binding a piece of muslin around his chest and over his shoulder, he put on his shirt and reached for his gun which, along with his ammunition, Virginia had brought him during his first day away from the cabin.

His .40 caliber Paterson pistol was a five-shot, single-action percussion revolver mass-produced by Samuel Colt in Connecticut for use by the United States cavalry, and known as a horse or dragoon pistol. It had a four and one-half inch barrel and no trigger guard. When the revolver was uncocked as it was now, the trigger guard folded back into the gun's frame.

Judah checked the gun's cylinder. Each chamber was loaded with percussion cap, powder, and ball. He picked up a separate cylinder and proceeded to fill each of its five chambers with cap, powder, and ball, which he then sealed with beeswax to keep the powder dry. He pocketed the loose cylinder, thinking that if he missed Grant with each of his first five shots, a possibility he considered unlikely, he could remove the gun's cylinder and insert the fresh, fully loaded one, thus giving himself five more chances to achieve his desired goal.

He shoved the revolver into his waistband and left the woods to walk somewhat warily across the fields toward his cabin. As he neared it, he carefully surveyed the surrounding countryside. There was no one in sight. He studied his cabin and shed as he walked. No sign of life near either of the buildings.

He entered the cabin and was surprised that its stillness bothered him. It never had before. But then Virginia had come to live with him, bringing laughter and an end to loneliness. Angrily, he left the cabin, slamming the door behind him, and went to the shed.

Inside it, he found his horse's feed bin nearly empty. He refilled it with oats and, when the horse had eaten its fill, he began to saddle and bridle the animal.

He led the horse out of the shed, swung into the saddle, and headed for Nauvoo.

He rode at a gallop, eager to get where he was going and as eager to find and kill Grant.

He skirted the edge of the city and entered it from the east, heading straight for Smith's house in order to avoid being seen by too many people.

Emma Smith answered his knock on her back door and she let out a little cry when she saw who was standing on her doorstep.

"I've got to see Brother Joseph," he said to her. "He here?"

"Yes," Emma replied, backing away as Judah strode past her and into the house.

He found Smith in the parlor, poring over a pile of what looked like legal documents. He looked up as Judah entered the room and gasped.

"Brother Judah!" he cried, rising. "I feared you might be—"

"I'm alive. And I'm looking for Simon Grant. You happen to know where I can find him?"

"Where have you been?" Smith inquired, consternation evident in both his voice and manner.

"Where's Grant?"

"He's not here. However, I do believe he might be found at the site of the Temple. He's been encouraging the men there. He's been asking them to work longer hours. I could ask if Mr. Kane knows where he is. He's out on the front porch, I believe.''

As Smith started to leave the room, Judah reached out, gripped the man's shoulder, and shook his head.

"What—"

Judah left the room, drew his pistol, and opened the front door. "Kane!"

As Kane turned and saw the gun, he raised both hands as if to ward off a blow.

"Inside, Kane."

As Kane entered the house, Judah rammed the muzzle of his pistol into the small of the man's back and said, "Step on into the parlor, Kane."

As the two men entered the room, Smith said, "Mr. Kane, do you know where—" Then he saw the gun in Judah's hand and he asked, "What is the meaning of this?"

"Tell him, Kane."

"Tell him what?"

"I can't miss you, Kane. I can blow your insides out with one, two shots at the most, at this close range."

Kane began to babble.

When he was finished, Smith sat down heavily and something not unlike a moan escaped his lips. He dropped his head in his hands. And then, looking up again, his face drawn, he said, "Mr. Kane, I find what you've just told me both astonishing and impossible to believe."

"It's true!" Kane insisted. "Every single word of it! Grant shot Bascomb. Then him and me—he made me help him—we dumped Bascomb in the river, figuring he'd drown if he weren't already dead."

"Now you know why I'm hunting Grant," Judah said to Smith.

"This is terrible," Smith muttered, pulling nervously at

his chin. "Should our enemies hear that I have been harboring a would-be murderer who has been serving me as both friend and counselor—" His words trailed away.

"I helped you, Bascomb, back at Beecher's," Kane whined. "You got no cause to kill me."

"You also pistol-whipped me," Judah reminded Kane and the man groaned. He withdrew the muzzle of his gun from Kane's back and the man's groan became a sigh of relief.

To Smith, Judah said, "You'd best get your gun."

"What for?"

"Hold it on Kane. I'll round up some men and send them here to take him into custody so's he can stand trial as an accessory to attempted murder."

Smith left the room and when he returned he had a pistol in his hand. His eyes were glazed. "Will I never have peace on this earth?" he asked rhetorically, aiming the gun at Kane.

"Now, I can go gunning for Grant," Judah said.

"Judah!" Smith cried. "Thou shalt not kill!"

"Reckon I shalt, Brother Joseph."

As Judah quickly left the room and made his way to the back door, he heard Smith cry out, "Judah, you dare not flout God's and man's law!"

Once outside, he stepped into the saddle and took the horse at a fast canter around the house. Then at a gallop, he rode down the middle of the wide street to the site where the Temple was being constructed. When he reached it, Grant was nowhere in sight. He rode up to a group of men who were busily stacking lumber beside an unfinished wall and, when they looked up at him, he asked, "Where might I find Grant?"

One of the men said, "I know you. You're Judah Bascomb."

Before Judah could say anything, one of the other men pulled off his hat, wiped the sweat from his forehead and laconically commented, "Told you he wasn't dead. Or disappeared either. Off minding his own business, I told you Bascomb was."

"Is Grant here?" Judah asked.

"He was," replied the man who had spoken first. "Telling us all how we ought to work twenty-five hours a day building the Temple. He doesn't seem to care that we got other things to do like our livings to earn and our businesses to run. He thinks we ought to donate all our time to building the Temple."

"You know where I might find him?"

"Try Nauvoo House," one of the men in the group suggested. "Like as not, he's over there haranguing the men working there just like he's been haranguing us."

"Some of you men," Judah said, "had best go to the Prophet's house. He's holding a gun on a man there and could use your help."

Judah turned his horse. It took him nearly ten minutes to reach the partially completed Nauvoo House which was to serve the Saints as a combination meeting house and entertainment center.

Grant was there and, when Judah spotted him, he reined in his horse and sat his saddle, staring hard at the man whose back was turned to him as he urged the workers to commit themselves—by signing a paper he waved in one hand—to working longer hours on the construction project.

"When I get back from my trip to Saint Louis," Grant declared, "I want to see every man's signature on this agreement."

"You men!" Judah shouted, drawing his pistol from his waistband and aiming it at Grant's back. "Move out of the way!"

Grant turned at the sound of the shouted order and he blanched at the sight of Judah and the gun in his hand.

As Grant began to back away from him, Judah cocked his pistol. His finger tightened on its trigger.

"He's going to kill me!" Grant screamed frantically, still backing away, the paper falling from his hand.

Judah walked his horse forward.

"Somebody shoot him!" Grant screamed.

Judah had scanned the workmen and seen that none of them were carrying guns. His finger remained tight on the trigger as he made ready to fire.

If you do what you intend to do, you will not be the man you are at this moment. I know I will not want to marry the man you will have become. I know I could never love such a man.

The devastating words Virginia had spoken before she left him roared in Judah's mind.

Grant, as Judah hesitated, turned and ran.

Judah dug his heels into his horse's flanks and galloped after him. As he passed him, he abruptly wheeled his horse and fired.

Dirt flew up in front of Grant's feet and he skidded to a halt, almost colliding with Judah's horse.

"Now then," Judah said to him, "turn yourself around and start walking. Next time I won't fire into the ground. Next time I'll fire into *you*. March, Grant!"

Wordlessly, his expression a bitter blend of fear and hate, Grant turned and began to walk up the street. Judah walked his horse, following Grant. They passed Nauvoo House and the crowd, drawn by the gunfire, that lined both sides of the street.

Grant walked on, looking neither to the right nor the left, planting one foot stolidly in front of the other, his shoulders hunched, his arms hanging stiffly at his sides.

Judah's eyes were on him as they moved past the shops on both sides of the street.

They had almost reached the end of the business district when Judah caught a flash of light out of the corner of his eye.

At the same instant, a shot sounded.

Judah's horse screamed and reared under him. The animal went down, throwing Judah, who rolled over and over as he hit the ground. And then, his pistol still in his hand, he was up on his feet. To his left, his horse thrashed on the ground, sending up billowing clouds of dust. It screamed again as Judah searched the rooftops for the man with the gun who had meant, he was certain, to shoot him but who had instead fatally wounded his horse.

Grant, who had been terrified, stood without moving a muscle in the middle of the street, his back to Judah.

Sunlight glinted again on a rifle barrel and Judah took quick aim and fired.

The man who had been kneeling on the rooftop slowly rose. His rifle fell from his hands. He clutched his throat from which blood was gushing and tottered backward, then forward. He fell from the rooftop. His body made a dull *thwump* as it hit the ground. He tried to rise and then collapsed to the ground.

Judah walked over to him.

It was Kane.

Blood still flowed from the wound in the base of his throat where Judah's bullet had entered and then exited, leaving a gaping hole in the back of Kane's neck.

It was obvious to Judah that Kane was dead. He quickly turned and walked over to Grant.

"We'll move along now," he said, and Grant set out down the street, Judah walking close behind him.

When they reached Smith's house, Judah was gratified

to see several members of the Sons of Dan gathered on the front porch along with some of the workmen who had been at the Temple site. When they saw Grant, one of the men called out to Judah.

"Kane got away from us!"

"Don't matter now. He threw down on me. I shot him."

"He's dead?" someone asked.

Judah nodded, prodded Grant in the back with the muzzle of his pistol, and then followed him past the men who made way for them and into Smith's house.

Smith was standing in the hall as if he had been expecting company. His face was solemn as he stared at Grant.

"Brought him here to tell you himself that what Kane told you was true, Brother Joseph," Judah said evenly.

"You didn't kill him," Smith said with genuine relief.

"Speak your piece, Grant," Judah ordered.

Grant said nothing.

Smith said, "Judah, some of the Sons of Dan were taking Kane to jail. He escaped from them."

Judah told him what had just happened, concluding, "Kane probably figured if he killed me, there'd be nobody to testify against him and Grant here. Grant, I told you to tell Brother Joseph what you and Kane did to me."

Grant hesitated a moment and then, speaking in a low voice, he recounted the story in clipped sentences.

"You tried to commit murder!" Smith exclaimed when Grant finally fell silent. "And yet you dared to urge me to excommunicate Judah for his behavior. You wanted me to expel Miss Delano from Nauvoo as a public nuisance!

"Hypocrite!" Smith bellowed, shaking a finger at Grant. "You shall stand trial for attempted murder!"

Judah called out to the men gathered on the porch and they

came into the house. "Take him to jail," he ordered the men. "And *don't* let him get away from you."

Several of the men grabbed Grant and dragged him from the house.

Judah shoved his pistol into his waistband.

"Judah, I owe you an apology," Smith said meekly. ":I really believed you intended to kill Grant."

"You don't owe me no apology because you were right. I did intend to kill him."

"But you didn't. Why not?"

"On account of Virginia Delano."

"I don't believe I understand you."

"No matter."

"Judah, I ask your forgiveness for having been such a fool. For dismissing you as my bodyguard on the advice of Grant and installing Kane in your place. Will you resume your position?"

"Maybe. But not right now. There's something I got to do."

"May I ask what that something is?"

"Got to take a trip. I'm heading for Saint Louis to pay Miss Delano a visit."

"She's not—ah, still visiting you at your cabin? She has returned to Saint Louis?"

"Yes, and I'm going there to bring her back here with me."

"This time—you and Miss Delano—you do intend to be sealed?"

"You don't have to fret anymore about us living in sin."

Smith breathed a heartfelt sigh of relief.

Judah grinned.

EIGHT

WHEN he arrived in Saint Louis on the last day of May, Judah went directly to the Delano house.

He used the brass knocker to announce his arrival and, as the door swung open, he was smiling broadly. His smile vanished when he saw Nelson, the manservant, staring at him. He had been expecting Virginia to open the door for him.

Music drifted out through the open door and dissipated in the damp evening air.

"May I have your invitation, sir?" Nelson asked coldly,

his eyes gliding down over Judah's flannel shirt and jeans to his dusty boots.

"Nobody invited me. I'm here to see Miss Delano."

"Mr. Delano is giving a reception to celebrate his daughter's return home. Admittance is by invitation only."

"That so?" As Nelson started to close the door, Judah kicked out at it and, with one blow of his booted foot, sent it flying open again.

Nelson, startled, said, "See here—"

But Judah was already past him and striding across the foyer and into the sitting room which he discovered was filled with women in evening gowns and men wearing formal attire.

Candles glowed everywhere. Flowers filled vases and their perfume sweetened the air. Brass fixtures gleamed. Crystal glittered.

The music came to a stop.

Judah took it all in: the five-piece orchestra, the people staring at him in surprise, the elegance that made him uneasy, and the manservant Nelson spluttering beside him.

When Nelson clapped a hand on his shoulder, he shook it off and shouted, "Virginia!"

Women gasped and busied themselves with their paper fans. Men murmured to one another.

Judah was about to shout Virginia's name a second time when he saw her suddenly appear in the doorway that led to the dining room.

She was wearing a floor-length white gown that was trimmed with French lace and embroidered on the bodice and hem with roses. In her free hand, she held a goblet that contained a pale liquid which bubbled. Her other hand rested on the forearm of a pale young man who was frowning at Judah.

Judah pushed his way through the crowd toward her and

when he reached her he took the glass from her hand and put it down on a table. Then he removed her hand from her companion's arm and said, "Got to talk to you, honey."

Virginia gestured, a command to the orchestra. Music again filled the room. To the man standing at her side, she said, "George, I just know you will be kind enough to excuse me for a minute or two."

George mumbled something and Virginia kissed his cheek. "You're really such a dear."

Then, almost angrily seizing Judah's arm, she led him out of the sitting room, through the foyer, and on into a small room off the foyer which contained a desk, chair, and an upholstered couch.

She closed the door of the room. "Judah, I wasn't expecting you."

"Well, I'm here. It's real good to see you again."

Virginia looked away from him.

Judah, watching her closely, felt the room grow cold. Or was the chill the product of his imagination?

"I didn't kill Grant."

Virginia looked back at him.

"Well, aren't you glad? I mean you said—you told me if I did—don't you want me to tell you what happened?"

"What happened?"

He told her.

"Then the matter is finished. How I did misjudge Simon. But all that is in the past now, isn't it?"

"All what's in the past?"

"Judah, you shouldn't have come here."

"Well, I could have wrote you a letter, I guess. But I thought it'd be best if I came for you and the two of us took the trip back to Nauvoo together."

Virginia dropped her eyes.

"How soon can you leave? Tomorrow?"

She looked up at him and there was a tenderness in her eyes which hadn't been there earlier. "Judah, being with you was wonderful."

"*Was*?"

"Since I've come home, I've had time to think. What I did—teasing Simon the way I did by going off with you—well, as I've said, I've had time to think and I've come to the conclusion that I made a mistake."

"About me you mean?"

"Yes."

"You didn't act like you were making a mistake when you and me—"

"Quiet!" Virginia warned, glancing at the closed door. "Judah, I truly believed I loved you. In fact, I'm sure I did. But our worlds are so very different. *We* are so very different from one another. I belong here in this world. It's the one I've known all my life. Our little idyll—"

"You trying to tell me you and me are through?"

"Yes, Judah, I am. I'm sorry. Frankly, I didn't think you'd come here. I really never expected to see you again."

"You tell your daddy about the baby?"

"No. In a day or two, I'm going to tell him that I want to take an extended trip East—to New York or perhaps Philadelphia. My maid will accompany me. I've already confided in Selena about my condition and we've made our plans. Once the baby is born and placed in a suitable institution—"

"By God, woman, you will not give away my son—or daughter. I'll be *damned* if you will!"

"Judah, stop shouting!"

"Maybe you don't love me anymore. I guess I can handle that, only it's not going to be an easy thing to do because I loved—I still love you, Virginia. But I'm not a man to make a woman stick with me if she don't have a mind to. But that baby you're carrying, it's as much mine as it is yours and I mean to have it to raise.''

"Be sensible, Judah. How could you raise a child? A violent man like you would—''

"Violent? What kind of man do you want? A man like that sly Grant slinking around in the night trying to murder me? You don't consider that violent? Or that George you had in there when I got here? All manners and no balls was what old George looked like to me.''

"How dare you speak to me like that?''

"We did some pretty plain speaking to each other when we were making love back in Nauvoo. You weren't so shocked at the words I used then and, as I recollect, you used a few randy ones yourself once I'd got you all worked up.''

"Please, Judah. Be reasonable. Go back to Nauvoo. Forget about me. You'll meet other women. Let got of the past. Don't let it drag you down.''

"Maybe what we had is past for you. It's not for me. I figured on a future for us, Virginia. I know I'm not educated and I don't know anything about how to behave in your kind of society. I know I'm a violent man at times. But I'd never lay a hand on you and that's a fact.''

Virginia seemed to weaken in her resolve. "You were very tender to me.''

As if he hadn't heard her, Judah continued, "But I'm a fairly decent man. At least I try to be. And I love you, honey. I did back in Nauvoo and I do right now. I'm a man who thinks it's a serious matter when two people pledge themselves to one another. *I* took it serious. I thought you did too.''

"Judah, please!''

"Well, I can't keep you if you won't be kept. But one

thing's certain. You're going back with me and you're going to—"

Virginia gasped as the door of the room suddenly swung open and her father appeared in the doorway.

"—have our baby and then you can come back here if you want to," Judah continued, unaware of Delano standing behind him. "But after you deliver our child, I'm keeping it. You can come on back here to your George or whoever you've taken a fancy to."

"Virginia!" Delano exclaimed, staring at her, shocked. He quickly shut the door behind him. "Who is this man?" And then, recognizing Judah, he said, "You're Smith's bodyguard. I'm right, am I not?"

"Mr. Delano, sir," Judah said, "I'm real sorry you had to bust in at a time like this."

"Virginia, is it true? Are you with child?"

"Father, let me explain."

"Answer me!" Delano thundered, his face reddening as he glared at his daughter.

"She is," Judah said, answering Delano's question. "But she don't want nothing more to do with me now and I've told her that's her choice. But she's not going somewheres to have our baby like she said she was planning to do and then give it away to strangers. No, sir, she's not going to do that. Because I won't let her."

"You had relations with this man?" Delano asked Virginia, his voice ominously low.

Virginia tried to speak but no words came. She nodded.

"You have gone too far this time!" Delano told her angrily. "You have flouted every convention and every rule of polite society practically since the day you were born. But this—now you have disgraced yourself, me, and the Delano name."

"Father, no one need know. I'll go to New York and

then, when the baby's born and placed in an orphanage, I'll come back home and everything will be all right again.''

"It won't be all right! What about the next time? And the time after that?"

"Father! How can you say such terrible things to me?"

"I can say them because of what you've done, Virginia. Go with this man who has gotten you with child. I don't care where. But go now. *Tonight!* I want you out of my house—and out of my life!"

Delano turned toward the wall. He leaned his forehead against it and began to sob.

Virginia went to him and tentatively touched his shoulder. He shook her hand away and whispered brokenly, "Get out of this house. Both of you. *At once!*"

Three days later, Judah and Virginia returned to Nauvoo and the following day Virginia was baptized in the morning and, in the afternoon, sealed to Judah, both ceremonies having been performed personally by Smith.

When, as husband and wife, they returned to the cabin following the sealing, Virginia remarked, "I hope now you are satisfied."

"If you mean am I glad my child will not be born a bastard, yes, I'm satisfied."

Virginia looked around the cabin. "The curtains are dirty," she observed. "The floor is filthy."

"Wash the curtains. Sweep the floor."

She glared at Judah, her hand planted firmly on her hips. "I will not! I agreed to come back here with you until the child is born. I agreed to marry you for the sake of the child. I shall live in your filth until I deliver your baby and then I shall return to—" She fell abruptly silent.

"You know your father won't take you back. So you'll have to find somewheres else to go." Judah paused a moment and then said, "Honey, you don't have to go. I don't want you to go. The two of us could try to be like we were before. It wouldn't be hard. Not for me, it wouldn't be."

"I'm your wife now," Virginia said sadly. "But I felt closer to you the first few weeks that I was with you than I do now." She began to cry soundlessly, tears streaming down her cheeks.

Judah went to her and put his arm around her. He drew her close to him and, as he did so, he felt the familiar surge of desire for her well up within him. "Honey," he whispered, smelling the sweet scent of her hair, "I love you a whole lot."

"Don't," she said and tried to push him away.

"I won't force you. But I figured maybe if we'd—you know, if we made love to each other again—things might work out for us."

Virginia sighed. "I'm your wife now." She freed herself from his embrace and began to unbutton her dress. "I have always understood that a wife is duty-bound to satisfy her husband's carnal desires."

Judah wanted to tell her that she didn't have to do anything she didn't want to do. But he couldn't bring himself to say the words. They would not come and so he merely stared hungrily at her naked body as she went to the bed and sat down upon it.

Then, as she lay back upon the bed, staring up at the ceiling, he could restrain himself no longer. He pulled off his boots and flung them into a corner and then began to tear off his clothes.

Minutes later, naked, he dropped down on the bed beside her, deliberately prodding her body with his stiffness as he caressed her breasts and then bent to kiss her mouth.

She did not return his kiss but accepted it passively, her lips closed, her arms at her sides.

Judah ran his left hand up and over the slight curve of her belly and let it come to rest, hotly grasping, between her legs.

She made no sound. She didn't move.

He felt himself softening and to prevent that from happening, he rolled over on top of her and abruptly entered her.

She turned her head to one side to stare at the unshuttered window.

He began to thrust and withdraw, thrust and withdraw. Still she did not move.

He slumped down upon her and moaned as he felt himself growing limp within her. "I can't," he said bitterly. "Not if you won't—not if you don't want me too."

"Are you finished?" she asked him coldly.

He withdrew from her and sat on the edge of the bed, his elbows propped on his knees, his head hanging in his hands.

She turned over to face the wall, drawing her knees up against her body and wrapping her arms about her breasts.

Smith called the Nauvoo City Council into an emergency session.

Judah, once again the Prophet's bodyguard, sat in a chair at the council table to the left of Smith who, as soon as the meeting opened, brandished a newspaper in his hand, his face florid, and then slammed it down upon the table. He shoved it away from him as if it were something foul which he wanted to avoid.

"You have all read this filthy piece of journalism," he intoned, pointing to the newspaper. "John Bennett, despicable apostate that he is, has outdone himself this time with the scurrilous lies he has printed about me and certain authorities of the church in that newspaper he has just begun to publish.''

Judah glanced at the newspaper: *The Nauvoo Expositor*. And at its date: June 7, 1844.

''And this is only the first edition of Bennett's paper!'' Smith exclaimed angrily. ''What will the next ones be like? What scandalous lies, what hideous speculations, will they contain?''

''Surely, Joseph,'' Hyrum Smith, Smith's brother and vice-mayor of Nauvoo, began soothingly, ''those who read the stories will see clearly that Bennett is maligning us solely because he has not agreed with your policies in the past and has therefore formed his own counter-organization of dissenting Saints here in the city.''

''With all due respect, Hyrum,'' Smith said, ''I think you are a fool to take that position. The stories in this newspaper will fan the fires of anti-Mormonism and none of those who faithfully follow me will be safe.

''Bennett accuses me of abusing the Nauvoo city charter. He casts doubt upon my revelations. He charges me with having used church money for my private land speculations. And, worst of all, he has printed affidavits by his cohorts, William and Jane Law, stating that they have personally seen a copy of the Lord's revelation to me in which He allows each faithful Saint ten virgins.

''As a direct result of all this villification, those who hate us have stepped up their attacks against us. Outlying Mormon settlements will be attacked again, mark my words. In fact, one was only this morning east of the city.''

''What would you have us do, Joseph?'' Hyrum asked.

Smith replied, ''I am not totally ignorant of the law. I have read Blackstone. He says that a community has a right to abate as a public nuisance anything that disturbs the peace. That is precisely what Bennett's *Expositor* has done. I want to recommend that we, as the legally constituted governing body of the City of Nauvoo, formally condemn the *Expositor* as libelous and also as a public nuisance which endangers the civil order.''

''That may be easily done,'' declared one council leader.

''Furthermore,'' Smith continued, ignoring the man's remark, ''I want this council to direct the city marshal to destroy all copies of this edition and the press that printed it as well.''

Murmurs of concern rippled through the assemblage.

Judah glanced at Smith, whose eyes were on fire as he shot glances at one after another of the hesitant council members.

''Is there a concensus?'' Smith asked impatiently.

There was a moment of uneasy silence before Hyrum Smith said, ''We will vote to so direct the city marshal, Joseph.''

''Good!'' Smith declared triumphantly. ''By so doing, we will have rid Nauvoo of a virulent pestilence!''

''All in favor,'' said Hyrum Smith, looking around at the men seated at the table, ''say—''

Judah interrupted him. ''Hold on a minute. Now I know I don't have a right to meddle in council matters, but there's something I think I ought to say and I hope you gentlemen will hear me out.''

Smith turned in his chair to stare coldly at Judah.

Avoiding Smith's eyes, Judah said, ''You go and wreck Bennett's press and you're asking for a whole lot of trouble. I can see it riding down the road. Now I'm no scholar of government, but I wouldn't be much surprised were people to start hollering about censorship and freedom of the press if you destroy those papers and that press. Why not just

fine him for creating a public nuisance? Or maybe for
inciting to riot? Something like that? You could make
things hot enough for him so that he might pull in his
horns some.''

"More drastic action than that is called for, Brother
Judah,'' Smith said. " 'If thine eye offend thee, pluck it
out and cast it from thee.' I would rather have the thing
smashed and die tomorrow than live and have it go on, for
it is exciting the spirit of mobocracy and will bring death
and destruction upon us.''

Judah said nothing more.

The council voted to invoke the law against Bennett and
the *Nauvoo Expositor* as defined by Blackstone and then
quickly adjourned.

That night, Judah was just leaving Smith's home when a
lieutenant of the Nauvoo Legion arrived at the house.

"What news?'' Smith asked the man eagerly.

"We stormed Bennett's place. We threw the type into
the street and smashed the press.''

"Good!'' Smith exclaimed happily, rubbing his hands
together.

Bad, Judah thought. But he said nothing.

In the days that followed, Judah's judgment proved to
have been correct. The destruction of Bennett's press by
the members of the Nauvoo Legion aroused severe reac-
tions among the Gentiles not only in Nauvoo and in the
state of Illinois but also throughout the nation.

Newspapers everywhere denounced the action. They con-
demned Smith as a despot and a tyrant. They declared the
Mormons and their religion a threat both to American
values and American morals. Editorial writers called for
action. For laws restricting the Mormons. For their banish-
ment from "civilized society.'' For an end to their threatening "theocracy.''

Smith and the church authorities were portrayed more than once as satyrs in their "vile practice of polygamy." They were accused of practicing lechery supposedly sanctified by divine revelation.

Smith fought back. Although he did not deny the charge of polygamy, he denounced his accusers as thieves, fornicators, and bearers of false witness against him and the other church authorities.

But to no avail, Judah noted sadly as he read, several days after the destruction of Bennett's press, an editorial in the *Warsaw Signal* written by the paper's editor, Thomas Sharp, who had returned to his attacks upon the Mormons with renewed vigor and seemingly tireless energy.

> *We hold ourselves at all times in readyness to cooperate with our fellow citizens to exterminate, utterly exterminate, the wicked and abominable Mormons.*

The words were flames and they had ignited more than one mob whose members had raged through Western Illinois, destroying Mormon property and attacking Mormons and severely beating them.

And all, Judah thought, under the guise of a respect for constitutional law and civil order.

Almost every Mormon-hater had taken upon himself the mantle of an avenger in the name of freedom of the press and the restoration of civil rights which, they claimed, had been violated by Smith when he ordered Bennett's press destroyed.

"They're right," Judah told Virginia one night in the cabin after they had eaten their supper.

"They're wrong!" she insisted. "They are nothing but

vicious vigilantes using fine words to disguise their foul deeds.''

"What I meant was they're right in saying Brother Joseph shouldn't've had that press smashed. Now they've got him on a charge of inciting a riot and they want to take him to Carthage to try him.''

"If he goes to the county seat,'' Virginia said, "they may kill or injure him. Carthage is a hotbed of Mormon haters.''

"He knows that. Today he got himself a writ of habeas corpus from the city court in Nauvoo and tomorrow he's supposed to appear in court.''

The following day, Smith did appear in court and was, to Judah's and Virginia's delight, acquitted of the charges against him.

"And the judge,'' Virginia pointed out to Judah as they left the courtroom, "was a non-Mormon. Justice, apparently, is not dead. Still, I don't see why the Sons of Dan don't retaliate against the men in those wolf packs who have been attacking us.''

"There's rumors that the Sons have done just that. Myself, I'm not so sure that's such a smart move if it really has happened.''

"Why not? We have to fight back! We can't just let ourselves be beaten and perhaps murdered and do nothing!''

"You talk like you're starting to take your new religion seriously,'' Judah said to her in surprise. "I thought you just did what you did—getting baptized and sealed to me—on account of you had to, more or less.''

"I've been reading the Book of Mormon. I take comfort in the faith. I just hope it's true because it's all I have now.''

"You have me.''

Virginia didn't respond.

*   *   *

The jubilation that arose in Nauvoo over Smith's acquittal quickly died and was replaced by fear as word spread that men from Illinois, Missouri, and Iowa were taking up arms and heading for Carthage. The fear deepened when the Mormons learned of the petitions that had been sent to Governor Ford of Illinois, demanding that Ford call up the state militia to end what was being called Smith's blatant defiance of the law.

In response to all this, Smith defiantly declared martial law in Nauvoo, mobilized the Nauvoo Legion, and wrote letters to Brigham Young and other Mormon missionaries asking them to come home immediately.

As mob violence directed at the Mormons spread like a fire in dry grass across Illinois and neighboring states, Governor Ford, on June twenty-first, traveled to Carthage in an attempt to put out the growing conflagration.

From there, he wrote to Smith, urging him to appear in a Carthage court to answer the charges leveled against him. It was, Ford wrote, the only way to avoid continued violence. Smith responded to Ford by writing that he would come only if he could be protected by a military escort drawn from the ranks of the Nauvoo Legion. Ford's response to this proposal was negative.

Virginia had changed her mind and now favored Smith's appearance before a Carthage court. "Brother Joseph," she told Judah, explaining the reasons for her change of mind, "can then adequately explain his behavior and make clear to one and all that the charges against him are nothing but an excuse to rouse the border scum against us."

Judah said nothing. But, later that day, he advised Smith to flee.

While Smith pondered his advice, Judah returned home

and, over Virginia's mild protests, set about teaching her how to load and fire his Hawkens rifle, which hung on wall pegs above the cabin's fireplace. He also taught her how to load and fire his pistol.

"Do you think I'll really ever have to use these guns?" she asked him during the grim lessons.

"I hope you won't have to."

When Smith sent word to Judah the following day that he had decided to go into hiding temporarily, Judah spoke to Virginia about what he had decided to do.

"I'm not keen on the idea of leaving you here by yourself," he told her. "But I feel it's my duty to do all I can to protect the Prophet."

"I'll be fine," she assured him.

"Maybe I ought to stay here with you till things die down some."

"You have a duty to perform."

"It's true that I have a duty to Brother Joseph. But I got a duty to you too."

"Nothing will happen to me. But, if something happens to Brother Joseph, what will the Saints do?"

Reluctantly, Judah left her, carrying his pistol but leaving the Hawkens rifle behind.

When he arrived late that night at Smith's home, he found the Prophet surrounded by friends, all of them deeply engaged in discussing what Smith should do to save himself from what they all now openly considered to be the possibility of certain death at the hands of either the unruly mobs of Mormon-haters roaming the countryside or at the equally deadly hands of the Illinois State Militia, the Carthage Greys.

As Judah sat down among the group, he heard Smith say, "I have considered going to Washington to lay my case directly before President Tyler. In fact, I wrote a letter to him a few days ago explaining conditions here. In it, I claimed the constitutional right of federal assistance because of the fact that forces from both Missouri and Illinois are planning an insurrection against us and the city itself.''

Then, sitting with bowed head, Judah heard him murmur, ''There is no mercy—no mercy here.''

No one in the room spoke.

Suddenly, Smith raised his head, his eyes bright and his lips parted in a smile, and announced, ''The way is open. It is clear to my mind what to do. All they want is Hyrum and myself. We will cross the river tonight and go away to the West!''

''Brother Joseph,'' Judah said, ''if that's what you've got in your mind to do, we'd best be about getting out of here. It's nearly midnight.''

''We'll go at once,'' Smith declared.

''How're you planning to get across the river?'' Judah asked him.

''Porter Rockwell and John Taylor,'' Smith answered, referring to two members of the church's Twelve Apostles, ''have hidden a rowboat on the bank of the river in case I chose to use it.''

Smith rose and kissed Emma, who had been sitting quietly in a corner, her eyes cast down. They embraced briefly and then Smith turned and gestured to Hyrum.

As the brothers left the house, Judah followed them outside. Moving as quietly as possible, all three made their way through the empty streets of Nauvoo and, when they reached the river bank, Judah found the boat which the two Apostles had hidden in some undergrowth lining the bank.

Judah, once the Smith brothers were seated in the boat,

pushed it away from the bank and jumped into it. The three men were silent as he rowed to the opposite bank.

The following afternoon, Porter Rockwell arrived on the western bank after rowing across the Mississippi.

"Prophet!" he called out excitedly as he dragged his rowboat up on the bank. "This morning a posse came to Nauvoo from Carthage to arrest you and Brother Hyrum. The Carthage Greys, they've threatened to destroy Nauvoo if you fail to surrender to the posse, and our people are in a panic. Governor Ford has promised you safety if you will but submit. Mrs. Smith sends her fond regards and urges you to return to Nauvoo at once and give yourself up."

"Don't do it!" Judah counseled Smith. "You do it and you're a dead man sure."

Smith seemed lost in thought. "Nauvoo the Beautiful," he whispered as if he were talking to himself. "It must not be destroyed. My dream must not die." And then, "Hyrum, you must flee to the West. I will surrender."

Hyrum Smith, his face impassive, said, "I will go with you, Joseph, to Carthage where we will place our fate in the hands of the Gentiles."

Judah gritted his teeth in silence.

Smith turned to him and said, "When we return to Nauvoo you must go home, Judah, and look after your wife. There is nothing more that you can do for me now."

"I plan on seeing this thing through," Judah stated flatly.

After recrossing the river, the Smiths and Judah returned to the Smith home where they spent the night. The following day, Judah accompanied the Smiths to Carthage, where they allowed themselves to be arraigned before Justice of the Peace Robert Smith, a man Judah knew to be not only the commander of the Carthage Greys but also a rabid anti-Mormon who had often expressed his sentiments about the Saints in public.

Justice Smith set a high bail.

The Smith brothers paid it and were released.

They jubilantly rented a room in a Carthage hotel, but had hardly had time to make themselves comfortable in it when there was a knock on the door. Judah answered it and found himself confronting a constable who announced the ominous news that he had a writ ordering the arrest of Joseph and Hyrum Smith on a charge of treason.

Judah could do nothing but accompany the Smiths and the constable on a return visit to Justice Smith who, to Judah's amazement which was blended with a sense of rage, ordered them—illegally because he did not hold a hearing—remanded to the Carthage jail.

When they arrived at the small, two-story jail, the constable herded the Smiths up the stairs and into the unbarred debtor's room on the second floor.

Judah asked the constable's permission to remain with the Smiths, and the constable, after hesitating for some time while Judah argued with him, finally granted it.

When news of the incarceration of the Smiths reached Nauvoo the next day, the jail was soon besieged by Mormons—both men and women—wanting to visit their Prophet. The constable at first tried to bar them from the building but at last he relented and admitted them.

As the day wore on and became hotter, Judah managed to take Smith aside. "Got something for you, Brother Joseph." He slid his pistol from his waistband and passed it to Smith, who took it gratefully and hid it in a pocket of the coat he was wearing.

Judah stood at the window of the jail with Smith's friend and confidant, Apostle Willard Richards. Both men watched in silence as Gentiles outside threw stones at the jail and shouted taunts and curses.

The constable reappeared and ordered the visitors to leave. "That's a hot-headed crowd out there," he said. "I'm just trying to do all you folks a favor."

As the Mormons reluctantly and, in some cases, tearfully, took their leave of Smith, Apostle John Taylor began to sing the currently popular inspirational song, "A Poor Wayfaring Man of Grief."

Judah stared out through the window at the jeering crowd and at the company of Carthage Greys who had been assigned the duty of guarding the jail and presumably, he thought wryly, the lives of Joseph and Hyrum Smith.

By four o'clock in the afternoon, the sweltering debtor's room on the second floor of the jail contained, besides Judah, only the Smith brothers and the two Apostles, Willard Richards and John Taylor.

The five men sat silently while the crowd outside the jail continued their stoning of the building and their shouting.

An hour passed.

The crowd outside fell suddenly silent.

Curious, Judah got up from his chair and went to the open window. The crowd had, he saw, vanished. Approaching the jail was a mob of men wearing the uniforms of the Warsaw militia, their faces daubed with mud so that they could not be identified.

"We're going to be attacked!" Judah yelled to the men in the room behind him. "Fire, dammit!" he yelled through the window to the company of Carthage Greys below.

The Greys, as if obeying his command, opened fire on the advancing militiamen and Judah watched incredulously as not a single shot found its mark.

The mob of militiamen, yelling Smith's name and curses, continued to advance steadily through the fire of the Greys.

"Blanks!" Judah said to himself as he suddenly understood why none of the men in the mob had been hit by the heavy fire. They're in on this, he thought. They've loaded up with blanks!

And then the first of the men were past the Greys and pounding up the stairs of the jail, shouting to Smith to surrender.

Judah left the window and hurled himself against the door of the room as the men outside began to hammer on it, still shouting loudly.

Shots tore through the door, one of them narrowly missing Judah.

He jumped back out of the line of fire, vaguely aware of his pistol in Smith's trembling hand and of Taylor's cane that was raised high above the man's head.

The door burst open.

The militiamen fired into the room.

Hyrum Smith was hit by several shots. He fell to the floor, killed instantly.

Smith fired Judah's pistol three times, hitting one of the militiamen.

Taylor's cane whirled through the air, striking the invaders on the shoulders and knocking down their gun barrels.

Smith dropped Judah's gun and ran for the open window.

Taylor fell wounded to the floor, his cane rattling against it as he went down.

Judah seized one of the nearest militiamen and hurled him against the others. Men stumbled, toppled, fell.

"Jump!" Judah shouted to Smith who had climbed up on the windowsill. Judah started toward the window, intending to shield Smith with his body so that the man could make his escape, but halfway across the room he fell over Taylor and hit the floor hard.

A shot zinged past him as he fell.

It entered Smith's back. Smith let out an agonized cry, his body snapping backward before he pitched forward and fell through the window to land on the ground below at the feet of the shouting militiamen.

Instantly, they seized him and dragged him to the well-curb in the yard where four militiamen gleefully fired into his lurching body.

Judah leaped to his feet and ran to the window as the invaders fled the debtor's room and pounded back down the stairs. He grimaced at the sight of Smith's lifeless body lying on the ground below. He suddenly remembered his pistol, which Smith had dropped before attempting to escape through the window.

He turned and ran back across the room. But, as he picked up the pistol, Richards grabbed his arm and said, "Taylor's hurt bad. Help me hide him, Brother Judah."

Judah hesitated, torn. He wanted to use the remaining two shots in his gun to bring down at least one of the men in the mob. But, at that moment, Taylor moaned and, in a barely audible voice, whispered, *"Help me!"*

Judah bent down and lifted Taylor to his feet. Then, with Richards' help, he got Taylor down the stairs and into a room off the hall.

Outside, a man shouted, "Christ, look at that, will you?"

Judah, leaving Richards to tend the wounded Taylor, ran to the door of the jail, the pistol still in his hand. As he reached it, he saw that clouds in the sky had parted and a shaft of sunlight was streaming through them to fall directly on Smith's corpse.

The militiamen seemed frozen for a moment. And then they fled.

Judah fired at them but missed.

Minutes later, the scene was deserted. Judah stared

through eyes that were blurred by tears at the dead Prophet. When Richards appeared at his side, Judah asked, "How's Taylor?"

"Bad," Richards said. "Would you get help—a doctor? I'll stay with him. My horse is tied out back."

"I'll go."

"The Prophet—is he . . . dead?"

Judah nodded and left the jail.

After stepping into the saddle of Richards' horse, he galloped away from the now eerily silent jail.

In Nauvoo, he stopped at the doctor's house and told him what had happened to the Smiths and to Taylor. When the doctor left to go to the jail, Judah remounted Richards' horse and headed south to his cabin, shattered by a sense of loss and tormented by a sense of despair as an image of Smith's broken body burned in his mind.

It was dusk when he came out of the trees bordering his fields and saw the flames rising from his cabin and shed.

Virginia! his mind screamed as he galloped toward the burning buildings.

She was nowhere in sight.

He leaped from the horse's back and, kicking open the blazing cabin door, raced inside.

He found her lying face down on the floor beneath the wooden table as if she had crawled there seeking refuge.

Not far from where she was lying was a portion of a broken broom handle. Almost its entire length was coated with blood.

Despite the heat of the fire, cold sweat suddenly slicked Judah's entire body. He ran to Virginia, picked her up, and cradled her in his arms.

And then, as the flames crackled around him and the roof heaved dangerously above him, he stood transfixed, staring down at the wet mass of organic matter that had been lying beneath Virginia's body.

The placenta.

And the fetus curled up on the floor, its tiny fingers forming fists, its undeveloped body looking peaceful in its sleep of death.

He ran from the burning cabin, carrying Virginia. He placed her gently down on the grass far from the cabin that was now collapsing in upon itself. And upon his dead child.

He placed a finger against the side of her neck, and heaved an enormous sigh of relief when he felt a faint pulse.

He didn't know how long he sat dazedly beside her but, when at last her eyes fluttered open, he bent down toward her to catch the words her lips were trying so hard to form.

"—men—wolf pack—"

Her eyes closed. And then they snapped open, brimming with horror as memory returned to her.

"*My baby!*" she screamed hysterically.

Over and over again.

BOOK TWO: ZION

NINE

IN September of the year eighteen forty-six, more than two years after the assassination of the Prophet, Judah was close to despair.

After the burning of his cabin, he had taken Virginia into Nauvoo and there rented a small house. As the months passed and Brigham Young continued to promise the Gentiles that the Mormons would leave Illinois, Judah had worked harder than most men in making preparations to head west to find a suitable site on which to once again attempt to build the heavenly city where the Saints could hope to be finally free of persecution and where they might live at last in safety and serenity.

Now, as Nauvoo lay nearly totally deserted, Judah thought he might never be able to persuade Virginia to leave the city. He had pleaded with her countless times but she had steadfastly refused to leave Nauvoo.

He had told himself while he worked and planned their departure during the preceding two years that she would surely change her mind. Any day now, he had constantly assured himself, she would agree to go west. Next week. In a month perhaps.

But she hadn't.

He had worked doggedly on, always hoping. He cut and kiln-dried oak for the wagon he was building. He cut hickory and soaked the wood in brine before using it to fashion axles. He constructed a forge and on it he tirelessly hammered out tires and chains for the wagon.

When the wagon was finished, it had enough room for two beds and space for the provisions he intended to take with him on the long journey. Judah's wagon had eight bows eighteen inches apart and he had sewn together two webs of thick drilling which he used to cover the wagon. But, because he was familiar with the heavy rains that spilled from the sky during the relentless thunderstorms that punished the prairie, and the snow that the land's terrible winters sent spilling upon the plains, he had covered the drilling with stout sheeting which he had then painted to waterproof it.

Weeks ago, he had harvested the squash he had grown and put them aside to dry. He had slaughtered the hog he had raised and then smoked and salted its flesh along with that of the fish he had caught in the river.

Virginia had watched his efforts without comment and without offering to help him.

He didn't blame her for her failure to help him or for her refusal to leave Nauvoo. He understood the reasons for her listlessness and vagueness that seemed to have turned her into a stranger. The violence of the attack upon her had left her in a state of shock that still persisted, and which kept her fearful of visitors and seldom willing to venture out of the rented house.

And the attack had left her terrified of Judah's touch.

When he had tried to soothe her in those first few weeks following the loss of their unborn child, she had recoiled from him in horror. Once she had screamed when he had accidentally and somewhat roughly touched her. She had never let him enter her bed after that awful night. He was forced to sleep in a bed of his own and forced finally to move that bed out of the room in which Virginia slept because, she claimed, she could not sleep when he was with her in the dark room.

Walking through the almost deserted city on a still-summery day in mid-September, Judah's despair deepened as he passed the abandoned houses of friends who had either sold them for little more than ten cents on the dollar to Gentiles anxious to take advantage of their owners' desperate plight, or who had simply fled, leaving behind all that they could not take with them to be plundered or destroyed by the wolf packs which still made frequent forays into the city in search of any unarmed Mormons unlucky enough to fall into their hands.

The sun shone down as brightly as ever, but it seemed to Judah that the city had shriveled beneath its warm rays. Stillness stalked the almost empty streets. An occasional carriage appeared as he walked aimlessly along, an occasional passer-by eyed him apprehensively as he approached, obviously wondering if he posed a threat to them. Was he a Gentile? If so, was he a member of a wolf pack? Relief showed on the faces of these infrequent passers-by when Judah greeted them politely and walked on.

He turned and retraced his steps, intending to go home and try once more to convince Virginia that they should leave the city and head west after those who had gone earlier. He would, he decided, tell her of the rumors he had heard of the threats being made by militiamen to destroy Nauvoo and the relatively few Mormons who still remained in the city.

He would tell her that neither the federal government nor the state government had made any efforts of any kind to stop the night riders who had invaded Mormon homes in Nauvoo and killed or wounded their occupants. He would tell her that a man he knew, a Mormon, had, only last night, been taken from his home by a wolf pack, stripped, and savagely whipped.

When he arrived at the house he shared with Virginia and gone inside it, he found her seated in the parlor, her hands folded in her lap, her eyes cast down. She did not greet him as he entered the room.

"You didn't go out," he said, his remark more of a statement than a question.

"I had no reason to go out. You said yourself that the city is threatened. Why would I risk going out?"

Judah allowed himself to hope. She seemed suddenly to have become aware of the danger of remaining in Nauvoo. She had never before given him any indication that she knew they were both taking a risk in remaining.

"Honey, we have to leave here."

She slowly shook her head.

"But, Virginia, if we don't we're liable to—"

She looked up at him. "Where would we go?"

"West. When Brother Brigham left last February with

the vanguard, he said they'd find a place where all of us can live in peace.''

"A wild goose chase.''

"We've got to take our chances,'' he insisted. "We can't stay here. There's only a few hundred people left in Nauvoo of all the thousands who once lived here. Most of them are old and feeble and sick, and if the mobs take it into their heads to destroy the city they'll be—maybe all of us'll be killed.''

"I've told you before, Judah. There is only one place I will go if I leave here.''

"But you can't go home! You wrote your father a whole lot of letters going on over two years now and he didn't answer even one of them.''

"I'll wait. He'll relent. I'm sure he will. In time.''

"We haven't got us that kind of time, Virginia!'' Judah declared, his voice rising to match his growing sense of frustration. "We just don't. You've got to believe me. It's right *now* that we should be going!''

"Are you hungry? Shall I prepare something for you to eat?''

Judah groaned. Wearily, he leaned against the wall and ran tense fingers through his hair.

Virginia rose and started for the kitchen at the rear of the house. Then, suddenly, she halted, listening. "Judah, do you hear something?''

Did he? At first, he wasn't sure. Perhaps what he thought he heard was only the pounding of the wild thoughts careening through his mind.

"Drums?'' Virginia said speculatively. "Maybe the Legion is drilling.''

The instant Judah recognized the sound of cannon booming in the distance, he snapped erect and went to the window. He stared out in the direction from which the ominous sounds were coming.

"Virginia," he said, forcing himself to speak softly, "the militiamen—they said they were going to destroy Nauvoo if we all didn't leave. That's them. That's their cannon you're hearing. They're attacking the city from the north. We've got to leave. Right now!"

He saw terror fill Virginia's eyes as she stood stiffly in the center of the room staring at him, shaking her head as if she were trying to deny the truth of his words.

Through the window, he saw an old man run out of a house across the street and begin shouting. He was quickly joined by a younger man from the same house and, as Judah watched, the pair began to throw up a makeshift barricade in the middle of the street consisting of wagons, odds and ends of furniture which they carried from their house, and cords of firewood.

Fools, he thought.

He saw the gray smoke begin to rise above the city in the north. They're burning us out, he thought angrily.

He turned away from the window and grabbed his Hawkens rifle and his Paterson Colt.

"What are you doing?" Virginia cried.

"Get those sacks I sewed. They're in the kitchen. Fill them with food. Crackers. Flour. Sugar. Anything you can lay your hands on. Bring them out and put them in the wagon. We're leaving!"

"No! I'm afraid!"

"You know what they'll do if they catch us. They won't rest until every last Mormon has been murdered." He saw the terror deepen in her eyes. "We can try to defend ourselves. We can shoot them if we have to. But there's lots more of them than there is of us. And if they see you—a pretty woman like you—" He didn't want to go on voicing the thoughts that were howling in his mind. But he did want to make Virginia see that she must leave with him immediately. "You remember that night when the wolf pack came—you told me what they did to you—how they—"

Virginia's hands flew up to claw at her face. She screamed shrilly.

Judah slapped her face.

She quieted.

"Now you go and you fill up all those sacks with as much food as they'll hold like I told you."

Relief flooded through him as she ran toward the kitchen. He went outside and around the house, where he began to put his team of horses into the wagon's traces. As he worked, he tried to drown out the sound of the distant cannon by whistling, tried not to think of whether or not he could get his wagon across the Mississippi—or whether he could even get as far as the river with Virginia before the mobs caught up with them.

When both horses were securely in their traces, he ran back into the house and helped Virginia fill sacks with food. Then he carried them out and loaded them in the wagon beside the barrels of smoked and salted meat and fish that he had previously stored in the wagon.

Then, hastily, making many trips back and forth between the house and the wagon, they filled it with linens, clothes, cooking utensils, and Judah's tools.

Thirty minutes later, Judah helped Virginia climb up onto the wagon's sturdy plank seat and then he climbed up beside her. He picked up the reins, slapped them across the backs of the horses, and clucked to the team.

As the wagon moved away from the house and down toward the river, the cannon continued to boom in the north and the smoke from burning buildings thickened in the sky overhead. Judah urged the horses into a full gallop, aware of the fearful faces peering from the windows of the few occupied houses they passed. He saw men, most of them aged, running north through the streets with pitchforks or old muzzle loaders in their hands.

"Get out!" he yelled to them. "To the river—make a run for it!"

They paid him no attention.

But, as they neared the river, they met other wagons of all kinds also heading in the same direction. Frantic men and women were driving them, children bouncing about in the wagon beds. A child in one of the wagons was crying and the child's mother, grim-faced, kept her grip on her horses' reins, ignoring the little girl's distress.

By the time they reached the river, its bank was crowded with refugees from the city and their wagons.

Some people, Judah noted, had no wagons. They stood in the throng, apparently dazed, holding their few possessions which they had bundled in sheets and tablecloths. A man was pushing a wheelbarrow which was piled high with household goods and threatening at any moment to topple over as he maneuvered it over the rough ground.

Horses whinnied and reared, their front legs flailing the air. Men and women cried out fearfully to one another.

"They've defiled the Temple!" a man shouted. "Those drunken men in their carousing vomited in the baptismal font. They urinated and defecated on every one of the twelve marble oxen that support it!"

"Have you seen my Harry?" an old woman wailed as she made her uncertain way through the crowd of people who were loading their wagons and possessions on lighters, scows, and skiffs of every kind. "*Harry!*" she cried, disappearing into the crowd.

An old man threw his arms up into the air and, as the

breeze whipped his long white beard, hurled the violent words of the psalmist at the unseen mob that was sacking the city:

> *"Remember, O lord, the children of Edom in the day of Jerusalem; who said, Raze it, raze it, even to the foundation thereof. O daughter of Babylon, who are to be destroyed, happy shall he be, that rewardeth thee as thou hast served us. Happy shall he be, that taketh and dasheth thy little ones against the stones."*

Judah wanted to cheer the old man on. He wanted to leap from the wagon and return to the city, not to dash the children of Babylon against the stones, but to seize and slowly slaughter, one by murdering one, their fathers who were sacking the city of the Saints.

But instead, he jumped down from the wagon after ordering Virginia to take the reins and remain where she was. He moved quickly through the crowd, asking people he met if there was a boat he could borrow—a boat big enough to accommodate his wagon—which he could use to cross the river. Some of the people he accosted ignored him, others merely shrugged helplessly. One man told him to forget about a wagon and to swim the river.

The sound of the distant cannon suddenly ceased.

The people on the river bank seemed to stiffen in the silence. For a moment, no one moved. And then, as they heard the cries and curses of the onrushing mob, everyone was instantly galvanized into action. Boats pulled away from the shore. One, when it was halfway across the river, suddenly tilted dangerously as the two oxen aboard it clumsily shifted position. One of them went over the side.

Men and women fell overboard after it, and they floundered desperately in the water.

Judah asked a man who was launching a flatboat if the man would return for him and his wagon. "I'll pay whatever you ask," he told the man.

The man shook his head. "I'm not coming back here once I get to the other side," he said firmly. "It's sure death to come back here. Can't you hear them, Brother? They're coming!"

Judah, suddenly remembering, turned and ran back to his wagon.

"Where were you?" Virginia called out as he approached her. "I've been so frightened."

He leaped up onto the seat beside her and turned the two horses.

"Where are we going?" she asked him, clutching his arm as the wagon rumbled along.

"South!" he shouted above the din the crowd was making. He didn't tell her why. He didn't try to explain that he had remembered the flatboat he had seen moored at the rotting wharf of Beecher's warehouse the night Grant and Kane had imprisoned him in the building. He wouldn't let himself consider the fact that the flatboat, like the wharf to which it had been moored, might also be rotting. He didn't let himself think that the boat might not be there any longer.

The wagon moved on through the noisy crowd, Judah shouting to warn people to get out of his way. To his left, he saw flames rising on the eastern edge of the city. He caught a glimpse of the white and gold dome of the Temple on the hill. What had that man said earlier? The mob had defiled the Temple. Judah's jaw set as he drove doggedly on.

It took him only minutes to reach Beecher's warehouse.

He jumped down from the wagon and ran out on the wharf, examining the flatboat that was, he saw with immense relief, still moored to the wharf. There was no water in its bottom. He turned and called out to Virginia and then beckoned to her.

When she had joined him on the wharf, he said, "We'll make the crossing in this. You've got to help me."

"How?"

He was gratified to see the spark that had been rekindled in her eyes. It had not been there since the night the mob had left her to die in the burning cabin. He had thought he might never see it flare in her beautiful blue eyes again. But now it was back and his heart leaped for joy at the sight of it.

He started to tell her what they must do to get the horses and the wagon aboard the flatboat, but before he could finish his instructions he heard a scream. He spun around to see several men dragging a gray-haired man along the ground at the end of a rope that bound the man's wrists together. Behind the man being dragged ran a young woman.

Judah was struck with her beauty, despite the fact that her long black hair was undone and her face twisted with fear and horror. Her dark eyes were large and glistening with tears as she cried out to the men and pleaded with them to release their elderly prisoner.

Suddenly, one of the men in the mob slowed his pace and seized the young woman. He threw her to the ground, then quickly dropped down upon her. Judah took his rifle from the wagon just as the militiamen hurled the man they had been dragging into the river. As the currents began to sweep their victim downstream, the woman struck the man who was trying to rape her on the side of the head with a stone she had found. He rolled off her, bellowing his rage, and she leaped to her feet and ran to the river bank.

When she saw the bound man vainly trying to swim in the swift current, she screamed.

Judah raised his rifle and fired.

One of the men on the river bank fell to the ground, clutching his arm.

The woman screamed a second time, dropped to her knees, and reached out helplessly to the man floundering in the river.

"Next time, I'll shoot to kill you!" Judah shouted at the militiamen, the rifle still braced against his shoulder, his finger tight on its trigger.

One of the men in the mob swore at him.

Then they all surged in a body toward him.

Behind Judah, Virginia gasped.

He fired. A man dropped and didn't rise. Or move.

The mob scattered, fleeing from the river bank.

Judah handed the Hawkens to Virginia. "If they come back, shoot them."

He leaped from the boat and raced to where the woman was still kneeling on the bank and weeping. He bent down and lifted her to her feet. He put an arm around her to steady her shuddering body as he stared out over the unbroken surface of the river.

The man who was the cause of the woman's weeping was nowhere to be seen.

Judah remained silent as the woman turned to him and buried her face against his chest. He stood there, holding her, wishing the mob would return so he could kill them all.

"He might make it back to the bank," Judah said to the woman in his arms. "Or maybe he's got over to the other side."

"He's dead," the woman murmured through her tears. "I know he is."

"Your husband?"

"My father. He had a bad heart. And rheumatism. When they caught us back in the city—they took him— you saw what they did to us."

"We've got to get out of here. We have a boat. Come on."

He led her by the hand as if she were a reluctant child. At the wagon, he said to Virginia, "That man they tossed into the river—he was her father."

Virginia lowered the rifle and handed it to Judah.

"This here's my wife," Judah said to the woman, who had stopped crying and now stood staring stonily out over the water. "We're the Bascombs; she's Virginia, and my name's Judah."

"I'm Olivia Ames," the woman said.

Judah, with Virginia's help, prepared to load the wagon and its team on the flatboat for the river crossing.

When they had disembarked on the western bank of the river, they found themselves in the midst of what Virginia correctly called "pandemonium."

People milled aimlessly about on the bank. Horses and wagons were mired in deep mud and their owners struggled to free them. Children cried. Oxen bellowed. A calf was accidentally killed beneath the iron tires of a runaway wagon whose team had suddenly bolted.

Judah, undaunted by the chaos surrounding him, drove his wagon away from the river bank to slightly higher and much drier ground. He looked back at the people on the bank and shook his head.

"They'd best get themselves organized or they're not ever going to get anywhere," he remarked to Virginia and then he suddenly jumped down from the wagon's seat and strode back to the river bank.

When he reached the edge of the throng, he yelled, "Get your wagons in a line. Everybody without one get ready to march alongside the wagons."

"Who are you?" a man shouted from the crowd.

Another man provided the answer to the question.

"That's Brother Judah Bascomb, the man Simon Grant tried to kill."

"Too bad that Grant was acquitted of the crime and allowed to leave Nauvoo," the man who had spoken first muttered. "That judge that tried him didn't know his ear from his elbow."

A woman asked, "Who gave you the right to order us about, Brother Bascomb?"

"Nobody did," Judah replied. "But it sure looks to me like you ought to elect yourself a leader else you'll all be still here come the day of resurrection."

"He was the Prophet's bodyguard," a man called out to the crowd. "A man like him has the makings of a leader."

"I'm not looking to be anybody's leader," Judah said quickly. "I'm just trying to give you folks a little advice. We should all move out of here now before it gets dark. We could make it as far as Sugar Creek by the time the sun sets if we get moving. It's not more'n seven miles or so and there's good water and timber to cut for cooking."

"I suggest we elect Brother Bascomb our wagon master," the man who had earlier identified Judah called out.

Judah listened to the people arguing among themselves and then, disgusted with their indecision, said, "I'm not looking to be your wagon master so there's no need for you all to fuss so about it. I'll leave you to settle things among yourselves." He turned and headed back toward his wagon.

But, as he was pulling out for Sugar Creek, a man came running toward him.

Judah reined in his team as the man, breathless, called out to him. "We put it to a vote. We want you to lead us to Zion, Brother Bascomb. We think you're the man best suited to do it."

"That's a fact, is it?" Judah pondered the development. He had intended to travel alone with Virginia. But now he had more or less committed himself to taking a third person—Olivia Ames. Could he, should he assume the responsibility for another few hundred, he asked himself. "If I'm to be wagon master," he said after a long moment, "I'll make the rules and you'll all follow them. Anybody breaks the rules, they'll have me to answer to. You'd best go on back and make that clear to everybody. Then, if they still want me to take charge, well, I'm willing."

The man left and, when he returned a few minutes later, it was with the news that the refugees had agreed to Judah's terms.

"I'll be right back," Judah told Virginia, and he left with the man to go back to the river bank.

"How many of you have wagons?" he asked. When he had his answer, he asked, "How many of you are on foot?" When he had the answer to his second question, he moved through the crowd assigning to wagons those who had none of their own.

"How many of you men have guns?" he asked, and when those owning guns stepped forward, he designated them guards for the wagon train and assigned each man a position on the train's flanks.

"My wife will lead the way in our wagon," he told the people. "Me, I'll scout on up ahead. We'll head for Sugar Creek. That's where we'll spend the night. Each wagon will rotate from the front of the train to the rear each day we're on the trail. That way, nobody will have to eat too much dust. Once we get to Sugar Creek, you—" he pointed to a man wearing a slouch hat, ''—will take an inventory of the stock we have with us. I want every cow, calf, ox, goat, mule, and chicken counted.

''What that's done, Sister Olivia Ames will go among you and take an inventory of how much food each of us has got. If anybody's sick, she'll tell me. If anybody's hurt, she'll tell me that, too.

''There'll be no thieving among us. Anybody caught thieving, well, I've got me a bullwhip in my wagon and I won't hesitate to use it. We'll share and share alike, and anybody caught hoarding'll be turned away from the train.

''We've got us many miles to go. Once Brother Brigham finds a place for us, he'll send somebody back with the news. Till then, we'll head west to Winter Quarters he's set up on the Missouri River. The snow'll be flying soon enough, so we'll have to hole up there till next spring. Now you know where I stand as wagon master. Maybe some of you'd like to change your mind about putting me in charge.''

Murmurs weaved in and out among the crowd.

''Well, speak up, any of you who've got any objections to what I've just said.'' Judah waited.

No one spoke.

''I'll need a good horse,'' Judah said. ''Anybody ready to turn one over to me?''

''I have a strong mule you can borrow,'' a man at the edge of the crowd volunteered.

''You can have one of our horses,'' a woman called out. ''My family has a wagon, three cows, and two extra horses. You can have one of the horses, Brother Bascomb.''

''Thank you, Sister,'' Judah said to the woman. ''I'll take good care of him and turn him back to you once we all reach Zion.''

As he went to get the horse, and as the wagons began to

form a long line behind his wagon, he heard a woman's voice burst out in song, a song he had heard sung in Nauvoo which had been learned from one of the messengers Young had sent back to the city from time to time, the song that had become the camp song of the emigrants on their way west.

> Come, come ye saints,
> No toil, nor labor fear,
> But with joy wend your way;
> Though hard to you
> This journey may appear,
> Grace shall be as your day.

The woman walking beside Judah also began to sing the song. Moments later, everyone was singing. Everyone, Judah noticed, except Olivia Ames. He glanced back across the river at Nauvoo and then joined in the singing.

> 'Tis better far for us to strive
> Our useless cares from us to drive;
> Do this, and joy your hearts will swell.
> All is well! All is well!

TEN

BEFORE dawn the next morning, Judah crawled out from beneath his wagon where he had spent the night, rubbed his eyes with his fisted hands, and fired his Colt—one shot, a signal to arouse the camp.

He immediately regretted his action when he heard a woman scream from inside a nearby wagon. "All is well!" he quickly yelled at the top of his voice. "It's time to move out!"

As people began to climb out of their wagons, he opened the drawstrings of his own wagon to find both Virginia and

Olivia sitting up on the two beds and putting their shoes on.

"We'll be moving out soon," he told them. "Start a fire, Virginia. Olivia, you help her cook breakfast for us."

"We left our sheet metal stove back in Nauvoo," Virginia reminded him. "How can we—"

"You'll have to learn how to cook outdoors," Judah told her. "Now, I'm going to check the night guards, and see that everything's all right. I'll be back real soon—and I'll be bringing my hunger with me. Ask among the women. Someone will show you how to build a fire."

He walked through the camp, nodding greetings to the people he met, occasionally stopping to offer words of encouragement to those who seemed to need it.

He moved through the camp, checking with each of the guards he had posted the night before and learning from them that nothing untoward had happened during the night. Then he searched through the camp until he found the man with the slouch hat whom he had told, while still on the western bank of the Mississippi, to make an inventory of the refugees' stock.

"You get it all down?" he asked, noticing for the first time that the man was young, not much older than he was himself, and boyishly lean-limbed with regular features that women would probably consider attractive.

"My name's Vernon Drake," the man volunteered as he handed the list he had made to Judah.

"Glad to know you, Drake." Judah scanned the list. "Looks like we have enough stock to last us. We'll take from those who have a lot and give some to those who have none."

"Some people," Drake suggested, "might take some persuading to part with what they correctly consider theirs."

"I can be a very persuasive man," Judah assured him

with a smile. "A forceful one where persuasion won't turn the trick."

"I'll be glad to help you any way I can."

Judah met Drake's appraising gaze and said, "You're figuring I'm going to need help, that it?"

"No, I didn't mean it like that. I just thought—"

"Appreciate your thought, Drake. Might be, I'll be calling on you for that help you've so kindly offered me." He paused. "I've seen you before, haven't I?"

"Probably. I was a member of the Nauvoo Legion. I stayed on in the city hoping for a fight."

"You get one?"

"I guess I did. Some of us were trying to keep the mob out of the Temple. We did—for a spell."

"Heard they made a mess of it."

"They did. But at least we tried to keep them out."

"It's all a man can do, Drake. Try his best." Judah started to leave and then he asked, "You got a family traveling with you?"

"No. I'm alone."

"Come along then. You can breakfast with me and my wife."

"I'd be pleased to do that, Brother Bascomb."

When the two men returned to Judah's wagon, they found Olivia kneeling on the ground and trying to fan into life a small fire she had made using twigs she had broken from the branches of the sheltering trees.

The fire went out.

Judah glanced at Virginia.

She looked up at him and said, "Well, I told you that I haven't the slightest idea of how to cook out in the open like this."

"I'm sorry," Olivia said as she stared in disgust at her dead fire. "I just can't seem to keep it burning."

"Green wood," Judah said.

"I'll dig a fire pit," Drake said.

"This here's Vernon Drake," Judah said. "He was one of our Legionaires till he got run off like the rest of us. Drake, meet my wife, Virginia. And this is Sister Olivia Ames."

Virginia smiled at Drake and Olivia rose and shook his hand.

Judah was pleased to see how quickly Drake got a fire burning in the pit he had dug and circled with stones. Above it, he had placed an iron spanner that rested in the notched and upright ends of two iron rods he had scavenged from somewhere.

Virginia hung her kettle by an S-shaped iron hook from the spanner, and soon the water in it was steaming. Drake placed another S-hook on the spanner and hooked it into the handle of Virginia's coffee pot so that the pot hung above the fire.

"I'll get plates and things," Virginia volunteered and climbed into the wagon. When she returned to the fire, she passed out plates, cups, and utensils to Judah and Olivia, who were seated on the ground near the fire.

As Drake began to spoon some of the contents of the kettle onto the plates, she asked, "Does this dish you have concocted have a name, Mr. Drake?"

"Yes, it does. It's called Spotted Pup." He grinned at her. "Maybe you can guess why." He filled her plate.

She looked down at the rice and raisins Judah had given him earlier and then up at Drake. "I'm afraid I'm not a very good guesser."

"Don't it remind you of a Dalmatian dog?" Judah asked her.

She laughed. "Why, of course. The raisins—black against

the white rice. But, Judah, how did you know what it's called? Or did you guess?"

"It's a trail favorite of most cowboys. Ate my fill of it time and time again."

"You Americans speak in such a colorful manner," Olivia commented shyly.

Judah glanced at her in surprise. "You're not an American?"

"I'm from Hereford, England," she replied. "I became a Mormon when the Prophet's missionaries came to England and visited us. Then I traveled to Nauvoo—with my father."

Judah turned to Drake, "Sister Ames lost her father when the city was sacked. He drowned. She's as alone as you are, Brother Drake."

Drake turned back to the fire.

Judah, behind his back, winked at Virginia.

"This is really quite delicious, Mr. Drake," Virginia said. "You shall have to teach me how to make it sometime."

"Nothing to it, Mrs. Bascomb. I'll be glad to."

"You can wash these dishes down in the creek," Judah told Virginia. "We just have time for a quick cup of coffee before we pull out."

Drake wrapped a cloth around his hand, gripped the coffee pot, removed it from the fire, and filled Virginia's cup.

When Judah's cup had been filled, he turned to Olivia and asked, "Did you find out if anybody's sick or hurt?"

"Yes, I did. I wrote down their names. Most people are fit. But Mrs. Petry has a fever and Mr. Slocum has something the matter with his arm. He can't seem to raise it. It may be broken."

"Is there a doctor with us?" Judah inquired.

"I checked, and I'm afraid the answer is no," Olivia said.

Judah emptied his cup and stood up. "I'll look in on Sister Petry and Brother Slocum before we pull out. Olivia, you finished your breakfast? Could you show me where to find them?"

"This way."

She led him to a Conestoga wagon near the creek and Judah climbed into it.

"Sister Petry?" he asked the woman who was lying on the pallet in the wagon bed.

"Who are you?"

"A friend." He placed a hand on her forehead. "How long you been feverish like this, Sister?"

"Days," the woman answered in a faint voice. "I must have taken a chill."

Judah opened a trunk in the front of the wagon and rummaged about in it until he found a bolt of gingham. He tore a piece from it and handed it out to Olivia along with instructions to soak it in the creek and then bring it back to him.

When she had done so, he folded the gingham and gently placed it on Mrs. Petry's forehead.

"That feels so soothing," she whispered. "Thank you."

"Anybody traveling with you, Sister?"

"My daughter, Daisy. She'll be back directly."

"When she gets back, you tell her to keep a cool cloth on your forehead. She can dip it in your water barrel from time to time."

"Daisy's a good girl. She'll do all she can for me."

"Where's your blankets?"

"We had to pack in such a terrible hurry—I'm afraid I forgot to bring blankets."

"You rest. I'll be right back." Judah climbed out of the

wagon and, with Olivia accompanying him, went to a nearby wagon beside which a man sat at a small fire.

"Your name, mister?" Judah asked him.

"Sidley."

"You got any blankets?"

Sidley nodded, and Judah said, "Give me two of them."

"What for?"

"Sister Petry's sick with fever and she's got herself no blankets. Now, are you going to give me two of yours or am I going to take them from you?"

Sidley, grumbling, got up. He emerged from his wagon a moment later and handed two blankets to Judah, who thanked him and turned to leave with Olivia.

"What's my family supposed to do for warmth when winter comes?" Sidley called after him.

Without turning around, Judah yelled back, "You can worry about that once winter's here."

"Take these to Sister Petry," he told Olivia, handing her the blankets. "And point me the way to the Slocums."

She did, and he made his way to the family group who were standing huddled together near the creek.

"Heard you had a bad arm," he said to the only man in the group of two women and six children.

"I think it might be broken," Slocum said as if he were apologizing for a personal fault. "I fell when we were running from Nauvoo. This arm of mine pains me something terrible, I can tell you."

"Let's have a look at it."

Judah examined Slocum's left arm, which hung limply at the man's side. Slocum winced as he touched it. "It's not broken," Judah said. "Just dislocated. Maybe I can fix it for you if you think you can stand some pain."

"You're a doctor?" Slocum asked hopefully.

"Nope. But I've cared for sick stock. Even a cowboy or

two who got themselves banged up a bit. I'll try not to harm you anymore than you're already hurt. Figure I just might be of some help. You willing to give it a go?''

Slocum hesitated a moment and then nodded, his decision made.

''It's your elbow,'' Judah explained. ''It's slipped its socket.'' He continued talking in an attempt to distract Slocum and then he suddenly seized the man's bicep in his left hand and Slocum's forearm in his right and pulled and then twisted.

Slocum gasped, gritted his teeth, and squeezed his eyes shut.

Judah crooked Slocum's arm at the elbow and asked the women for a piece of cloth he could use to make a sling.

When he had the sling in place, he said, ''Don't use your arm. Let it hang there like that for a week or so.''

''Friend,'' Slocum said, opening his eyes and visibly relaxing, ''I couldn't use this arm of mine to so much as pick the last rose of summer.''

Judah returned the man's smile, then turned to the staring children. ''You tads help your daddy all you can. You can see he's hurt and needs your help bad.''

''Yes, sir,'' said a small boy who looked to Judah to be no more than six or seven years old.

When Judah got back to his wagon, he found Virginia sitting on the plank seat with the reins held lightly in her hands.

''How far is it to Winter Quarters?'' she asked him.

''About four hundred miles.''

''How long will it take us to get there?''

''Depends.''

''On what?''

''The weather mostly. We can make up to twenty miles a day, I reckon, if the weather's fair. Rain'll slow us down by turning the ground muddy. Storms might stop us for a spell. Where's Olivia?''

''I haven't seen her since the two of you went off together.''

Judah went around to the rear of the wagon, untethered the horse he had borrowed, and swung into the saddle.

He let out a yell and gestured to the people when they turned toward him. ''Move out! I'll pick the spot for our nooning. Follow me!''

He trotted west while behind him Virginia drove their wagon and the others followed in a long line, flanked by guards with guns.

Behind them, to the east, the sun was rising and the shadows of the people stretched out in front of them as if they too were yearning to reach out and touch the promised land that lay somewhere ahead of them in the faraway West.

Before the sun had reached its meridian, Judah called a halt and the train nooned on the grassy prairie.

He left his horse, its reins trailing to keep it from wandering off, to graze under the warm sun and walked through the camp, dodging running children and an occasional barking dog that was eager to join the childrens' games. People he knew and many he didn't spoke to him as he passed. Some offered to share their dinner with him, but he thanked them and moved on, his eyes roving over the camp, searching for Olivia.

He found her feeding grass to a goat that was tied to the endgate of a wagon near the rear of the train.

''Oh, hello!'' she said cheerfully as he came up to her. ''It's a lovely day, now isn't it?''

''Fine,'' he agreed. ''Why aren't you up front with Virginia?''

Olivia dropped her eyes and absently petted the goat

before answering, "I didn't want to inconvenience you, so I asked Mrs. Petry if she would mind if I shared the wagon with her and Daisy. That way, I can tend to her while Daisy drives the wagon." She looked up, but avoided Judah's gaze. "She's a bit better, I do believe. Perhaps its only because we're moving. I know I feel so hopeful now. I daresay you think it awful of me to say such a terrible thing with the Prophet . . . gone, and my father so recently lost to me, but I can't help it. I do feel hopeful. I feel as if we've left all the horror and persecution behind us forever. I'm confident that the Lord will open the way ahead for us and that He shall bless us in the days to come."

"What did you mean when you said you didn't want to inconvenience me?"

"Well—" she began and fell silent.

Judah watched her closely. She was a very attractive young woman. Even in her sorrow, she seemed to sparkle. Her brown eyes glistened. Her black hair was soft and, although she had parted it in the middle and bound it severely in a bun at the nape of her neck, it looked luxuriant. Her nose was small and upturned above her full and faintly sensuous lips.

Her figure was full, especially her hips and breasts, but she nevertheless gave an impression of supple slenderness.

"Well," she repeated, "you have only two beds in your wagon and I hated to force you to sleep out last night. So I really did think it best that I make other arrangements for myself. I hope you don't think I didn't appreciate your kindness and hospitality, Brother Bascomb."

"I'd like it fine if you'd call me Judah."

"I shall then."

"I wasn't inconvenienced by you sleeping in my wagon," he said, suddenly aware of the tantalizing scent of her that made him think of a thousand flowers in full and beautiful bloom. "Virginia and me, we—" He tried to stop himself from speaking but something compelled him to go on. "We haven't lived together as man and wife for quite a spell. A wolf pack attacked our cabin back in fourty-four and it left her fearful of men—of me too, seems like."

"Oh, I'm terribly sorry. What an awful thing to have happen."

Why wouldn't she use his first name? he wondered. Why did he long to hear her speak it in that faintly husky voice of hers? "So you see, it wouldn't be any real bother to either of us were you to decide to sleep in our wagon."

"That is really very kind of you . . . Judah."

He felt himself relax, and a warmth that was not born of the sun coursed through him.

"But," she continued, "I can be of service to Sister Petry here."

He couldn't insist that she return to his wagon. He wanted to. He wanted to very badly. But he didn't dare. She would wonder about the reason for his insistence. And, after all, Mrs. Petry needed someone to watch her on the trail.

"You suit yourself," he said, trying to keep the frustration out of his tone.

As he walked away from her, he wanted to look back, to absorb and store in his memory the sight of her, the graceful way she moved that was so innocently provocative, the way she smiled, seeming to dim the sun as she did so. He forced himself to stare straight ahead as he walked on, feeling as if he had just lost something he had never really possessed.

When he came to his wagon, he was surprised to find Vernon Drake sharing the wagon seat with Virginia. He looked up at her, a question in his eyes.

Virginia smiled down at her husband. "Brother Drake

has graciously offered to drive our wagon for me. Isn't that nice of him, Judah? I mean, it is for me. I'll have nothing to do now but just sit up here beside him and see all the sights that there are to see.''

Without a word, Judah turned and headed for his horse.

Virginia enjoyed the first few days on the trail. The weather remained autumnal with glorious sunlit days and cool fragrant nights. As the wagon train moved over the prairie, she had a sense of floating in time and space as if she were suspended in a safe and dreamy limbo. No trees split the boundless horizon. The land seemed limitless, without beginning or end, the horizon forever unreachable. She felt at times as if she were drifting in a serene space between two worlds—the ugly one she had left behind her, and the unknown one that waited for her somewhere in the distance.

Drake, those first few days, drove the wagon while she sat, sometimes quiet and sometimes animated, beside him. She enjoyed his company. Although he was a strong man—it was obvious in the purposeful way he walked and in the steadiness of his hands on the reins—he was, she thought, so unlike Judah. Judah was just as strong, but in a completely different way. Drake, she decided, had the quiet strength of a steady wind while Judah—the comparison that came to her mind both startled and amused her—had the wild and raging strength of a storm. She wondered what kind of man would emerge if she could, in some mysterious manner, blend the two men to produce one entirely different being.

One morning, when they had been on the trail for nearly a week, Drake did not appear at her wagon as usual while everyone made ready to move out. Shielding her eyes with her hand, she scanned the bustling scene. Drake was nowhere to be seen. It was not until late in the afternoon of that day that he joined her on the wagon seat and explained that Judah had ordered him, along with several other men, to leave the train to hunt for whatever game could be found.

She drove the wagon alone the next day as well. Judah told her that he had sent Drake to the rear of the train to aid stragglers.

The following day they remained in camp because Judah had sent a dozen men into a nearby settlement to help the people there harvest their corn. The men would be paid in needed corn and other foodstuffs. Drake was among the men Judah had sent.

When Drake returned that night, he offered Virginia a large bucket of honey, part of the mens' payment.

Judah was present and he ordered Drake to divide the honey among as many members of the train as possible.

Virginia protested. She told Judah how much she longed for something sweet. She reminded him that they had run out of sugar days ago. He remained firm, and Drake went away carrying his bucketful of honey.

Another week passed.

Virginia visited often with the families of the wagon train, helping them when she could and accepting their help when it was needed. She learned how to construct an earth oven and how to cook sourdough bread in such an oven. She learned how to milk cows and how to find prairie peas and how to dig wild turnips. She learned how to help deliver babies when a young woman traveling with the train went into labor, a woman she had befriended and who, at the first onset of her pains, had asked that Virginia stay with her.

Virginia not only stayed with her friend but had held out her hands to receive the baby as it emerged from the woman's body, fighting the onslaught of memory that made her want to weep. She cut the cord, bathed the baby—a girl—and gave it to its profusely sweating but overjoyed mother. Then, after helping mother and child move to the opposite side of their wagon, she stripped the bed where the lying-in had taken place, took the soiled linen outside, and washed it in a tin tub.

When Judah came to inquire about the condition of mother and child, Virginia tried to hide the tears that were dripping from her eyes into the soapy water.

But he saw them and he saw her give way to the pain that lay locked within her and weep openly for her lost baby.

Another dawn.

Sun and sky. The horizon seemingly forever out of reach. The monotony of the treeless prairie, the gently rolling hills, the waving hip-high grass.

Virginia, as she drove her wagon, thought of her home in Saint Louis. But she forced herself to face the fact that she had no real home. Her father had driven her from her home. He had not answered the many letters she had written to him. And her home in Nauvoo—that little rented house which had been her home for too short a time—now seemed like a nest that she, a frightened bird, had vacated when the season of violence had descended upon the city.

She began to feel lost. Rootless. A woman unanchored anywhere with no place to call her own except a springless wagon that lurched for long hours beneath her and made her buttocks ache.

At night in the wagon that was lighted by a coal oil lantern, she read the Book of Mormon and the Bible while the crickets in the tall grass outside sang their mating song that would be stilled when death seized its singers in the first icy fingers of frost. She prayed, but never for worldly goods such as those she had possessed most of her life. She prayed that God would at last grant her a place where she could stop and rest—and really belong.

It was on a night when they had been more than three weeks on the trail that Judah interrupted her silent prayers.

He had pulled off his boots and was sitting cross-legged on the wagon bed staring at her as she sat with the Book of Mormon resting in her lap. She could feel his eyes on her and she could feel the familiar anxiety rising within her.

"It's late," he said.

"I'm not tired."

"It'll be another long day tomorrow."

She said nothing. The words on the page in front of her blurred before her eyes but she did not look up.

He reached out, took the book from her, and set it aside. Then he got up and blew out the lantern.

In the sudden darkness, Virginia tensed and shut her eyes. She felt his callused hand close around hers.

"Honey," he whispered.

Flames danced in the darkness behind her eyelids. Wood blazed, sending off sparks.

"I love you, Virginia."

In her waking nightmare, a man, burly and bearded, gaped at her, slack-jawed and leering. He licked his lips. They gleamed in the darkness and then parted to reveal crooked, tobacco-stained teeth.

"I've never stopped loving you," Judah whispered to her.

She tried to free her hand from his. She couldn't.

Words then, remembered words, words she was sure she would never forget, never stop hearing, drummed in the inferno that her mind had become:

"Now that she's taken us, maybe she'll take this too.

It'll really loosen her up. Maybe give her an even bigger thrill than we did.''

The bearded man was laughing in the darkness and only Virginia could hear him.

She saw the broken broom handle in his hand—its long stiff shaft. He was moving toward her . . .

"Honey, I need you so bad!" Judah moaned.

The bearded man's hands—someone's—were on her breasts. Gentle hands. Warm and caring hands.

She screamed as the broom handle was thrust inside her and shoved upward.

"Virginia!" Judah exclaimed, drawing back swiftly and then fumbling about as he nervously tried to light the lantern.

Light yellowed the interior of the wagon.

Virginia was on her knees, bent over, her hands covering her face as she sobbed, her shoulders shaking, her hair that had grown long falling over her shoulders to rest in a golden pile on the wagon bed.

Judah reached out to touch her and then hastily withdrew his hand. "What's wrong? I didn't mean to hurt you. Did I hurt you, honey?"

The bearded man's loud laughter began to weaken. It finally faded away.

Virginia remained hunched over for another minute and then she crawled onto her pallet and turned her face to the drilling.

She heard the sounds Judah made as he lay down across from her. She wanted to turn and reach out to him. She heard him fumbling with his clothes. A moment later, she heard his soft breathing grow more rapid. And then she heard his sigh. And then—stillness.

I'm sorry, Judah. Oh, Judah, I am so very sorry. You shouldn't have had to do that. I shouldn't have forced you to seek that lonely and joyless release. But I'm afraid. I'm so frightened.

She lay rigidly on her pallet, biting down on her knuckles, as the crickets sang their instinctive demands in the night outside. Her tears now were not only for herself and what had happened to her, but also for Judah and what she knew she was doing to him because of that long-ago night and the brute with the broom handle in his hand.

It began to rain, slowly at first, and then with increasing intensity. Virginia lay curled up on her pallet listening to the wind as it rose, lashing the drilling tnat covered the wagon, and rocking the wagon itself.

She heard Judah rise and tighten the drawstrings that closed the drilling at the rear of the wagon. But rain, driven by the wind, found its way into the wagon. Its cold touch chilled Virginia as she lay sleepless, trying to think of nothing, as the wind howled and the rain drummed.

She was still awake hours later when dawn came and Judah left the wagon. She got up, wondering how fires could be built so that breakfast could be cooked while the rain continued to fall. As she peered out of the wagon, the cold rain slapped her face. She could see people in slickers moving about, mostly men. Did Judah expect them to move on in this downpour?

She heard him shout instructions and orders and then he was standing before her.

"You'll have to drive the wagon. Your friend Drake's going to see to the loose stock."

Her friend Drake?

Well, it was true, wasn't it? He was her friend. But why had Judah made the word sound so ugly?

She found a hat and a sheepskin jacket of Judah's and put them on before venturing out onto the wagon seat. Rain pelted her. Wind lashed her face and body.

The team was in its traces, standing with their heads hanging down, rain running in thick rivulets down their glistening bodies, their manes and tails sodden.

Virginia, blinking away the water that streamed down her face, gripped the reins and slapped them across the horses' rumps.

Most of the grass had been flattened by the continuing downpour, the ground beneath it turned to mud. The wagon lurched forward, its tires making sucking sounds in the thick gumbo that the ground had become.

The rain soon soaked through Judah's coat that Virginia was wearing. It ran down her neck and down her back, chilling her. She called out to urge the horses on and as she did so rain ran into her mouth, almost choking her. She spat and pressed her lips together in a thin line.

The wagon swayed from side to side as the horses plodded forward. They sank to their hocks in the mud and Virginia found herself pitying them. She relaxed her grip on the reins and let the horses set their own pace.

Suddenly, the wheels on the left side of the wagon sank into a gully that the rain had gouged out of a stretch of grassless ground. The wagon lurched, then leaned and Virginia started to slide along its steeply slanted seat.

She seized the seat with her left hand and then cried out in pain as wooden slivers sliced into the flesh of her palm. Reflexively, her hand left the wagon seat. As it did, she lost her balance and fell to the wet ground, Judah's hat flying from her head. Almost at the instant of impact, she fought hard to regain her feet, slipping and sliding as she struggled in the muddy gully. Mud was in her shoes. In her hair. It covered her hands and dripped from her dress and coat.

The wagon, she thought. It's going to go over. She struggled through the mud which seemed to be trying to drag her down into it and, when she reached the wagon, she braced her back against it, trying to right it. Although she strained against it as hard as she could, her efforts were fruitless.

She was about to give up when Judah galloped up and jumped down from his horse. He planted his boots in the mud and leaned forward toward the side of the wagon bed, pressing his palms flat against it.

"The horses!" he yelled through the relentless rain and whirling wind. "You lead them. I'll hold the wagon up till we get it out of this gully."

Virginia made her way around him. Flinging her hair out of her eyes with a toss of her hand, she seized the harness of the two horses. Pulling on it as hard as she could with both hands, she walked backward, step by slow step, the horses straining to follow her.

She could barely see Judah through the sheets of rain as he walked sideways, his hands still pressed against the wagon bed. She continued to pull on the horses' harness, determined to resist the bizarre impulse to turn and flee. Somewhere. Anywhere. Out of the rain that was like a wind-borne sea in a world it had turned a mournful gray.

"Pull!" Judah shouted at her. "Pull *hard*!"

She did, causing the horses to suddenly spring forward.

She saw Judah lose his grip on the wagon bed as his boots slid in the slick mud. She saw the wagon begin to list. She saw it fall.

On Judah.

ELEVEN

"Stop it!"

The spoken command filtered through a deep darkness into Judah's consciousness.

What, he asked himself dimly, had he done wrong?

He tried to move, but his body resisted his efforts. After what seemed to him like an hour or more, he was finally able to open his eyes, and they sensed more than actually saw a light flickering. He squeezed his eyes shut and then opened them again, blinking in an attempt to bring his blurred vision into focus. The light suddenly seemed dazzling. He managed to turn his head slightly and discovered the source of the light—a tallow dip burning in a hollowed-out turnip that sat on top of a cracker barrel.

He heard a door open.

"Get out!"

He raised his head slightly and saw two vaguely familiar figures outlined in the doorway.

The door slammed.

He realized that he was lying in an unfamiliar bed. Above him was a sod roof. Log walls surrounded him. He tried to raise himself up on his elbows and was surprised by his weakness which kept him lying flat on his back in the strange room. He turned his head slowly and saw a fireplace with a turf chimney. Above its flames a blackened kettle was suspended.

"Judah!"

He recognized the voice. It was Virginia's voice. "Honey," he mumbled thickly.

And then he saw her crossing the room, moving quickly away from the closed door of the log cabin. She knelt beside the bed and placed a cool hand on his forehead.

"What place—where—" His voice died.

"Judah, we're in Winter Quarters on the western bank of the Missouri River."

"Winter Quarters," he repeated. "How—the last thing I remember—the rain—what happened?"

Virginia reminded him that their wagon had fallen on him. "One of the wheels struck you on the head. We righted the wagon and put you in it. When we arrived here, Brother Brigham assigned us to this cabin. You've been unconscious most of the time since you were injured."

"Who's the "we" that put me in the wagon?"

"Vernon and I."

Judah was silent.

"You woke up—just for a minute or so from time to time. I was able to feed you some barley soup and some bits of bread I'd soaked in it. I was so afraid you might choke because you weren't fully conscious and could barely swallow."

"Am I broken anyplace?"

"We don't think so. Not as far as we can tell."

"We," he repeated tonelessly. "You mean you and Vernon Drake." Suddenly he remembered the two dim figures he had seen at the door when he had regained consciousness. One, he realized, had been Virginia, and now he was sure that the other had been Drake. Why had Virginia ordered Drake out of the cabin? What was it that she had earlier ordered him to stop doing?

Virginia dropped her eyes now, and said, "Oh, Judah, I've been so terribly worried about you. We—I was so afraid that you might not ever regain consciousness again. You were in such a deep coma at times that I feared—but you'll be back on your feet now in no time at all. I just know you will be."

"Is Sister Ames all right?"

"She's staying with Brother Brigham until more cabins can be built. She brought some wine for you on one of her several visits here since you were hurt. There's an American Fur Company post at Pointe aux Poules and another one at Bellevue. One can buy many things at them. If one has the money, of course. Not many of the Saints do. But Olivia apparently is not wanting on that score."

"And here all along I thought she was a devout Mormon." Judah smiled weakly.

"Oh, you're thinking that wine is forbidden by the Prophet's Word of Wisdom. But she said she thought it would give you strength. She confessed to me that she also drinks tea when she can get it, another item forbidden by the Word.''

"Seems like she's a dyed-in-the-wool sinner."

"Oh, I don't think so. Olivia's far too prudish for that."

"You think she is, do you?"

"She keeps to herself, that one." Virginia abruptly changed the subject by asking, "Would you like some wine now?"

"First, some food. I feel like I'm starving."

"I've got stew in the kettle. I'll only be a moment."

Later, as Virginia spooned meaty stew into Judah's mouth, there was a knock on the cabin door. "Come in," she called out. "Now, Judah, please don't eat so fast."

"I've got some lost days to make up for."

"Ah, Brother Bascomb!" said a deep voice from the doorway.

Virginia rose from the bed and turned around. "How nice of you to pay us a visit."

"Brother Brigham," Judah said when he saw who their visitor was, "I'm real glad to see you again."

"And I am most happy to see that you are awake and eating heartily. You look, though peaked, as if you might be ready and willing to travel another four hundred miles. But on the next leg of your journey you must take more care, Judah. You must keep an eye out for falling wagons."

Judah grinned. "I'll most surely do that from now on. I'll watch out with *both* eyes. What news have you, Brother Brigham? Have you found the place where we will build Zion?"

Young shook his head. "We of the vanguard traveled toward the valleys of the mountains, but then Captain Allen came from Fort Leavenworth to visit us and convey President Polk's order that we must raise a Mormon battalion of five hundred of our men to join General Kearney's Army of the West to fight in the Mexican War and—''

"You didn't turn any men over to him, did you?'' Judah asked, frowning.

"I did. A few more than five hundred, all volunteers."

Judah's frown deepened. "It's not my place to question your leadership, Brother Brigham. But I'd have not handed over even a single man. What right does Polk have to ask us to help fight his war against Mexico after he let those bloodthirsty mobs run us out of our homes without so much as lifting a finger to try to stop them? We sent people to him for help and he said we had a just cause but there wasn't a thing he could do, damn him!"

"Patience, Judah," Young said, holding up a hand. "I gave the matter much thought and I consulted with the Apostles before making my decision. Consider this. The men will be provided for by the army, which will be better than having them try to scrape through a long winter as we must all do here. Their pay will benefit us. When they are mustered out next year in California—well, that is a place I have thought some of us might ultimately settle. In any event, with most of our vanguard gone, we had no choice but to return here to spend the winter."

"You know this is Indian land, don't you?" Judah said uneasily. "Here on this side of the river it is."

"Captain Allen gave us permission to remain here for the winter although—" Young's eyes danced mischievously, "—he had no authority to do so. Only the Bureau of Indian Affairs has that authority. But, you see, he wanted our five hundred stalwart Mormon men and, when I asked him if we might remain here, he gave his approval. I didn't question his authority to grant it. But I did take the precaution to meet with the half-breeds and French at the two nearby American Fur Company posts and with Big

Elk of the Omahas. As a result of that meeting, I was able to obtain the Omahas' agreement to allow us to stay here for as long as two years. In exchange, I promised that we would teach the Indians to farm and offer them protection against their enemies, the Pawnees.''

"No wonder you're called the Lion of the Lord," Judah remarked, giving Young another grin. "You sure know how to do battle for Him and His people.''

"Not do battle, Judah. Negotiate.''

"Do we have enough provisions to see us through the winter?''

"I hope so. And we have built cabins like this one. Some sod dugouts. Some of the Saints have been using their wagon beds propped up on posts and covered with drilling for shelter. We have cattle down in the rushes along the river. But there is no point in denying that the winter ahead will be difficult for us.''

"We will put our trust in the Lord," Virginia said. "We will work hard and we will help each other. Spring will be here before we know it.''

Judah stared up at her. For a brief moment, he saw a stranger. She had changed, he realized with a mild shock. She was no longer the girl she had been not so very long ago. Now he found himself looking into the face of a woman. A woman whose face was still beautiful, but who now wore upon it an expression of mature determination. It was evident in her steady gaze and in the firm set of her lips. She seemed, he thought, to have grown in some subtle way. Grown strong, he decided. She had endured a great deal of suffering, as had most of the Saints, and like iron in the hot fire of a forge, she had been tempered but not broken.

"—no fear.''

"Beg pardon?" Judah said to Young, whose words had been lost to him as he was studying Virginia's face.

"I was telling Sister Bascomb," Young replied, "that her attitude is one truly worthy of admiration and that if all the Saints had her faith and determination we could face the coming winter and its trials with no fear."

He continued, "We will all do our very best to survive whatever might lie ahead to test us. We must. I know that the Lord will not hide His countenance from us. I am certain of it."

"But, Brother Brigham, should He do so," Virginia said, and Judah caught the impish glint in her eyes, "we will pray loudly and without ceasing, and I am sure the holy racket we will raise will not go unheard by Him."

"You intend to storm heaven then, Sister Bascomb?" Young asked in a teasing tone.

"If I must."

"Brother Bascomb," Young said cheerfully, "you have chosen your first wife well and wisely. A good woman. And, if I may be so bold as to say so, a very lovely one." He bowed to Virginia and said, "I must go now. I have been making the rounds of the wards looking in on our people. I have many more visits to make. Let me repeat, Judah, it is good to see you on the mend. May the Lord be with you—with both of you."

"First wife indeed!" Virginia snapped when he had gone.

Judah said nothing. He was thinking of Olivia Ames.

Winter came, bringing with it bitterly cold winds and blinding snowstorms. With it too came disease and suffering that decimated the Saints. When there were no longer fresh fruits available, such as the Pottawattamie plums and wild grapes, scurvy and pellagra seized its victims. The faces of the Saints grew sallow. Their gums grew soft and their teeth began to fall out. They suffered from dizziness, raging fevers, and whooping cough. Their bodies were scourged relentlessly by the bloody flux.

They survived on cornmeal and flour from the mill that Young had established. And on their own stock that they killed in the slaughterhouse built by Brigham Young's brother, Lorenzo.

They traded their rings and brooches and pocket watches for food at the two American Fur Company outposts but, when the jewelry and valuable trinkets were gone, they made soup from oxhides and their meals sometimes consisted only of cider and pickles drawn from the dwindling supply in their household crocks. Succotash was a rare treat. So were boiled turnips that had been carefully hoarded. New potatoes became a delicacy because of their scarceness.

Suffering came too, not only from the biting winds of winter and the blizzards that sometimes nearly buried the settlement, but also from the Omaha and Oto Indians who stole badly needed food from the Saints. And from the wounds the men suffered in the battles they fought on behalf of the Omaha Indians against the Pawnees, who raided the Omaha villages and indiscriminately killed their inhabitants.

By the time April breathed its sweetness over the land, scores of Saints of all ages, from infants to centenarians, had died and been buried in the cemetery on the desolate hill overlooking the middle fork of the Grand River.

As the soft breezes and the warming sun of April gentled the land, women thinned the blood of their families with carefully hoarded sorghum and molasses. Children were sent out to forage for the first wild greens and pieplants. Men repaired wagons and harnesses. Everyone bought and borrowed and bartered to obtain most, if not all, of what they would need on their impending journey to the valleys of the western mountains.

And on the day that the first of the pioneers were due to depart, they danced.

After first listening to the rousing strains of melodies played by Captain Pitts' brass band, wind instruments took over and began to play French Fours, Copenhagen jigs, and Virginia Reels, themes by Henry Proch and Mendelsohn.

Although few jewels glistened in the women's ears or on their fingers or around their necks—almost all of them having long ago been traded for the stuff of survival—and although dresses were threadbare and trousers patched, feet skipped and hearts leaped as the Saints danced on the ground that was not yet green.

The musicians began to play a cotillion.

Virginia took Judah's hand and he let himself be drawn forward to become half of the first couple to lead the other dancers eagerly pairing off behind them.

The typically fast beat of the cotillion's waltz seemed to invigorate Virginia. Her face glowed as she moved through the intricate patterns of the dance with the other three couples who had joined her and Judah. She might have been once again at home in St. Louis at the Delano mansion. This might have been just one more party she was attending.

But there were differences.

The hem of the gingham wrapper she wore was ragged despite her repeated mendings and she wore no delicate gloves over her work-roughened hands. She had patched the hole in the sole of one of her shoes with a folded piece of calico.

"Be careful on your journey," she said to Judah and he nodded absently, his eyes on Olivia, who had also joined the dance with a man Judah knew only slightly.

"I'll be with the first group to leave here later this month," Virginia reminded him. "We won't be apart for very long."

And then he was gone from her as the dancers changed partners and the dance continued.

Minutes later, Judah found himself partnering Olivia.

"I'm going to miss you," he told her.

"And I shall miss you, Judah."

"Ask Brother Brigham if you can come with us."

"He wouldn't hear of it."

"There's three women coming with us already. He's bringing one of his wives—Clarissa."

The kaleidoscopic pattern of the dance changed again and Olivia was gone.

When, a little later, she was once again Judah's partner, he asked, "Have you made up your mind yet?"

"I told you, Judah. A man must obtain permission from his first wife before he can be sealed to another. You know that. Have you asked Virginia's permission so that we may be sealed?"

Before Judah could reply, Olivia's original partner claimed her.

Judah danced on. He hadn't asked Virginia's permission to take a second wife. Should he ask her now? Before the vanguard left Winter Quarters? What if she refused?

By the time the music stopped, he had made up his mind to say nothing to Virginia of his intention to make his marriage polygamous. There would be time enough for that once the vanguard had found the site where the Saints would build Zion.

Suddenly the bell, which had been removed from the Nauvoo Temple and brought to Winter Quarters by several zealots, began to ring.

When its tolling stopped, Young cleared his throat and began to address the crowd.

"I want you, brothers and sisters all, to pray for the success of our quest. I want you each to look to the other and render what help you can. Remain firm in the faith and continue to revere the memory of the Prophet. You have all been given your assignments to the parties which will leave here later this month and in the months to come. Until we are all reunited in Zion, may God watch over you and keep you."

"And keep you and those of your party!" a man called out from the assembled crowd.

Young acknowledged the man with a curt nod and then gestured to the others, Judah among them, to make ready to leave the settlement.

Judah turned to Virginia who was standing beside him. He bent to kiss her. She avoided his lips and stepped stiffly back.

"Take good care of yourself," he told her.

"I shall. And I shall pray for you, Judah."

He joined the throng of men and boys, more than a hundred of them, and within minutes the vanguard was heading west, driving their wagons or mounted on horseback as Judah was. Traveling with them were extra horses, pack mules, oxen, cows, and chickens.

Judah turned in his saddle as he rode away and looked back.

Virginia waved to him. As he returned her wave, he caught sight of Drake moving through the cheering crowd toward her. Olivia was nowhere to be seen.

That night, when they had made camp between the Elkhorn and Platte Rivers, Young designated men to stand guard. He also appointed men, Judah among them, to hunt mounted and on foot during each day of their journey to keep the party supplied with fresh meat.

"Tomorrow," he said, "we will set out on the north side of the Platte in order to avoid any possible confrontations with hostile Missouri Gentiles who might be traveling along the Oregon Trail on the south side of the river. Once we set out, I want every man to walk beside his wagon with his loaded gun in his hands. We will rise at five o'clock in the morning. A bugle will awaken us. We will move out promptly at seven o'clock. We will stop at noon for no more than one hour.

"No man may go more than twenty rods from camp without first obtaining my permission to do so. At night, we will corral our wagons as we have done here, tongues pointing outward, left hind wheels interlocked with the right wheel of the next wagon. Our stock will be kept inside the circle formed by our wagons. At eight-thirty each night the bugle will sound, and when it does I expect every man to retire to his wagon to pray. At nine o'clock all of us will be in bed with our fires extinguished."

When Young had finished speaking, Judah approached him. "I'd like to take a look at what Fremont wrote about the valley of the Great Salt Lake where we're heading if I could, Brother Brigham."

"Come with me."

At his wagon, Young handed Judah Charles Fremont's *Report* and also a copy of Lansford Hasting's *Guide*.

Judah took them back to the campfire he had kindled and sat down to read them by the light of the flames.

He learned from Fremont's *Report* that the valley of the Great Salt Lake was a harsh environment but, Fremont had written, it had "valuable, nutritious grass." Fremont also had come to the conclusion, Judah read, that the valley could be adapted to "civilized settlement."

Then, after turning to Hasting's *Guide* and reading of
that man's extensive explorations of the western mountains,
Judah sat alone by his fire as the stars glittered in the thick
black velvet of the sky above him. Later, as he slept on the
ground beside the fire that had turned to embers, wrapped
in a blanket and using his saddle for a pillow, he dreamed
of a gleaming white and gold city by a blazing blue lake,
its many tall spires piercing the powdery clouds in the sky,
its clean streets filled with heavenly music, its dwellings
built of marble that glowed in the sun that never set upon
the city whose name, Judah dreamed, was Zion.

During the days and weeks that followed, he dreamed
both night and day of Olivia, as the vanguard made its way
through the dusty valley of the muddy Platte River. She
was on his mind when they rested at Alcove Springs
before they crossed the Big Blue River, and she rode
beside him in his eager imagination as they reached and
then left behind Fort Kearney. It was her cheer, blended
with his own and those of the rest of the party, that he
heard when they sighted Chimney Rock looming tall against
the empty amethyst sky because they knew now that they
were halfway to their destination.

Behind them now was the sandy country. Now they
rode and drove through a land covered with short curly
buffalo grass. They saw busy prairie dog towns. They
hunted the white-rumped antelope and buffalo.

They stopped for a time at the adobe-walled and turreted
Fort Laramie, which was surrounded by the lodges of
many Sioux, and there they repaired wagons and shoed
those of their horses that needed it. And then they moved
on again, pausing briefly at Independence Rock where
Judah and many other members of the party chiseled their
names into the gray fissured surface of that huge mounded
rock.

And then they moved on again, at last reaching the south side of the Sweetwater Valley, above which in the north stood the great snow-summited chain of the Wind River Mountains. They were forced to cross and recross the Sweetwater as they climbed into higher country and the Sweetwater became a narrow ice-cold creek fringed with willows.

Judah saw to his surprise as they nooned that day that wild strawberries were blooming at the foot of five-foot high snowbanks. It was during that nooning that he was finally able to broach to Young the subject that had been troubling him for nearly a year.

"Brother Brigham," he began, "I've been thinking of taking me a second wife."

"Splendid idea! When are you and Sister Ames planning to be sealed?"

Judah was shocked. How had Young known of his interest in Olivia? He had tried to be discreet. He had been, he thought, almost secretive about his meetings with her.

When he didn't answer immediately, Young said, "It's been plain since last fall, Judah, that you had your eye on her. She's a lovely woman. She'll make you a fine wife, I'm sure."

"I got to tell you though that I got some doubts about the doctrine of plural marriage. Somehow it don't seem right to me to love one woman and then to go running off after another one. And maybe even another one or two after that. Now I know you've been sealed several times and I don't mean to criticize. It's just that I don't know for sure what's the right thing for me to do."

"I'll tell you the truth, Judah. I did not enter into multiple marriage lightly. I did much praying and soul-searching first. But the Prophet did receive a Divine Revelation from our Lord on the matter. That, in the end, is what matters. A good Mormon, the Lord has commanded, is bound to take unto himself as many wives as his heart and purse will permit him to take. In that way, God revealed to Brother Joseph, will we build the mighty nation of Israel through our increase.''

"I've always tried to be an honest man," Judah said, his voice low. "My wife—Virginia, she won't have none of me. Not since that night—'' He told Young what had happened when the wolf pack attacked and burned his cabin.

When he finished, Young stroked his chin thoughtfully for a moment and then said, "All the more reason for you to take Sister Ames as your second wife, Judah. You'll want a child to make up for the one that was so cruelly taken from you. You'll want many children!''

Judah, as the journey continued and May became June and June drifted monotonously into July, pondered the conversation he had had with Young. Was it indeed his religious duty to take another wife—maybe more than just one? Or was it the demands of his own aching and for so long deprived loins that had driven him into the arms of Olivia Ames? Olivia had let him hold her, had let him kiss her and even fondle her on more than one occasion, but had never let herself commit sin with him.

He reached no conclusion.

But, when they began to climb the mountains, their progress painfully slow and back-breakingly difficult, and Young fell ill with fever, he wondered if Young's illness might possibly be a sign of the Lord's displeasure with the advice Young had given him. Judah rejected the idea even as he hotly remembered the touch of Olivia's smooth hand

and felt once again his overpowering desire for her. But, he asked himself, what if Virginia had not turned away from him? Did he love her still? He knew that he did and deeply. Would he still want to marry Olivia if Virginia would have him—and their children?

Before he could formulate answers to his questions, they began to descend into a little dell and then to climb up Little Mountain from which they began their precipitous wheel-locked slide down what one of the vanguard jokingly dubbed 'Last Creek.'

"Brother Bascomb!"

Judah turned his horse and rode back to the wagon from which Young had summoned him.

"Scout ahead," Young directed him. "We must be nearly there."

Obediently, Judah rode out ahead of the others, and then out of the canyon through which they were traveling. He urged his stumbling horse up a steep hill. When he reached its summit, he sat his saddle, almost breathless with excitement, and stared down at the magnificent valley below that was shimmering in the summer heat. The mountain on which he stood ran southward and, in the north, it almost completely enclosed the valley. To the west rose the crestline of the Oquirrhs and north and west of the Oquirrhs lay the dark blue vastness of Great Salt Lake glistening in the sunlight.

He was finally able to tear himself away from the impressive sight. He quickly backtrailed until he reached the wagon in which the stricken Young lay. He told him about what he had just seen.

"Take me to see it!" Young commanded and the driver of his wagon obeyed the order.

Later, as Young gazed down into the valley from the wagon, he whispered, "Hosanna!"

"Hosanna!" Judah shouted to the heavens. His cry was joyfully taken up by the men and boys gathered behind and around him.

Their hosannas thundered in the clear mountain air above the valley that seemed to lie waiting for them to come down into it and make it their own.

TWELVE

VIRGINIA arrived in the valley of the Great Salt Lake with a party of fifty emigrants in early September.

Judah, when word reached him by way of the party's advance scout, that the emigrants were coming, rode out to meet the wagon train. He saw no sign of Olivia before he discovered Virginia near the rear of the long line driving her wagon, her face pale and drawn.

"Judah!" she cried when she caught sight of him. She reined in the team and, brightening, climbed down from the wagon seat and ran to meet him. She surprised him by throwing her arms around him and holding him tightly. "I've missed you so," she whispered, her cheek pressed against his chest.

He tentatively embraced her, pleased by the warmth of her greeting, and said, "I've sure missed you too, honey."

Then, after tying his horse to the endgate of the wagon, he drove it along the trail that led through the canyon, which had been partially cleared of willows and underbrush by the men of the vanguard, and then down into the valley.

"Judah," Virginia said in dismay as she sat beside him and studied her surroundings, "this is a desert."

"Won't be for long," he assured her. "We're going to turn it into fertile land. You wait. You'll see."

He drove to the cabin he had built of adobe bricks, which was located inside the fort. The men of the vanguard had constructed the fort, which enclosed twenty-eight other cabins in addition to Judah's.

They got down from the wagon and Judah, after borrowing a horse from a neighbor for Virginia said, "I'll show you all we've done—or are you too tired to take the trip to see it?"

She smiled faintly. "I am tired. But show me. I want to see what our new home is like."

As they rode their horses out of the fort, Judah pointed and said, "We strung up eleven miles of that fence all the way around the city we're starting to build. We put in roads and bridges—over there, see? We built a sawmill and a flour mill and look off there to the south—there's five thousand acres we got planted in radishes, potatoes, and turnips. We built dams up in the mountain creeks—with a little help from all the beavers that're up there." He laughed heartily. "Then we used go-devils and Jacobs' staffs to make canals to channel the water down here into the desert to irrigate the crops. Oh, honey, I tell you true. This place is going to be a marvel. It'll be the eighth wonder of the world!''

"I hope so."

"To me, it's home. A place I feel I belong. I haven't felt like I've ever had a real home since my ma died when I was but a boy. But *now* I have one!"

"*We* have one," Virginia amended.

"There's Salt Lake!" Judah declared, pointing to the west where the lake lay shimmering under the sun with seagulls circling above it.

When they reached it, they dismounted and walked along its shore.

"Judah, I—there's something I want to tell you but I don't exactly know how to go about it."

"Try starting right in."

"We met Brother Brigham on the trail as he was heading back to Winter Quarters. I had a long talk with him—about you and me, the way things have been between us of late and why. He was very kind and he gave me some advice. I've wronged you, Judah. I realize that now, although actually I've known it all along, I guess. I haven't been the wife—and certainly not the woman—I should have been for you—and for myself."

"Well, after what happened to you back in Nauvoo at the hands of that wolf pack—it's no wonder you couldn't act womanly with me. It can't be helped, I reckon."

"Judah, it can be helped. It can be if you'll help me help myself. Judah, I want to be able to love you again the way I did in the beginning. Not with just my heart and mind as I do now but also with— Do you understand what I'm trying to say?"

Judah gently touched her face and then ran a finger along the curve of her cheek. "You and me, it was awful good back then when we were in Nauvoo together in that cabin of ours.''

"It will be good again, Judah. I promise you that it will be.''

He drew her close to him and kissed her lips. ''I want you so bad. Have for so long I've taken to hurting over it.''

"Does anyone come by here?''

"Nope. We're too far west.''

"Shall we sit down?''

They did.

"I've wanted you too, Judah. But I've been afraid. And yet I remember how gentle you were with me that first time when I was still virginal. Do you think you could be that way with me again?''

He felt desire rising within him. At the same time, he felt his flesh begin to harden and rise as well. ''You mean here? Now?''

"Yes.''

Judah watched her for a moment as she began to undo the fastenings of her dress and then he got up and quickly undressed. He lay down on the warm sand beside her, gazing hungrily at her lithe body as she lay on her back staring up into the sky. When she turned her head and smiled at him, he leaned over and kissed her lips, the base of her throat, then her lips again as her arm slid beneath him and she drew him toward her.

With his lips still pressed against hers, he eased over upon her and her legs parted. He felt a tremor pass through her body and he remained motionless as her other arm slowly encircled his body.

Their lips parted and Judah buried his face in her neck, hoping, almost praying, that he would make no wrong move, that his raging passion would not betray him now when he knew he could so easily crack the fragile bond that existed between them on this carnal level—because of the fact that she had been hurt badly on that level and had learned to dread it. Her fear had exacted a terrible price from both of them during the now dead years. He did not want to continue paying that price and she had suggested that she did not want to continue paying it either.

"I'm all right, Judah. But please. Please tell me that you love me. Even if it isn't true anymore, say it."

"It is true, honey. I do love you. Always have. Always will, looks like to me."

He eased himself into her. She made no response. He lifted his hips slightly and then lowered them.

Her lips parted and she exhaled. And then she sighed. She began to moan and grip him tightly. "You're not one of those men," she said as if she were teaching herself a lesson. "You're Judah Bascomb. My husband. The man I love."

"I'd never hurt you. Oh, honey, I thought I'd lost you for good and all."

As his thrusting increased in intensity, her legs rose and encircled his thighs. He slowed, gauging her responses, aware of her wetness and of her body heaving beneath his as the desert around them vanished and the heat of the sun on their bodies was cool compared to the fires raging within them both.

Suddenly she lunged upward and seized him.

When she cried out her ecstasy moments later, he plunged down into her, letting himself go completely and, after only moments, he burst within her and then lay shuddering upon her, breathing hard, elated.

They lay locked together, neither of them moving or speaking for several minutes, and then Judah gently withdrew from her and flopped on his back beside her. He took her hand in his.

Still stiff, he wanted to jump up and run. To shout. To call out to the world and let it learn that this wonderful woman lying next to him was his just as he was hers. For the first time in his life as a Mormon, he fully appreciated the doctrine of celestial marriage. He could truly believe now that he and Virginia had been sealed together not just for this life but for all of eternity.

He could not imagine life without her. He knew that he would not want to live it without her. Why would a man want to live a life that merely masqueraded as life when it's true name would be death?

Virginia suddenly scrambled to her feet. "Judah!"

He was on his feet immediately, his face and body tense. "What's the matter? What's wrong?"

"Nothing!" she cried, flinging her arms up into the air, her full breasts rising as she did so. "The lake!" she cried. "Let's swim!"

She didn't wait for his assent but went running down the sand and into the bright blue water. It splashed up around her as she entered it, sunlight glinting on its droplets, and then he was running after her. Into the water he went, reaching for her and missing her as she playfully eluded him, and then she was in his arms but both of them were off balance and they fell, laughing happily, into the water.

"Judah, look. I can float!" She lay on her back on the surface of the water, her arms and legs spread wide.

"It's the salt in the water that does it," he explained. "You couldn't sink in this lake if you tried to. We haul water from here sometimes, boil it, and keep the salt that's left. It takes four barrels of water to make one barrel of salt."

"Silence, Judah Bascomb! We will not speak of practi-

calities like salt. Instead, we will speak of meadowlarks
and rainbows. Of wildflowers and our love.''

''About how beautiful you are.''

''Of how strong and gentle you are.''

''About happiness—ours.''

''Yes, oh, do let us speak of our happiness.''

Virginia rose and Judah took her in his arms. They
stood there in the lake, their bodies dripping, and then,
without another word, they ran to the shore together where
they lay down and let their rejoined bodies speak of love
again in an eloquent and ancient but wordless language as
the sun dried them, leaving tiny white grains of salt on
their naked bodies.

Later, as they rode back to the fort, Virginia told Judah
of the trail and its hardships, of how she had wanted more
than once to simply stop and turn back.

''Judah,'' she said, ''I had a letter from Father before
we left. It was brought by a man from the American Fur
Company in Saint Louis who had made a trip to the
trading posts at Bellevue and Pointe aux Poules.''

''What'd he have to say for himself?''

''He said he wanted us to come home to Saint Louis.
Not you and me, Judah. He meant me and our baby. I
never told him what happened to it in my letters.''

They were silent for several minutes as their horses
plodded along.

And then Judah said, ''You could have gone back by
yourself.''

''But as you can see I didn't.'' Virginia gave him a
brilliant smile. ''I wrote and told him that I was coming
here to be with you.''

''I'm real glad you didn't go back to Saint Louis. Hope
I showed as much back at the lake.''

''You most certainly did.'' Another smile.

"Did Vernon Drake look out for you after I left Winter Quarters?"

"I looked out for myself," Virginia answered sharply. And then, more gently, she said, "By the way, I've learned to be something of a seamstress. I've sewn myself two new dresses. Just wait till you see them!"

"Did Drake come west with your group?"

"I don't want to talk about Vernon Drake, if you don't mind."

Judah decided to let well enough alone, pleased at her reaction to his questions about Drake although he didn't know the reason behind her strong, almost angry, responses.

"Did Sister Ames come west with you?" he asked as nonchalantly as he could manage.

"No. Olivia fell ill not long after you left and she was still bedridden when I left. She's become terribly frail and no one seems to know just what is the matter with her. A young man, Paul Tyler, and his sister, Wealthy, have been caring for her. Perhaps she'll soon become well and will be able to join the rest of us here in our desert paradise."

"It's sure no paradise, not yet it isn't. But hard work will turn it into one. And no Gentiles are going to drive us out of here. This land is ours. It's our home.

They rode on then without speaking, and it was not until they entered the fort that their contented silence was broken by Virginia who exclaimed, "Lamanites!"

Judah studied the two Ute Indians who were standing at the edge of the crowd of people inside the fort.

"We saw other Lamanites on the trail," Virginia said. "Someone told me they were Sioux. They frighten me so."

"It's the duty of every Mormon to try to redeem the fallen Lamanites," Judah remarked. "Even though God punished them by giving them their dark skin for their transgressions, He left the door open for their redemption. So what say you and me march on over there and try a little proselytizing on those two Lamanites?''

Virginia shuddered. ''Are those girls their children?'' she asked, referring to the small child and the older girl standing with the two Utes.

''Not likely. See how the girls' hands are tied? Those Indians are slavers.''

''Slavers?''

''A lot of the Lamanites out west here raid one another's villages and carry off young female captives if they can. Sometimes they keep them and use them in ways we wouldn't think fitting. Sometimes they sell them.''

They dismounted and, leading their horses, joined the crowd clustered about the Indians.

''You buy?'' one of the Utes growled at the crowd and pointed first to the child and then to the older girl. ''They work hard. Please man.'' Grinning, the Ute grabbed his buckskin-covered genitals with both hands.

The crowd began to disperse.

''Those poor children,'' Virginia said, her eyes wide with horror. ''They've been tortured. Look at their arms and legs, Judah.''

''You no buy, they die!'' the Ute roared at the departing people who had begun to hurry toward their cabins.

He grunted an order in his language to the Ute standing next to him and the man bent down, seized the younger child by the ankles, swung her up over his head, and then dashed her on the ground, shattering her skull.

Virginia screamed as the child's blood and brains spattered her dress.

The Ute dropped the dead child and quickly seized the arm of the older girl who stood mute and too terrified to struggle.

"Judah!" Virginia cried. "Don't let him—"

Judah was already striding toward the Ute who was holding the girl's arm. "Let her go," he commanded.

When the Indian's hand dropped from her arm, the girl took a step in Judah's direction and then froze.

"How much?" Judah asked the Ute who had impassively watched his companion slaughter the child. He pointed to the girl.

"You have big heart," the Ute said, grinning again. "Them—" he gestured contemptuously in the direction of the people who were watching horrified in the distance, "—they have no hearts. So we kill girl. Like we kill girl's mother. Father. Brother. We kill all but keep sisters to sell. People no want to buy girl, so she die."

"How much?" Judah repeated, pointing again to the girl standing between him and the Utes.

"Good horse. Good gun."

Judah went and got his horse which he led up to the Ute. As the Indian began to examine the animal, Judah told Virginia to go to his cabin, get his rifle, and bring it to the Ute.

When she had done so, the Ute nodded. "I take horse. Take gun. You take girl. She good for strong man like you. I know." He caressed his genitals and leered at Judah.

"Take the girl to the cabin," Judah directed Virginia.

As she led the girl away, he stripped the gear from his horse and the Ute tied a rope halter on the animal and then, carrying Judah's rifle, led the horse out of the fort, followed by his still silent companion.

Judah, carrying his gear, made his way to his cabin and, once inside it, found Virginia on her knees examining the wounds that covered the young girl's arms and legs.

"What could they have done to her, Judah? They're awful, these wounds."

"Looks like they hacked her with knives and then stuck burning brands into the cuts they made. You can tell by the way the flesh is all seared."

"And her hair. Almost all of it has been burned off."

"Shoshone?" Judah asked the girl.

She merely stared mutely at him, her eyes glazed, her scarred arms hanging limply at her sides.

"Paiute?"

No response.

"Gosiute?"

The girl's eyes brightened momentarily and then went dead again.

"My guess," Judah said, "is she's from one of the Gosiute villages south of here. But that Ute said he killed her family, so I guess there's no use taking her back there. Honey, you'd best strip those filthy rags off her. I'll take the bucket and go get some water from one of the irrigation canals. You can heat it and wash her up. We'd best clean her wounds so's they don't get infected."

He started for the door but before he reached it, Virginia called out to him. "Judah, she's a godsend. The Lord has sent her to us to replace the baby I lost."

"She's no baby though," Judah observed. "She looks to me to be about twelve, thirteen maybe."

"I'm going to call her Rebecca," Virginia announced, drawing the girl toward her and embracing her tenderly. "Her name from now on will be Rebecca Bascomb."

Winter came to the valley of the Great Salt Lake that lay cupped in the desolate mountains, and by January starvation was stalking among the cabins of the emigrants as the wind whistled around them and snow filtered through the cracks in their doors and windows.

Virginia, five months pregnant as a result of her September idyll with Judah on the shore of the lake, went out daily with a shovel to dig for sego lily bulbs to supplement the marble-sized potatoes that had been their share of the pitifully meager crop that had been harvested in October of the previous year.

On one bitterly cold day, Rebecca joined her and, taking Virginia by the hand, led her across the snowy ground. Virginia watched as Rebecca studied the ground and then knelt and began to burrow in the snow that had partially melted in a sunny spot. When Rebecca straightened she held in her hand some wild wood-pea seeds she had robbed from the field mouse nest she had found.

As the days passed and Rebecca found no more nests to rob and Virginia found not a single bulb, the pair, in desperation, began to gather thistle tops which they brought back to the cabin.

They found Judah waiting for them. "I didn't sight any game," he said, his expression strained.

"Not even a crow?" Virginia asked him.

"I spotted one. But it was too high up to bring down with my Colt. I sure could have used that rifle I handed over to that Ute."

"You saw no wolves?"

He shook his head. "That wolf we ate last month may be out last for awhile. But I'll go out hunting again tomorrow. Maybe I'll get lucky and find a jackrabbit. Or a hawk. Kendricks next door downed a hawk two days ago. What's that you've got?"

"Thistle tops. I'll boil them. They'll make a thin broth."

As Virginia proceeded to prepare the thistles, Rebecca watched her from a corner of the room. Noticing the girl's black eyes on her, Virginia spoke to her. "Are you hungry, Rebecca? You are, aren't you, child? Well, we'll have soup soon." She continued talking to Rebecca, who had not spoken a single word since the day Judah had bought her from the Utes who had captured her.

She was still gaunt, her thinness a mute testament to the little food that she, like Judah and Virginia, had had to eat during the past several months. The wounds on her tawny arms and legs had healed, leaving ugly scars to which she paid no attention. Her straight black hair had grown in and now reached almost to her shoulders.

"I've got something for you, Rebecca," Judah said to her. "Got it right next door. I'll go get it for you."

When he returned carrying a box, Virginia said, "Look, Rebecca. Judah has brought you a present."

Judah put the box down on the floor.

Rebecca stared, wide-eyed, at the puppy it contained.

"The Kendricks next door," Judah said to Virginia, "their bitch dropped a litter. The pups all died except this one. Cy Kendricks can't feed that big family of his let alone feed pups. I thought Rebecca might take to this youngster."

Rebecca walked slowly toward the box and stood staring down at the puppy it contained.

"Take it, Rebecca," Virginia said. "It's yours."

Rebecca bent down and then slowly rose, the puppy clasped in her arms. It licked her face.

"Oh, Rebecca," Virginia exclaimed sorrowfully as she watched the girl begin to weep as she rubbed her cheek against the puppy's fur.

"She's happy," Judah commented. "She's got something to love now."

"Will she ever love us?" Virginia asked him plaintively.

"Give her time. She's got to learn to trust us. She's

been through hell and is just now starting back from its rim. It'll take time."

Before Judah had finished speaking, Rebecca began to whisper Gosiute words to her puppy. She stopped crying and, cuddling it, began to smile, talking faster, stroking the puppy, letting it lick her face.

Virginia broke into a smile at the sound of Rebecca's voice and hurried over to the girl, touched the puppy, and said, "Dog."

Rebecca looked up at her for a moment and then her lips moved. "Dog."

Virginia hugged her. "Yes, dear. Dog. Your dog."

Rebecca's English lessons continued throughout what remained of the terrible winter and Judah found himself listening closely to Virginia, paying strict attention to the way she phrased her sentences, trying hard to learn how to speak more correctly and not in his former manner which he had begun to recognize as being little more than cowboy-crude.

As the weeks passed, Virginia and Rebecca were finally reduced to digging roots and stripping bark from the trees that grew on the mountain slopes for food. More than once during those dark days, Judah refused to eat.

"I'm not hungry," he would lie and glance at Virginia's thin face and growing girth.

Although he hunted daily, he rarely came home with game.

Rebecca, using the limited but growing English vocabulary that she was learning daily from both Virginia and Judah, would try to cheer him up on such occasions. "Soon we eat," she would say. "Leaf Moon come. Then crickets come. We eat crickets. Soon."

But as the months dragged on and Judah could finally find no game at all, he made a decision one morning as he sat alone with Rebecca in the cabin while Virginia was next door helping to nurse one of the Kendricks' sick children.

"Rebecca," he said, "we have no food."

"Dig roots?"

"No, I don't want you to dig roots." He pointed to the puppy.

She understood almost at once. "No!"

"It's got to be done, Rebecca. Virginia—she's going to have a baby. She needs her strength." As he picked the puppy up by the scruff of its neck, Rebecca came at him with her small fists flying.

She pummeled his body and clawed at his face. He thrust her from him and carried the puppy outside. Pulling his Colt from his waistband, he pulled back the hammer with his thumb and, as Rebecca ran out of the cabin after him, he threw the puppy to the ground and fired once.

The puppy yelped, convulsed, and died with Judah's bullet in its brain.

Rebecca began to cry hysterically as she fled back into the cabin.

Judah pulled his knife from his boot and, after severing the puppy's head, proceeded to skin it.

Virginia had heard the shot and rushed out of the Kendricks' cabin in time to see the puppy die. She cried out in anguish to Judah. "How *could* you? That poor puppy was all Rebecca had!"

"She has us," he responded, continuing to skin the small carcass. "We can make this meat last a few days, maybe as long as a week. You need some meat to eat. I made up my mind to get you some in the only way that seemed possible."

"I won't eat Rebecca's dog!"

But that night, at Judah's insistence, she did.

Rebecca would eat only some parched corn Virginia had accidentally found lying forgotten in the bottom of one of Judah's saddle bags.

Aware of the girl's accusing glances, Judah said, "Rebecca, Virginia told me how you taught her to rob the nests of field mice. Why did you rob those nests?"

"For food."

"You did it so we could live. As a result, maybe some mice will die. The way your dog did at my hands. Rebecca, I killed him so we could have the food we all need to help us survive this winter."

Rebecca met his steady gaze. After what seemed to Judah an endless time, she said, "It is good what you did. I know that."

"I hated to do it," Judah admitted. "But I had to do it."

"I do not hate you," Rebecca said. "I love you." She glanced at Virginia. "I love you too. Utes kill my mother. Father too. And brother. You my family now."

It was that love, that sharing together as a family, that helped sustain them until, after the end of the long winter, Rebecca's predicted Leaf Moon arrived. The snows began to melt as did the ice crusted on the creeks' surfaces. The first delicate green buds began to open on bushes and trees. The sun turned from a pale yellow disc to an orange orb that warmed the earth and the people of the valley who went out, Judah among them, with their plows to till and plant it.

April ripened into May as the earth awoke and another part of Rebecca's prediction came true. The crickets came.

Wingless, they marched—thousands of them—into the fields in which wheat was sprouting, its green and vulnerable shoots inching above the ground.

The black, thick-headed insects had grotesquely bulging

eyes and fat bodies longer than a man's thumb. They marched, as any invading army marches, into the fertile fields—relentlessly. The growing grain began to fall victim to them.

Judah fought them, standing shoulder to shoulder with scores of the others. Women flailed wildly at the massed crickets with broomsticks. Booted men stamped on them.

''Ditches!'' a sweating Judah suddenly shouted. He explained what he had in mind and ditches were dug in the path of the crickets after which water was channeled into them to drown the enemy. Many did drown. But too many did not. The survivors floated across the surface of the water, climbed up out of the ditches, and marched on through the fields they were so surely devastating.

A day passed during which the apparently hopeless battle continued. Men and women, many of them still emaciated from the hungry winter they had endured, nevertheless fasted and prayed for deliverance from the plague.

The crickets continued to swarm over the fields.

Virginia came out to the fields with Rebecca at her side. ''Judah,'' she said thoughtfully, ''why not burn them out?''

''Worth a try,'' he said wearily. He shouted to the people nearest him. ''Gather rushes from the marshes. Spread them on the edges of the fields. The crickets always take cover at night. It's likely that they'll head into the rushes tonight and, if they do, then we'll set the rushes on fire.

That night Virginia, carrying a torch, helped to set fire to the rushes.

''I told you to stay in the cabin!'' Judah said to her. ''You're due next month. Have some sense, woman!''

She ignored him, touching her torch to the pile of rushes and stepping quickly back as they blazed up in front of her. When Judah demanded that she return home, she responded calmly. "I must do what I can so that our son or daughter to be does not starve next winter, Judah."

He finally gave up trying to argue with her.

An hour later, the fields were ringed by flames which flung their fiery fingers at the stars, withdrew, and then thrust them upward again.

Virginia stood next to Judah, holding Rebecca's hand, as they watched the fires burn. And then, suddenly, she felt it. Pain. Sharp, biting pain. It passed. Came again.

"What's wrong?" Judah asked as he saw her twisted features, illuminated by the flickering flames.

"I've got to get back to the cabin," she whispered as the pain gripped her again. "It's my time."

"But you aren't due till next month!"

"Judah, help me." She reached out to him, staggered, and he picked her up and began to carry her in the direction of the fort.

"Baby come?" Rebecca asked as she hurried along beside them.

"It's coming!" Virginia cried. "Put me down, Judah."

"You can't have it here!" he protested, anxiety in his eyes and his heart beginning to pound.

But, while the flames continued to paw the night sky, casting their glow over the valley's fields, Virginia, moaning and straining on the hard ground, delivered her baby less than an hour later.

"It's a boy!" Judah told her happily.

He used his knife to cut the cord that bound his son to its mother and then deftly tied it. He took off his shirt and wrapped the baby in it before handing the child to Rebecca.

"Take the baby to the cabin," he ordered her. Then, bending over, he again picked up Virginia and carried her through the glowing night as dawn began to break.

He stopped in amazement a little later as the last of the

fires went out and the sky was suddenly filled with seagulls flying toward them from Salt Lake. He watched as the crickets again appeared in the fields, apparently undaunted by the fires that had been set to destroy them.

The seagulls swooped down. They settled on the fields. They feasted.

When they were gone some time later, so were the crickets.

"A miracle!" someone shouted in the distance.

"The Lord has delivered us!" someone else exulted.

A miracle, Judah thought, as he listened to his son crying in Rebecca's arms as the girl stood, awed, some distance away.

"Is he all right?" Virginia asked weakly.

"He's a small little fellow but, yes, he's fine. Are you?"

"Just tired."

"Honey, as far as I'm concerned, you can rest up for the whole summer that's coming. I'll do the cooking. I'll clean the cabin, me and Rebecca will. I'll work hard enough for both of us. For a whole army of men, I promise you." He bent down and kissed her and then turned and headed for the cabin.

"Judah?"

"What?"

"Let's have lots more."

"I thought you said you were tired," he commented, grinning down at her.

"I didn't mean that we should start having them right this minute!" she said, pretending indignation, as she smiled up at him.

THIRTEEN

TURMOIL spread throughout the burgeoning community of people who were living and working in the valley of the Great Salt Lake in the summer of eighteen-forty-eight.

It was caused initially by a man who had been a member of the Mormon Battalion which had joined General Kearney's Army of the West to wage war against Mexico. When the man was mustered out of the army, he headed over the Sierras to the valley, and when he arrived he spread the news to anyone willing to listen to him of what he had seen and heard during his recent months in California.

Judah told Virginia of the news that the man had brought on the day following the former soldier's arrival in the valley.

"He says you can practically pick gold up off the ground. The first of it, he said, was found in John Sutter's millrace at his fort near the place where the Sacramento and American Rivers meet. That was back in January. He says some of the Battalion members stayed to dig for gold and that some of them are already rich men as a result."

"Do you believe him?" Virginia asked sceptically.

"I see no reason for him to lie about something like this. He says men are already flocking to California to try to strike it rich. He says there's already a small town near Sutter's Fort that they're calling Coloma."

"Our next door neighbors," Virginia said, referring to the Kendricks, "are talking about leaving the valley and heading for California. I don't like the idea, not one bit. If many of us leave here, what will become of our plans to build Zion?"

Instead of answering her question, Judah said, "Kendricks showed me a copy of a San Francisco newspaper—*The Californian*. It was dated March 15, 1848 and it said a gold mine had been discovered near there."

Virginia went to the cradle Judah had carved from a log. She picked up the baby they had named Joseph after the Prophet and then sat down. Opening her dress, she let the baby nurse.

"The Marshal family has left the valley already—for California," Judah remarked.

"I didn't know that," Virginia said as she watched Joseph suckle contentedly at her breast. "Have any other gone?"

"Three other families and a few of the single men. Maybe they'll all strike it rich."

Virginia looked across the room at Judah. "You're not thinking of going to California, are you?"

"Well, I have to admit that I've been doing some thinking about it. It's hard not to let yourself think about a land where you can just step out and take a stroll and stop every now and then to pick up a nice shiny nugget of almost pure gold."

Thinking such as Judah's spread rapidly among the people in the valley as the weeks passed. Everyone talked of gold. Some claimed it was the religious duty of every able-bodied Saint to head at once for the gold fields to get rich and then return to the valley. They argued that the tithes then paid to the church would be enormous. But there was, Judah noticed as he listened to the people talk, the glint of greed in more than a few eyes.

Sadly—and not without a barely buried sense of envy—he watched wagons leave the valley and head west. Men and women he knew and liked left, lured by the stories trickling into the valley from both east and west. The men who came from the west brought more than stories. Many of them brought gold—dust or flakes or nuggets—which they proudly displayed. Some brought money they had gotten in exchange for the gold they had found along the banks of California's creeks and rivers where, some said, a man could pan a hundred dollars worth of gold before breakfast.

The men who came into the valley from the East—from New York and Boston and from the rocky farms of New England—brought second-hand stories and high hopes. They traded extra clothes and gear of all kinds to the Saints for food. And then they were gone. Over the mountains. On their way to what they had called El Dorado, which less than a year ago had been known by the more prosaic name of California.

From the East, too, came more Mormons from Winter

Quarters and, as they came, Judah scanned the faces of the women, searching for Olivia. In late September he finally saw her, as a party drove its wagons into the fort. He wondered why he felt so calm as he went to welcome her.

She turned just before he reached her and began to walk toward a young man who was talking with a young woman some distance behind her.

"Olivia!" Judah called out to her.

She turned around again at the sound of his voice and smiled when she saw him.

But she did not run to meet him. Had he expected her to do so, he wondered. He walked toward her, remembering how much he had once wanted her. *Once?* She was thin now but he found her to be still as desirable as when he had last held her in his arms.

"Hello, Olivia."

"It's good to see you again, Judah."

The young man and woman joined them and Olivia introduced them both to Judah. "This is Brother Paul Tyler and his sister, Wealthy. They cared for me while— did you know that I have been quite ill, Judah?"

"Virginia told me." He nodded to Wealthy and shook Tyler's hand.

"But she's fit as a fiddle now," Tyler declared cheerfully, giving Olivia an affectionate hug. "I do believe she could have walked the entire way here had we let her."

"How goes things here, Brother Bascomb?" Wealthy asked.

Judah described what had been accomplished and what was being planned, concluding with, "this will be a great city one day. It will be a place we'll all be proud to call home."

"You've all done so much in such a short time," Wealthy observed, looking around.

"We Saints have two things that set us apart from most people," Judah said. "Discipline and the ability to cooperate with one another to get a job done. Those two things have served us all very well so far here in our valley."

"Come, Wealthy," Tyler said. "We'll have to see what we can do about getting ourselves some kind of shelter."

"Olivia, are you coming?" Wealthy asked as she began to walk away with her brother.

"Soon," Olivia answered and waved them on. Then, turning back to Judah, she asked, "How is Virginia?"

"Fine. We have a little boy now."

"How wonderful for both of you. And you, Judah? How are you?"

"I'm well. And I'm glad to see you looking so well, Olivia."

"Have you spoken to Virginia?"

Judah didn't have to ask her what she meant. He shook his head. "I thought it would be best to wait until you got here first."

"Do you still have it in your mind to marry me?"

Judah hesitated a moment and then nodded. "I gave you my word—my pledge that we'd be sealed."

"Judah, it's been a long time since we last saw each other. Things have happened to both of us. Perhaps now— well, I thought perhaps you might have changed your mind."

"I am not a trifling man, Olivia."

"It would be quite all right with me if you had changed your mind. I'd understand."

"Well, I haven't changed my mind." A thought occurred to Judah. "Have you? Changed your mind, I mean?"

She looked into his eyes. "No. I gave you my word." She smiled faintly. "And I am not a trifling woman. But there is still the matter of obtaining Virginia's consent, you know, and you've told me that you have not yet spoken to her about me.''

"I'll do so."

"What if she were to refuse to grant you permission to enter into a multiple marriage?"

"Brother and Sister Tyler are calling you, Olivia."

"Judah, you look so fine—so very handsome. I don't know why I should be surprised because I thought of you so often while I was sick and then later on the way here."

The Tylers called to Olivia again.

"I must go now."

Judah watched her walk briskly across the compound to join the Tylers and tried not to face the unpleasant fact that he was wishing she had not come to the valley. He was happy now with Virginia, with his son, with Rebecca, and with his monogamous marriage. He was dismayed to realize that he now saw Olivia as a threat to his happiness.

But, he told himself, his reaction made no sense. Many Mormon families, he knew, were happy in their polygamous marriages. Monogamy did not necessarily guarantee happiness, he reasoned. And polygamy did not automatically destroy the happiness or the harmony of a man's home.

He turned, feeling decidedly uneasy, and made his way back to his cabin. As he neared it, he saw the wagon standing in front of it. The wagon's team was in its traces. The cover of the wagon was painted a bright red.

He found Rebecca seated on the wooden bench outside the cabin. In her arms she cradled Joseph.

"Whose wagon is this?" Judah asked her.

"The man's."

"What man's?"

"He is inside. Virginia say for me to wait out here."

Judah opened the door of the cabin. And saw Vernon Drake holding Virginia in his arms and kissing her.

"Judah!" Virginia cried as she caught sight of him over Drake's shoulder. She hastily disengaged herself from Drake and stepped back, her hands nervously smoothing her bodice.

Judah was across the room in an instant. He seized Drake before the man could turn, spun him around, and landed a clenched fist against his chin. He followed his right uppercut with a left jab that caught Drake just below his ribs, knocking the breath from him and doubling him over. Then Judah brought his right fist down, smashing it into the base of Drake's skull.

"Judah!" Virginia cried again as Drake hit the floor and lay there groaning.

"Sorry to interrupt this pleasant reunion between two old friends, but I'm a man who doesn't take kindly to sharing what's mine with the likes of him."

Virginia dropped to her knees and cradled Drake's head in her lap. The blood that was flowing from Drake's broken lower lip seeped onto her skirt. "I'm sorry, Vernon," she said.

"Get him up and get him out of here," Judah barked at her, his fists clenched at his side, his body quivering with rage. "Or do you want me to do it?"

Virginia shifted her position so that she was between Judah and Drake. "Can you stand up, Vernon?"

He let her help him to his feet.

Judah, as the two of them edged around him toward the door, did not turn to watch their progress. He stared at the far wall of the cabin, breathing heavily. Only when he heard the door close did he turn around.

"That was a stupid thing to do!" Virginia declared angrily. "A perfectly stupid thing to do!"

"You two must have had a fine time of it together back in Winter Quarters after I left."

Virginia sighed and made an aimless gesture. "You don't understand."

"I understand what I saw, and what I saw was another man pawing my wife and kissing her. That's easy to understand."

"You behaved like a stallion might have if it saw another stallion nuzzling one of its mares. Not like a civilized human being. Certainly not like a gentleman."

"And what do you call how you were behaving with Drake?"

"He took me by force. I was trying to push him away when you came in."

"Like you tried to push me away that night in your father's house when you came downstairs and practically raped me?"

Virginia's features hardened. Her face was expressionless as she stared at Judah. "I told you what just happened. Vernon Drake has been after me, if you must know, almost since the day we first met. The first time it happened—it was after you'd been shot by Simon Grant in Nauvoo. He came to the house pretending to be concerned about your welfare. He tried to . . . but, Judah, I made him stop and I ordered him out of the cabin."

Judah, listening to her, remembered the day in question, remembered Virginia's angry *"Stop it!"* and the slamming of the door. He recalled her angry responses to his questions about Drake, the questions he had asked her as they made their way back from Salt Lake on the day she had arrived in the valley.

"—and he continued to pester me in Winter Quarters," Virginia was saying. "I would have nothing to do with him. Then, today when he arrived here—well, you saw what he was trying to do."

The anger generated by what he had seen arose in Judah again and the words spilled from him before he could think or try to stop their bitter flow. "I know what I saw and I've just heard the way you tried to explain away what I saw."

"Damn you, Judah! I've told you the truth!"

"You've told me what you thought would settle me down so that you could start sneaking around behind my back with Drake."

"Judah, I'm warning you!"

"Woman, I'm telling you now and once and for all. You stay away from Drake. If I catch you two together again, I'll—" He couldn't go on. He didn't dare utter the thought that had flown unbidden into his mind.

"You'll kill him? Me? I believe you might be capable of doing it. Well, I'll tell you something. If I choose to see Vernon Drake, I will see him. You will not tell me what I may or may not do." Virginia's eyes blazed as she stood, hands planted firmly on her hips, glaring at Judah.

"Then do it!" he roared at her. "It won't matter to me. Take Drake as your new stud." He paused, drew a breath, and added, "Drake isn't the only person we know who arrived with the wagon train. Olivia Ames has also arrived. I've just been talking to her. Back in Winter Quarters when you wouldn't let me touch you, Olivia and I. . . . Woman, I'm going to be sealed to Olivia Ames!"

Shock registered on Virginia's face and for a moment she couldn't speak. But then, recovering herself, she said, "You are not!"

Judah turned and headed for the door.

"If you marry her," Virginia shouted from behind him, "I'll leave you!"

"Suit yourself because I am going to marry her!"

*   *   *

Late the following night, when Judah returned from hunting in the mountains, he found only Rebecca and Joseph in the cabin. He wanted to ask about Virginia's whereabouts, but a perverse pride prevented him from doing so.

"She is gone," Rebecca announced bluntly.

Judah stiffened. "Who's gone?" he asked, knowing the answer to his question but using it to forestall the terrible knowledge that he was sure was about to be revealed to him.

"Virginia went away with the man."

"What man?"

"The one who was here yesterday. The one you hit."

"When will she be back?" Judah wanted to beg Rebecca not to answer his question.

"She won't come back, I think."

"What do you mean by that, Rebecca?"

"Man came here to cabin again. Same man as came yesterday. I was sleeping. They talk and I wake up. Then Virginia tell me she will go away with man. I want to know where she will go. She say to California to look for gold."

"I don't believe it! She wouldn't just go away like that. She wouldn't just walk out and leave Joseph behind like that."

"She did."

Judah sat down at the table, his arms hanging limply at his side.

"Why did she go, Judah? She really go to look for gold?"

He shook his head sadly. "She's in love with the man she went away with, I guess." He didn't believe it. He knew that the truth was that he didn't want to believe it.

In his cradle, Joseph began to cry, his tiny fists balled and waved in the air.

Rebecca went to him, picked him up when she discovered he was wet, and placed him on the table. She began to change him.

When she had finished, she returned him to his crib where he promptly fell asleep again and then, turning to Judah, she asked, "Virginia not love you now?"

Judah remained silent.

"I was outside yesterday with Joseph. I saw you hit the man. I heard what you said. What Virginia said. Maybe she told you truth about the man."

"No, she didn't. The fact that she went away with him proves that she lied to me."

"Maybe she not in love with him. Maybe she go to stop you from bringing new wife to cabin."

"It's the Mormon way for a man to take more than one wife."

"Indian way too. But for me—wrong way. I will have husband someday. One man. He will have only me for wife. Maybe Virginia think same way."

"She had no right to do what she did!" Judah bellowed and pounded both fists down on the top of the table.

"But you have right to take two women?"

Fury coursed through Judah as he thundered, "She left her baby behind! What decent woman would do a thing like that? Abandon her own flesh and blood?"

"She ask me to take care of Joseph. I will do it."

Judah got up and stormed out into the night. He prowled through it like the wolves he heard howling in the surrounding mountains, his thoughts chaotic, conflicting emotions surging within him.

She had lied to him all along, he told himself bitterly. She had bided her time and waited for Drake to arrive in the valley so that she could be with him whenever the opportunity presented itself. But then the news of the discovery of gold in California had been brought to the valley. Drake must have heard the news. Everyone was talking about it. So when I made it clear to him, Judah thought, that he didn't have a chance with Virginia while I was around he decided to pull out. And he talked Virginia into going to California with him.

Maybe, Judah thought as he walked through the wolf-haunted night, the idea of finding gold had appealed to Virginia. She'd once been rich. She'd thrown it all away to come west and be with me. Judah laughed, a sad sound in the dark night. Maybe she'd taken to regretting what she'd done. Her actions had lost her the Delano fortune, that was certain. But if Drake found gold, she'd be rich again, maybe even richer than her father was.

She had been clever, he decided. There was no doubt about that. When he had told her he was going to marry Olivia, she had pretended to object. Probably, he thought, she and Drake had already made their plans to leave for California together.

He made himself face the fact that she didn't want him. That she was gone. That it was over between them.

He found himself wandering outside the fort. He leaned his forehead against the adobe wall surrounding it, folded an arm against it, and squeezed his wet eyes shut.

He forlornly whispered, "Virginia."

And then he gritted his teeth. He would not let her destroy him. He knew she could by her decision to leave him. He had seen men destroyed by similar actions of women they had loved and lost. He would not let himself be one of those men. He would survive and, if the loss of the only woman he had ever loved was now a sharp pain that lurked within him, it would, he knew, in time become little more than an ache that he would learn to live with, as an injured man learns to live with less than the full use of one or more of his limbs.

And there was Olivia.

The thought of her did nothing to lessen the pain he was feeling. But the thought of her did make him realize that he would be able to go on. If not with Virginia, then with Olivia. There would be other children, he promised himself. His and Olivia's.

He straightened up and returned to the cabin where he found Rebecca rocking Joseph in his cradle.

"Go to bed," he told her softly.

When she had done so, he picked up his son and held him close to his chest, looking down at the child's serene face as it slept in his arms. "You won't have to grow up motherless, Joseph," he whispered. "You'll have a mother. You'll not know—not for a long time anyway—that she isn't your real mother. And you've still got me. I'll do all I can to make up for the hole you'll find in your life once you learn that your real mother ran off and left you before you were even a year old."

He sat there for a long time, holding Joseph and thinking. His son made him feel purposeful. The child needed him. He could only wish, down in a deep part of himself where he was silently grieving, that the boy's mother had also needed him.

Days passed.

Judah, during them, continued to hope that Virginia would return. He tried for a time to convince himself that Rebecca had been mistaken in what she had told him. Perhaps Virginia had not gone with Drake to California or anywhere else for that matter. She might still be in the valley. Maybe she was staying with friends somewhere.

Maybe she was trying, by remaining away from him temporarily, to make him realize how much he needed her. Maybe she was, by her absence, trying to make him concede to her demand that he not take a second wife.

But, by the time a week had passed, Judah knew that she was really gone. He realized that there was no point in his delaying any longer. He had an obligation to Olivia. He intended to fulfill it.

He found her one hot afternoon hoeing in the fields. He took the hoe from her hands and began to cultivate the earth around the growing plants.

"Have you spoken to her yet?" Olivia asked as she knelt and began to pull weeds.

"You haven't heard, then?" Judah said, surprised.

"Heard what, Judah?"

"She's gone."

Olivia looked up in surprise. "Gone? Virginia?"

"To California. With Vernon Drake."

"But what—why—Judah, Vernon Drake of all people! On the way here he was caught stealing from other people's wagons. He was punished—given twenty lashes. Why would Virginia go anywhere with a man like Vernon Drake? I don't understand."

Judah explained to her what had happened and why, concluding with, "So there is no longer any necessity for me to ask her permission for us to be sealed."

Olivia bent and busied herself with the weeds growing between the furrows.

Judah said, "Things always work out for the best." But he didn't believe it.

"I wonder," she said.

"Well, we can marry now with no problem. Virginia can't stop us now."

"Can't she?"

"What do you mean by that?"

"She's gone away. But that does not necessarily mean that you have stopped loving her, does it?"

"She didn't just go away. She went away with another man. That's what's to be borne in mind."

"Do you no longer love her, Judah?"

"I don't know."

"I think you do know."

"All right! Yes, I still love her. But you're missing the point, Olivia. She no longer loves me. She's gone. You're here. Do *you* still love me?"

Olivia used the sleeve of her dress to wipe away the sweat from her face before answering, "I love you, Judah."

"Then we'll marry."

"If you wish."

Her remark—her uncharacteristic passivity—puzzled Judah. "You don't sound very pleased about the plan."

"That is because I'm not sure we'll be happy together."

"What makes you think we won't be?"

"I think you know."

"Virginia?"

"Virginia."

"She can't come between us now."

"She'll always be between us. But I suppose we will find a way to live with that unhappy fact."

"She probably thought that if she left me for awhile I'd give up the idea of wanting to marry you. Well, she was wrong. I intend to marry you and, if and when she should ever come back, she'll see how wrong her tactics were."

Olivia rose. "You don't want to marry me. You want to prove to Virginia that she made a mistake. Do you think that is a good way to begin a marriage, Judah?"

"I do want to marry you."

"I think you feel you must marry me. To prove that you

are a man of your word, a man of honor. One who stands by the pledges he makes.''

"Sure, that's part of it. After all, I gave you my word back in Winter Quarters.''

"And I gave you mine.''

Judah caught the note of resignation in her voice. He frowned. "You don't want to go through with it, do you?''

"You make it sound like a battle we were about to engage in.''

"Why don't you want to marry me?''

"I didn't say I didn't want to marry you.''

"But it's true, isn't it?''

Olivia looked into his eyes. "Yes, it's true. I don't want to marry you.''

"But you said a little while ago that you loved me.''

"I do. I'll always have love in my heart for you, Judah. As I know you will have for me. But I told you when I arrived here that things change. That things happen to people—''

"What's happened to you, Olivia? There's another man?''

"While I was sick in Winter Quarters for such a long time, the Tylers—Paul and Wealthy—they were both very kind to me. If they had not helped me the way they did, I might have died.''

"It's Tyler? You're in love with him?''

"Yes.'' Olivia spoke so softly that Judah was barely able to hear her answer. "It happened before I was really aware that it was happening. Then I thought about us and I had a lot of time to think, Judah. I'll tell you what I thought. I thought that you wanted me not so much for myself because your relationship with Virginia was not the best at that time. She had turned away from you. You told me so yourself. So you turned to me in loneliness and a kind of desperation. I'm not blaming you. I can readily understand why you thought you were in love with me then."

"I didn't *think* I was in love with you. I was—*am* in love with you."

"In a way, I believe that's true. But not in the way you believe it is true. You're in love with Virginia and you always will be. I'm sorry she has hurt you by deserting you, but you must face what you know in your heart to be the truth. She is the only woman you truly love."

Judah knew what Olivia had said was true. He tried to think of what to say to her. "You would have married me, but only because you promised to do so before you met Tyler."

"Yes. Just as I know you were willing to marry me now for the same reason. But we would be making a mistake. Surely you can see that now. I've been honest with you as a woman should be with a man she cares deeply about. And I do care deeply about you, Judah. You are a fine man, a good man. You are strong and yet tender. You are capable of loving a woman in ways that most men can only imagine.

"Judah, you want only one woman. I want only one man. You're still in love with Virginia and only with Virginia. You want her back."

As if admitting defeat to an adversary, Judah murmured, "I do."

"Then go after her. Go to California. Find her and bring her back here with you."

"No!"

"Pride, Judah, goeth before a fall."

"It's not pride that's stopping me. It's—"

"It is! Face it! And don't be a fool! Will your life in the

years to come be richer if you live it with your pride—
your false pride—intact but without the woman you love?''

''I can't bring myself to beg her to come back to me.
Even if I could find her, which I may never be able to
do.''

''You needn't beg. Find her. Talk to her. Make her
understand how you feel about her. Tell her that you're not
going to marry me. Tell her that you want only her, as you
so obviously do. Tell her the truth, Judah, and then have
hope.''

''I don't know how I can go on without her,'' Judah
admitted, staring at the ground. ''And *that's* the truth.''

''Go to California then. Try to find her.''

Judah looked at Olivia. ''Paul Tyler is a very fortunate
man. I cannot help envying him.''

''I shall pray that you will find Virginia and that all will
once again be well between the two of you.''

''Rebecca is doing a good job of taking care of my son.
But I'd be much obliged if you'd look in on them from
time to time after I'm gone to see that they're both all
right.''

''I'll be glad to do that, Judah.''

Judah gently kissed her on the cheek.

''Goodbye, Judah. May you have a safe and successful
journey.''

FOURTEEN

VIRGINIA stood on the hill outside the tent that was her home in San Francisco late one morning in mid-October and stared out over the bay. It was littered with steamboats and sloops, most of them marooned there because their crews had deserted them to head inland to prospect for gold.

She shivered and drew her ragged shawl around her shoulders as the wispy streamers of fog that were drifting off the water and climbing the hill touched her with their clammy fingers. All around her were shelters made of bolts of cloth draped over up-ended wagon beds propped on wooden stilts, canvas tents similar to her own, and small adobe huts, mere hovels.

She gazed out at the island in the bay and watched the hordes of pelicans rising from it like a winged fog to further obscure the already half-hidden sun.

Laughter drifted out through the open door of a shack near her tent. Drunken laughter. She grew cold, not from the fog, but from fear because Vernon Drake was in the saloon from which the laughter had come.

Someone inside the saloon began to play a fiddle. She heard the dull thudding of boots on the saloon's earthen floor.

As if stimulated by the sound of the fiddle, a band began to play, unseen, in one of the buildings down in Portsmouth Square, its notes drifting up the hill to her where she stood, her eyes closed and her lips quivering, as the damp fog fondled her.

She opened her eyes and they fell upon the lopsided wagon that belonged to Drake, the wagon that had brought her here to this hell, the wagon that was listing because of a broken axle, its team long since sold to pay for food, its wood beginning to rot in the damp October air.

She cried out in alarm as a rough hand suddenly seized her by the nape of her neck and another one gripped her wrist. As she lost her balance and almost fell, she realized that it was Drake who was dragging her away from the tent and toward the saloon.

"Dance," he muttered drunkenly. "You're going to. I have friends—they want to dance."

And then she was thrust inside the saloon, into the thick smoke, the raucous laughter, the crowd of crude men. Someone slapped her buttocks. Her shawl slid from her shoulders and was lost.

"Who's the soiled dove?" a man bellowed to Drake.

"She's not soiled yet!" he yelled back. "But I'm working at it—*hard!*" He laughed, picked up a tankard and brought it to his lips, tipping his head back as he emptied it. "Come on!" he yelled. "Come and get her!" He gave Virginia a shove and she went stumbling deeper into the dank lantern-lit room.

Someone's arms caught her before she could fall. Then someone else pulled her out of those grasping arms, turned her around, and pressed his lips which were bordered by a mustache and beard against her neck.

She seized the man's beard and jerked hard. The man let out a startled yell and backed off. She fought her way past faceless men. She slapped their groping hands aside. The door! She made for it.

But Drake managed to block her way to it. "These are my friends," he told her. "You won't be nice to me, maybe you'll be nice to them."

The fiddle began to play again. Drake, holding Virginia's forearm tightly, began to stamp his feet in time to the music and to move in an awkward circle, hauling Virginia with him. Her hair flew in her face and got in her mouth. She collided with a wooden table and pain flared in her hip.

She kicked hard, catching Drake in the shin. As he howled in pain and anger, he lost his grip on her and she ran.

Once outside the saloon, she hesitated. Where could she go? There was nowhere to go, no refuge where he could not find her. She ran back to the tent and ducked down beneath its pinned-back flap. She threw herself on the straw that served her as a bed and bit down hard on her knuckles to keep from crying out.

"*Bitch!*"

Drake stood hunched over and swaying inside the tent, his fists raised as if he were facing an opponent. "You insulted my friends. Didn't dance."

Virginia didn't look up. Maybe he would go away. Back to the saloon. She prayed that he would, not moving a muscle, not until she felt his heavy hand come to rest on her thigh. Then she quickly turned over and drew herself up in a tight ball in the far corner of the tent. As he stumbled toward her, she whispered, "Don't. Vernon, please don't."

"Don't!" he repeated in a mocking tone. "Vernon, please don't. What the hell do you think I brought you with me for? To look at? To just stare at and admire? No, by God! I intend to have you. All those times in the mountains on the way here when you wouldn't—" He seemed to become suddenly sober as he stared hungrily down at her. "And God how I want you! You've got no god damned right fending me off the way you've been doing.

"What the hell's wrong with the way I feel about you? Nothing! What's wrong with doing what you know I want to do with you? Nothing! But you won't. The bitch won't."

He seemed to be talking to himself. "Well, by God, you *will!* I've waited long enough. I've said soft words to you and I've treated you nice but nothing's worked. You won't let it work! But you're here and you're mine now and—" He lunged at her.

"Vernon," Virginia said, eluding him, "I'm here because you forced me to come with you." She tried to think of the right thing to say as she pushed his hands away.

He grabbed her and crouched upon her like some clumsy animal as his hands began to tear at her dress.

"I didn't want to come here with you. I tried to explain to you." She managed to slide out from under him and, as he fell to the ground, she started to rise.

But he caught her ankle and she fell, her elbow hitting the ground. Pain raced up her arm and into her shoulder.

He knelt, straddling her, his hands pressing her shoulders against the ground, saliva slipping from between his lips. "I thought it'd be all right," he said. "Once I got you away from Bascomb, I thought it'd be all right. I figured you'd get to liking me and then maybe love'd come along later."

"Vernon, you can't make a woman love you by threatening her and the people she loves." Virginia stared up into his dull eyes, almost pitying him. "How could I ever love a man who made me come away with him by threatening to kill my baby and Rebecca if I refused, as you did?"

"But I wanted you so bad!" he cried in anguish. "I want you so bad right now. *And, by God, I'm going to have you!*"

He tore at her bodice until her breasts were bared. He thrust his head down between them, making wordless sounds. He pulled her dress down over her hips and began to rip her petticoat.

Virginia succeeded in crossing her legs as he fumbled with the buttons of his trousers. When his loins were naked, he tried to pry her legs apart. His sweat dripped down upon her. He began to moan and then to whine as his hardened flesh desperately tried to probe her and could not.

Sobbing, he slapped her face. His hand swung back and struck the other side of her face.

She took the blows in silence as she fought him, trying to squirm out from beneath him, determined to keep her legs locked together. His fingernails clawed her thighs and she felt the blood from the scratches he had made on her legs begin to flow.

He slapped her viciously again, and then his eyes widened in surprise as her hand suddenly enfolded him. A trace of a smile appeared on his sweating face as she manipulated him, her hand moving rapidly back and forth along the length of his erection.

"Stop that!" he screamed as he realized what she was trying to do. "Not like that. *Don't!*"

But, before he could free himself from her, he erupted and, as he did so, Virginia pushed him backward and scrambled to her feet. She gathered her torn dress about her and, staring down at him, said in a cold voice, "I'm pregnant. I'm sure of it now. I wasn't sure when you forced me to leave the valley. I'm going to have Judah's baby. I won't let you hurt me or the baby I'm carrying. I'm leaving!"

Drake looked down at his limp flesh and then up at her. "Leaving? Where are you going? Back over the Sierras? It's snowing up there by now. You've heard what happened to the Donner Party. They got trapped up there in the mountains by the snow and they ended up eating their dead.

"You'll go to the diggings? You saw what those men in the saloon were like. They're the same in the diggings. Some of them haven't seen a woman in almost a year. No, you'll stay right where you are—right here—because you've got no place to go and no way to get there if you did have someplace."

Virginia sat down on the ground and slumped forward, her hair falling about her face. "When spring comes . . . when the snow melts in the mountains . . . some of the men who have come here to California came overland. Some of them *walked* over two thousand miles. I can walk back to the valley."

"By spring I'll have you tamed and taught. I'll teach you tricks you can perform on me that you wouldn't have thought possible. And I'll try a few I have in mind on you, too. Mrs. Bascomb, come spring, as a result of my special tutoring this winter, you'll be wanting to spend twenty-four hours of every day on your back begging me to come get you. And in one or two other positions I have in mind to teach you, as well.''

As Drake pulled up his trousers, he was laughing. He was still laughing a little later as he left the tent, leaving a distraught Virginia behind him, wondering what she could do and trying to convince herself that she would be able to think of some way to escape from him and return to the valley and Judah.

Drake made his way down the hill, weaving between the shacks and tents clustered on it and soon found himself among the much larger frame buildings of Portsmouth Square. He strolled, his hands in his pockets, around the plaza, listening to the shouts and the laughter spilling from the numerous casinos which were the only business establishments in the square.

As he walked, he fingered the drawstring of the buckskin pouch he carried in his pocket. He hesitated in front of the entrance to Sloane House. He had never been in the relatively new casino. He wasn't known there. So there was a chance, he thought, that he might be able to succeed there where he would very probably fail in the El Dorado or the La Souciedad where his face was as familiar by now as was his unsavory reputation.

He pushed open the door of Sloane House and went inside, barely glancing at the bouncer who stood with brawny arms folded over his chest just inside the door.

He peered through the thick smoke at the red plush drapes on the windows, glanced at the painting of the female nude hanging above the long oak bar, looked up at the many glass globes of the coal oil lamps suspended from the ceiling, and then down at the sawdust-strewn plank flooring.

The casino was crowded with men of every description. There were foppish men wearing tailored suits and shiny top hats, roughly clad men in worn boots who looked as if they had just arrived from the diggings, soft-capped and canvas-jacketed sailors, Mexicans wrapped in colorful serapes.

He walked through the crowd, stopping once to watch the men who were tossing metal discs onto the wooden surface of a board which had holes cut into its surface. The board topped a series of upright trays—four in all—into which a metal disc might fall if the man who had thrown it succeeded in getting it past the metal loops arching above the holes, which were designed to make the task as difficult as possible.

Slots in the four trays bore such numbers as thirty, six hundred fifty, and three thousand to indicate the amount of money a player would win if his disc succeeded in finding its way through one of the holes and down into one of the trays below.

On impulse, Drake handed the game's attendant a coin he drew from his pocket and took the discs the man handed him. He tossed one. It bounced off the board. He aimed for the gaping mouth of the metal toad which sat in the center of the board and which gave the game its name—El Sapo. The disc clinked off the toad. So did his next disc. Disgusted, he moved away from the game, glancing in the direction of the bar. He decided he wouldn't take a drink. Not now. Lately, when he drank, his fingers had developed an annoying tendency to tremble and he knew that trembling fingers could spell disaster for him because of what he was planning to do. No, he would not have a drink. Not now. Later. When it was all over and he was safe. Then he'd have one. Maybe more than one. To celebrate.

Music suddenly erupted.

A man with pipes fastened to his shoulders was playing them while he did a vigorous clog dance, the cymbals that were attached to his wrists clanging, the drum he was beating resounding throughout the large room.

Drake eased up behind a crowd of men who were surrounding a table where a faro game was in heated progress. He listened carefully to the bets the men were making as the dealer deftly exposed one card after another. Within minutes, he had identified the high bidders in the crowd.

He shifted position until he was standing directly behind a jovial player whose buckskin pouch lay on the table in front of him. Drake noticed the few flakes of gold that had fallen onto the table from the drawstringed pouch and his heart began to thud against his ribs. He watched the man bet and, when he won, place a white chip beside his pouch and, when he lost, a red one, so that he could keep track of his wins and losses and thus be able to settle his account upon the conclusion of the game.

Drake stepped up closer to the man, edging his body between his intended victim and the man on the unsuspecting player's right. He reached into his pocket, palmed his pouch, and withdrew it. Then, pretending to stumble, he fell against the man he had singled out. His left hand seized the man as if to support himself. At the same instant, his right hand shot out toward the table and then quickly withdrew. He thrust his right hand into his pocket and pretended to regain his balance, apologizing profusely to the man he had fallen against.

Then he backed away from the startled player and melted into the crowd.

It was time to get out. Time to find out what kind of a haul he had made when he had stolen the man's pouch and replaced it with his own.

But, as he was passing the bar on his way out of the casino, he hesitated. He wanted a drink. Badly. A drink would wash away the nervousness that was causing his entire body to break out in a chilly sweat despite the room's warmth.

He stepped up to the bar and ordered whiskey while the one-man band continued to deafen every patron in the place.

Almost immediately, the drink began to drain away his nervousness. The second one he hurriedly downed relaxed him completely.

He was about to order a third when he heard the shout. It had come from the faro table. He tensed, his glance darting toward the door.

"This isn't gold!" the faro dealer yelled. "Mr. Kenilworth, there's just a sprinkling of flakes in your pouch. The rest's brass filings!"

"That is not my pouch." The man the faro dealer had called Kenilworth shouted. "I've been robbed. Somebody—" He spun away from the table, his eyes sweeping the room.

Drake headed for the door, walking slowly, keeping his head turned away from the faro table.

"That's him!" Kenilworth shouted, pointing at Drake. "Grab him, somebody! That man robbed me!"

Drake made a dash for the door, shouldering his way through the thick crowd.

He never made it, because the bouncer blocked his path. The huge man seized Drake and, holding him by his collar in one hand, marched him, protesting loudly, toward the faro table.

"Search him!" Kenilworth demanded. "I guarantee you'll find my pouch on him!"

"I don't know what the hell you're talking about," Drake declared as calmly as he could.

The bouncer pulled the pouch from Drake's pocket and held it up in his free hand.

"That's mine!" Kenilworth said triumphantly. "I don't try to cheat the house by adulterating my flakes with brass filings. Get the proprietor. He knows me. He knows very well that I would never cheat. He knows I'm no scoundrel like he is!" Kenilworth pointed directly at Drake.

Drake struggled to free himself from the bouncer's firm grip but was unable to do so. Sweat poured down his face. He could feel it sliding down his back.

Silence dominated the room. The one-man band had disappeared. No glasses clinked at the bar.

A man was moving through the crowd toward the faro table. When he reached it, he asked, "May I inquire as to the cause of the commotion, gentlemen?"

"That man—" Kenilworth pointed at Drake again, "—stole my pouch and put his in its place. It contains some gold flakes, but mostly brass filings!"

Drake stared at the man Kenilworth had addressed, apparently the proprietor of Sloane House. He was wearing a white shirt with blue pinstripes, pinstriped gray trousers, a frock coat, black string tie, and shiny black shoes. "I know you," Drake said. "You're—"

"Simon Grant, at your service, sir. Now what have you to say about Mr. Kenilworth's charge?"

"I deny it. Just because I happened to lose my balance and stumble against him—I deny his charge!"

"This is not my pouch, Mr. Grant," Kenilworth maintained.

"They are both buckskin pouches," Grant observed pointedly.

"Mr. Grant, you know I do not cheat," Kenilworth declared.

"My competitors," Grant said, "have been kind enough to inform me of a man who has practiced the same sort of theft in their establishments so that I might be warned. They told me the man was named Drake. "May I ask your name, sir?"

"Ralston," Drake snapped.

A man in the crowd hooted. "That's Drake, Mr. Grant. I know him. Me and my partner live up near his tent on the hill, the one he shares with his whore."

Grant turned to the bouncer who was still firmly gripping Drake's collar. "Oscar, take Mr. Drake out into the plaza. I'm sure your fists can convince him that he would be unwise to return to Sloane House."

As the bouncer handed Kenilworth's pouch to Grant, Drake whispered, "Wait, Grant. Don't turn me over to him. Call him off and I'll give you some information you'll find interesting. Some information about Virginia Bascomb."

Grant's eyes narrowed as he studied the cringing Drake and then he said, "Let him go, Oscar." As the bouncer released Drake, Grant handed the pouch he was holding to Kenilworth. "I'm sorry for the trouble you've experienced, Mr. Kenilworth. Whatever you order at the bar will be free of charge during your stay here. I trust that will help to make amends for this unpleasantness."

"Thank you, Mr. Grant," Kenilworth said and, smiling, turned back to the faro table.

Grant glanced at Drake. "Come with me."

Drake followed him to the staircase at the rear of the

casino and then up it and into Grant's office on the second
floor.

As Grant seated himself behind his polished desk, he
pointed to a chair that sat in front of it and Drake sat
down.

"I didn't know you owned this place, Grant. I didn't
even know you were here in San Francisco. Looks like
you made out pretty well since you beat that murder
charge back in Nauvoo."

"Drake, you said you had some information for me
about Virginia Bascomb."

"That's right, I did say that. And I do." Drake leaned
back in his chair and smiled. "I bet you'd be willing to
pay for it, wouldn't you, Grant?"

"You'd lose your bet, Drake. You'll give me the information and you'll give it to me now or I'll summon Oscar
who will be able to obtain it from you quite quickly I can
assure you."

"She's here."

"Virginia is here in San Francisco?" Grant was clearly
incredulous.

"It's the truth," Drake assured him. "She came out
here with me. When I realized who you were downstairs—
well, I figured you'd want to know that. At your trial in
Nauvoo, it was clear to me at least, if not to the judge, that
you tried to kill Judah Bascomb so you could get your
hands on Virginia. Now, I can't blame you for that, Grant.
She's a woman most men would want to get their hands
on."

"And you, Drake? Have you gotten *your* hands on
her?"

"I've tried to. More than once, I can tell you. But she's
a fighter—fought me off every time. Downstairs before—I
figured I could save myself a beating over what happened

and get even with her for the way she's fended me off at the same time."

"Do I understand that you think I would attempt to harm Mrs. Bascomb?"

"Well, you've got a score to settle with her, too, the way I see it. She wouldn't have you any more than she'd have me."

Grant propped his feet up on his desk and said, "You might say that I have a score to settle with the lady. Yes, you might say that."

"If you intend to have her, Grant, you'd better be ready to have somebody help you hold her down. She's still stuck on Bascomb. What's more, she's carrying his kid."

"Virginia's pregnant?"

"With Bascomb's second kid. She's already got a baby back in Salt Lake Valley."

"And you say she is still in love with Bascomb?"

"That's right."

"And she is pregnant with Bascomb's child," Grant mused. He swung his feet off the desk and leaned over it toward Drake. "Where is she?"

"I've got a tent pitched up on the hill. She's up there. I could go and get her for you."

"That won't be necessary. I'll have Oscar get her and bring her here. How can he identify your tent, Drake?"

"Well, it's just a canvas tent like most. But my wagon's parked right next to it. Tell him to look for the wagon. It's got a broken axle. And it's cover is painted red."

Drake rose and started for the door. He halted before he reached it and turned around to face Grant. "I'd like to know something."

Grant waited.

"I'd like to know what you're planning to do to her."

"What makes you think I'm planning to do anything to her?"

"I saw the look on your face downstairs when I told you I had information about her. That look on your face was one of pure hate. So I'd like to know what you're planning. After all, Grant, it would give me no small amount of pleasure to know she's going to get what she deserves for the way she's treated me lately as well as the way she's treated you in the past."

"I'll say this much, Drake. I do not want Virginia the way she is. I have no use whatsoever for a pregnant woman. But I will have use for her when she is no longer pregnant. I do not intend to wait for her to come to term before putting her to the rather amusing use I have in mind."

Drake smiled broadly. "Well, I'll be damned! You mean you're going to see to it that she has an abortion?"

Grant nodded solemnly.

"But there's no doctor in San Francisco, not as far as I know there isn't."

"That's correct." Grant smiled for the first time since entering his office. "But I happen to know of a veterinarian here in town. The man is in my debt. I'm sure he'll be willing to use his skills on Mrs. Bascomb."

Later that day, Grant was in the process of lighting a cigar when a knock sounded on his door. "Come in!" he called out.

The door opened and Oscar entered the room carrying Virginia, who was both bound and gagged, over his shoulder.

"I take it you had some trouble with the lady, Oscar," Grant observed laconically.

Oscar set Virginia on her feet and said, "She screamed

when I grabbed her. Tried to run. So I trussed her up. Shut her up too.''

Virginia, her ankles bound and her wrists tied behind her back, stared in surprise through wide eyes at Grant, unable to speak because of the gag Oscar had tied around her mouth and knotted at the nape of her neck.

''I have no doubt that you are surprised to see me, my dear Virginia,'' Grant said to her. ''I've been here in San Francisco for months now, thanks in large part to you. You see, after my trial in Nauvoo I returned to Saint Louis hoping to reestablish myself with the American Fur Company, but unfortunately for me I was unable to do so because of a letter you wrote to your father in which you told him that I had been tried for the attempted murder of your husband.

''It seems that your father spread the news among his wealthy and influential friends and, as a direct result, Mr. Astor, who happened to be visiting his office in Saint Louis at the time of my arrival there, refused to employ me again.

''The years that followed were difficult for me. I went to New York, but Mr. Astor, I soon learned, had made my name and background known there as well and I could not have been more scorned in the society where I had once been welcomed had I been *convicted* of the murder of Bascomb. When word reached New York of the gold strike at Sutter's Mill, I saw a way for me to make a new start. I took a steamboat down the east coast, crossed the Panamanian Isthmus, and took another steamer up the west coast. I soon found that grubbing in the ground for gold was not quite to my taste. Oh, I did find some gold—enough to enable me to come here and invest it prudently. As you know, Virginia, I have always been a most prudent man.'' Grant smiled slyly.

"I saw many ways of making money without having to dirty my hands or break my back panning the creeks and streams of California for gold.

"Now I own several stores which sell general merchandise—foodstuffs, mining implements, and the like. I also own this casino. What money I don't manage to take from the miners for supplies and provisions, I acquire at my gaming tables and the bar downstairs.

"And I'm expanding. Just as San Francisco itself is. Who would believe now that San Francisco was just a sleepy little village called Yerba Buena only a year ago? Or that, arriving here practically penniless, I would attain the position I now enjoy?"

Grant gestured and Oscar removed the gag from Virginia's mouth.

She started to speak and then swallowed hard. She moistened her dry lips with her tongue. "Why did you have this—this oaf—bring me here, Simon?"

"Oscar is not an oaf, Virginia. How unkind of you to call him that. You seem to have forgotten the manners you learned in Saint Louis. Oscar is a trusted and valued employee of mine. But to answer your question. I had Oscar bring you here because I learned from your—ah, friend, Mr. Drake, that you had come to San Francisco with him. Now I have a question for you. Why did you desert Judah Bascomb? I ask because I noted an inconsistency in Mr. Drake's account of your recent behavior. He told me that you came here with him but he also told me that you are still in love with Bascomb. I didn't question him concerning that apparent inconsistency. Instead, I thought I would ask you to explain it to me."

"I'll explain nothing to you. Now order this man to untie me. At once!"

"Ah, Virginia," Grant said and sighed deeply. "You

have not lost your disagreeable habit of giving orders to other people, have you? But may I point out to you that you are not now in a position to give orders to anyone.''

''I'll scream.''

''Should you do so,'' Grant said mildly, ''Oscar will replace the gag. Now isn't it much more pleasant this way? We two old friends have so much to talk about. If you are gagged, I will be the only one who can talk, and I've always hated one-sided conversations. They are so biased, I've found.''

Grant glanced at Oscar. ''Did you stop on the way to Mrs. Bascomb's tent and ask Mr. Sheridan to join us here in my office?''

''Yeah. Sheridan was doctoring a sick mule. He'll come once he's done, he said.''

''Good. I want him to correct Mrs. Bascomb's unfortunate condition as soon as possible.''

''Simon, what are you talking about? Who is Mr. Sheridan?''

''Mr. Sheridan, my dear, is a veterinarian. He will relieve you of the burden you are carrying.''

''The burden I'm—'' Virginia gasped as she understood the meaning of Grant's remark. She stared in horror at him.

''You see,'' he said, ''we have no doctor as yet here in San Francisco so I thought we would enlist the aid of our local veterinarian to rid you of Bascomb's brat. I gather you have become something of a brood sow, Virginia. Drake said you have had one child already by your cowboy.''

''Simon, don't,'' Virginia pleaded, fear chilling her. ''Don't hurt my baby!''

Grant emitted a snarl. He stood up quickly, knocking over his chair as he did so. ''I *will* hurt your baby!'' he said, his voice cold. "And I'll hurt you! I despaired of ever having the chance to do the latter. But I've longed for the opportunity to revenge myself upon you—and upon Bascomb for taking you from me. Well, fate it seems, has been kind to me. What better way to injure you both at the same time than to destroy the fruit of your fucking." He began to laugh, his head thrown back, his cigar lying forgotten in an ash tray on the desk.

Virginia, forcing back the tears she felt beginning to flood her eyes, moaned. "You can't hate me—us—that much, Simon. Surely you can't."

His laughter ceased. "I've hated you both since the night Bascomb came to your house in Saint Louis with that supercilious prophet of his in tow. I tried to kill him in Nauvoo and failed. But this time I won't fail in what I intend to do to you."

Virginia, desperate, said, "You loved me once, Simon. Untie me and I'll make love to you. And later, when we can't have intercourse, I'll—I'll satisfy you in other ways. I'll be good to you, I promise I will be. But let me bear my child. Then I'll send it back to Judah—to Salt Lake Valley." She hesitated briefly. "And I'll stay here with you."

"A most interesting and, if I may say so, a most magnanimous offer, my dear. A rather titillating one too."

"Then you will? You will let me—"

"*I won't!*" Grant roared and banged a fist down on his desk. "Once Sheridan gets here and gets rid of your baby, I'm going to turn you over to Oscar and my other employees. As a kind of reward for their faithful services. Do you really believe I'd want you now after you've been with Bascomb and Drake?"

"I have not been with Drake, as you put it."

As if he hadn't heard her denial, Grant continued, "But

I shall watch you service my employees—one after the other. And let me inform you that I happen to know that Oscar, for one, has rather peculiar, that is to say, perverse, sexual preferences. I think you'll be surprised, if not at all pleased, to discover—and satisfy—them."

Oscar grinned and began to chew on his lower lip, his glittering eyes on Virginia.

"Perhaps," Grant continued, "you will then have become professional enough to entertain the casino's customers as well—for a suitable fee which I shall collect, of course."

"The instant you free me, Simon, I'm going to kill you."

Someone knocked on the office door.

Oscar opened it and spoke to the man who had knocked. Then, closing the door again, he turned to Grant and said, "That mule died."

"What the hell are you talking about?" Grant asked him.

"That mule Sheridan was doctoring. That was the swamper I sent after Sheridan at the door just now. He went to fetch him, but apparently the owner of the mule shot Sheridan when the animal died. The vet's nursing a bullet wound in his right arm, and says he can't come here just now."

"Damn him!" Grant muttered. "Well, we'll just have to wait until he's fit to operate on our fertile little lady. Take the slut out of here, Oscar."

"What do you want I should do with her?"

"Take her down the hall and lock her in the storage room and then bring me the key to the door. And Oscar— gag her. If she were to start screaming, it might unsettle our patrons downstairs.

As Oscar gagged Virginia and then picked her up and carried her from the office, Grant touched a match to his dead cigar. He smiled contentedly as he puffed on it.

FIFTEEN

AFTER leaving the California Trail, Judah rode southwest and arrived in San Francisco as the sun was dipping down toward the bay. Its light gilded the water, turning it from blue to a burnished amber.

He rode in among the buildings that were sprawled in random patterns along the bayfront, all of them wooden, all of them showing signs of their hasty construction. Some leaned slightly. Many were unpainted. Signs sprouted from them at right angles or hung, in some cases lopsidedly, above their entrances.

'Merchandise,' one said. 'Counselor-at-law' said another.

Judah dismounted in front of a one-story frame building that had the word 'EATS' printed on its plank door. He left his horse, its reins trailing, in front of the building and went inside. He took a seat at a small oilcloth-covered table and, when a man in a dirty apron approached him, ordered steak and potatoes.

"We're all out of potatoes," the aproned man said gruffly.

"Then I'll have a double order of steak."

Later, when the man returned with the food, Judah asked him if he knew a man named Vernon Drake. The man said that he didn't and when he had gone Judah began to devour the two steaks on his plate, glancing around the room at several other men who were also eating. None of them was Drake.

After paying for his meal, he left the restaurant and, leading his horse, walked down the dirt street that was bordered by buildings, some sharing a common wall between them, others standing isolated and seemingly aloof from their neighbors.

He went into a building that advertised itself by means of a chalked sign as 'The Miner's Friend.' He had expected it to be a saloon. Instead, he found himself staring at piles of merchandise stacked haphazardly about the dark interior of the building—shovels, rockers, pans, spades. A tallow candle burned on a plank that had been laid across two barrels. At one end of the makeshift counter where the candle burned was an open keg of blasting powder. At the other end lounged a shaggily mustached man, obviously drunk.

"Help you, mister?" the man asked Judah.

"Maybe you car. I'm looking for a man named Vernon Drake."

"Never heard of him," the man replied, and hiccupped. "But men come and go so fast through here, it's hard to keep track of them, let alone get to know them by name."

"What about a woman named Virginia Bascomb?"

The man swayed and stumbled against the counter. Regaining his balance, he said, "There are no women in San Francisco. Not yet. But we're growing by leaps and bounds. They'll be along, no doubt about it. Whores at first. Ladies later."

Judah left the store and led his horse down toward bay. When he came to Portsmouth Square, he glanced around at the many casinos scattered about the plaza. He visited several, asked about Drake, and found no one who knew him.

He began to worry. He had not been able to find either Drake or Virginia during the many days he had roamed through the diggings, asking everyone he met if they had seen or heard of them. He had gone to Tuleburgh and found no trace of them there. He had ridden for endless miles along the banks of the American River, searching, questioning prospectors—and failing to find them.

And now the man in The Miner's Friend had told him that there were no women in San Francisco. He thought about the size of California, its immensity. He thought of how slim were his chances of finding Drake and, most importantly, Virginia.

Perhaps he had missed them during his travels. They could be anywhere. Perhaps they had not even come to California.

He stood there, growing more and more worried, close to despair, as the sun drowned in the bay which became blue again to match the cloudless sky arching above it.

A man came out of Sloane House and Judah asked him where he might find lodging for the night.

"Try Clancy's Hotel," the man advised. "See that path that goes up the hill over there? It's up at the end of it, Clancy's Hotel is."

Judah led his horse up the well-trodden path that served as a street and stopped in front of the building the man had directed him to. He entered it and found himself in a dirty warren of muslin-draped cubicles, some empty, some occupied by sleeping or card-playing men.

He asked one of the card players the cost of a night's lodging.

"Twenty-five dollars," the man answered without looking up from the cards he held in his hand.

Judah let out a whistle, surprised by the high price.

One of the other players idly scratched his chest. "It's steep, the price is," he said. "Like everything else here is. But Clancy don't charge extra for either the quicks or slows."

"Quicks or slows?" Judah prompted, puzzled.

"Quicks," the man answered with a wink, "be fleas. Slows, they's lice."

Judah left the hotel, having decided to spend the night in the open. He stepped into the saddle and turned his horse, heading away from the maze of buildings toward the sloping hills behind them. The wind that had arisen after the sun set ruffled his hair as he rode in among the clustered tents and adobe huts.

As he approached a party of men in the distance, he scanned their faces, disappointed to find that Drake was not among them.

As he rode closer to them he realized they were engaged in burying a coffinless corpse. Riding past them, he caught one man's bitter comments: "It's the damned spring water that's killing us. It'll give us all dysentery till there won't be anybody left to do the burying."

Judah headed for an open space beyond a cluster of tents which cast their blunt shadows on the ground behind them. He was about to dismount when something attracted his attention. He sat his saddle, reconnoitering. What was it that he had seen? He had received a vague impression of color among the white huts and tan tents. Where? He turned his head.

There. Off to the right. Excitement gripped him as he stared at the listing wagon beside the tent not far away, the wagon which had a cover that was painted a bright red.

Drake's wagon? He suppressed the excitement he felt. Other men might have painted their wagon's drilling red.

He heeled his horse and trotted toward it. When he reached it, he dismounted and stood staring at the wagon for a moment. Then he shifted his attention to the tent, his hand easing toward his Colt which hung in a holster from his wide leather belt.

Moving cautiously toward the tent and drawing his pistol as he did so, he listened but could hear no sound coming from within the tent. He reached out and carefully folded back the tent flap. He crouched and, in one swift movement, entered the tent. As his eyes became accustomed to the darkness within it, he spotted Drake sprawled on his back on the ground, his arms flung out, his mouth open.

Judah looked around the tent's interior—and saw the torn dress he recognized as belonging to Virginia lying crumpled in a corner.

He reached out with one booted foot and nudged Drake. The man merely snorted sleepily and turned over on his side. Judah's boot prodded him again.

Drake turned back. He opened his eyes and blinked. "Who—"

"Where's Virginia?"

Drake propped himself up on his elbows and shook his head from side to side.

"Where is she, Drake?"

"Who the hell are you?" Drake muttered, rubbing his eyes with his balled fists.

"Judah Bascomb."

Judah watched Drake's fists fall and his eyes widen. He saw fear in Drake's eyes.

"I just want to talk to her," he said reassuringly. "Where is she?"

"Gone."

"Gone where?"

"Listen, Bascomb, she wanted to come with me. If that Indian kid of yours back in the valley said I made her come with me—well, the kid's a liar."

So that's how the land lies, Judah thought. That's why Drake has so much fear of me showing in his eyes. Because he forced Virginia to come here with him.

He began to exult as he warily scanned the interior of the tent again. No sign of any weapon. Drake wasn't wearing a gun. He was dressed only in longjohns. Judah holstered his pistol.

He reached down and seized Drake's longjohns in both hands and hauled him to his feet. With his face only inches from Drake's, he said, "You forced her to come here with you, didn't you?"

Drake started to shake his head.

Judah shook him. "The truth, Drake."

"I wanted her but—"

"But she didn't want you, did she? That's it, isn't it?" Judah was silently cursing himself for not having believed what Virginia had told him before having been forced to leave the valley with Drake. He turned the fury that he had been directing toward himself upon Drake. "That's the truth of the matter, isn't it?"

"Yes."

"Now, you're going to tell me where she is. If you've hurt her, I'll—"

"I don't know where she is!" Drake cried, trying to break Judah's hold on him.

Judah released him. He landed a swift left uppercut on Drake's chin. He slammed a hard right fist into Drake's chest. As the man went down, Judah reached for him and again hauled him to his feet. Holding him with his left hand, he drew his right fist back.

But, before he could deliver his blow, Drake cried, "Don't! I'll tell you. Simon Grant's got her!"

Judah released his hold on Drake, momentarily stunned by the man's revelation. "Where is Grant?"

"Here. Here in San Francisco. He owns a casino down in the plaza—Sloane House."

"Grant's got her there?"

"I don't know. I don't and that's the truth! He sent Oscar, his bouncer, up here two days ago to get her. I don't know if Oscar got her or not. She's gone. That's all I know."

A sudden loud roar tore through the deepening darkness outside the tent.

Judah felt the ground tremble beneath his boots. He let go of Drake and ducked out of the tent. Down below where he was standing, a building had exploded. Its debris was still flying through the air above the bayfront's buildings. As Judah watched, another explosion occurred in what remained of the building and flames followed it, shooting up to extinguish the first faint stars that had appeared in the evening sky.

Judah remembered having been in the building that had

just exploded. For a moment, he wasn't sure exactly which building it was. But then, mentally retracing his earlier journey, he realized that the building that had exploded was The Miner's Friend. He remembered the drunken man with the shaggy mustache. He remembered the tallow candle that had been burning on the plank counter next to the open keg of blasting powder.

He leaped into his saddle and, digging his heels into his horse's ribs, galloped down the hill in the growing darkness, Drake remaining forgotten behind him.

Men were pouring out of Clancy's Hotel, most of them half-dressed, as Judah rode past the building. A man shouted to him, wanting to know what had happened.

Judah rode grimly on without answering. He turned at the intersection of the narrow path and the broader dirt street and a moment later reined in his horse. As the animal reared under him, he fought to stay in the saddle, his eyes on the burning debris littering the street ahead of him. His horse wheeled under him and he struggled for control of the animal while simultaneously searching for a way past the fire that was blocking his path. Buildings lined both sides of the street, he noted, and the one on the bay side of The Miner's Friend had also begun to burn.

He was about to turn his horse and head back the way he had come when he spotted a break in the ragged line of flame ahead of him. He urged his horse forward. The animal, its eyes wide and rolling with fright, strained at its bit. Judah savagely slammed his heels into the animal's flanks and the horse sprang forward. He gripped it tightly with his knees as the animal left the ground and went flying through the temporary rent in the flames. He galloped on until he reached Portsmouth Square where he leaped from the saddle, barely aware of his horse fleeing from the plaza as if the flames it so greatly feared were pursuing it.

Judah ran to Sloane House and bounded through its entrance, yelling, "Grant!", only to be seized by Oscar the instant he did so.

"Let me go!" he bellowed, battling the bouncer.

"You come in here like that, you're going right back out till you learn how to act like a gentleman!" Oscar picked Judah up and hurled him through the door.

Judah hit the ground outside but was instantly up and running again. This time, as he came through the door, he was ready for Oscar. As the bouncer lunged toward him, Judah side-stepped and, as Oscar hurtled past him, brought both of his clenched fists down hard on the back of the big man's neck.

Oscar fell and lay without moving at his feet.

And then Judah was at the empty bar and he leaned over it, panting. When he got his breath back, he asked the bartender where he could find Simon Grant.

"Upstairs," was the man's abrupt answer.

Judah took the stairs two at a time. He stood on the upper landing a moment, looking down the hall in both directions.

He saw several doors. He turned left and grabbed the knob of the first one he came to. He swung it open and found only an empty room behind it. He moved on to the next door across the hall. Locked. He tried the one next to it and, when he opened the door, he found himself facing Grant who was seated at his desk leafing through several sheets of paper.

Grant looked up. And froze.

"I want my wife!" Judah said, his voice ominously low. "I've been told you've got her."

"You should be more careful, Bascomb," Grant said.

"You really shouldn't let her run off with other men. But that does seem to be one of her bad habits, as we both know."

Judah ignored the jibe. He strode across the room and, planting the knuckles of both of his hands on the desk, asked, "Where is she, Grant?"

"Now that I've finally gotten her back, I have no intention of telling you where she is."

Judah hurdled the desk and seized Grant from behind, locking a forearm around his neck. "You'll tell me or I'll kill you."

Grant gagged.

Judah relaxed his hold on the man but only slightly—just enough so Grant could speak.

But Grant said nothing as his fingers tore at Judah's forearm in an effort to free himself.

Judah jerked his arm, and Grant's body lurched in the chair. His face reddened.

When Judah again relaxed his hold, Grant said, "I'm told there's a fire in town. Why don't you go and try to put it out instead of wasting your time here."

"I don't intend to waste my time." Judah lifted Grant out of his chair and, using both hands, slammed him up against the wall behind the desk.

Grant's head rocked back and forth on his shoulders.

Judah drew his pistol and placed its muzzle against Grant's Adam's apple. He didn't speak as he slowly drew the hammer back to full cock. But his eyes did.

And, as Grant stared into those hard eyes, his mouth opened. At first, no words came but then they rushed out in a steady stream. "I'll tell you. Let me go and I'll tell you where she is."

Judah slowly withdrew his pistol from Grant's throat.

"—sit down," Grant muttered. "Let me sit down."

Judah backed up as Grant made his way to the desk and flopped in the chair behind it.

Judah walked around to the front of the desk, the pistol still in his hand and still cocked.

"Your wife is—" Grant rose and took a step to the left. "What do you want?" he asked, staring at the door behind Judah.

Judah turned quickly, his pistol rising.

There was no one in the doorway.

He heard the sound of a desk drawer opening, and then the sound of a shot the instant before he felt the bullet rip into the flesh of his upper left arm.

The searing pain almost caused him to drop his Colt. But he held onto it and, turning, fired rapidly.

Once. Twice.

Grant, the smoking revolver he had taken from his desk drawer in his right hand, was hurled backward by the two shots Judah had sent burning into him. He hit the wall behind him. The revolver fell from his hand. Both of his hands clutched convulsively at his stomach. Blood began to redden his white shirt. He looked down at it. And then, grimacing, up at Judah. He staggered forward and fell face down on the desk. He began to slide off it. He clutched at the smooth surface of the desk but finally fell to the floor, taking papers and an ink well with him.

Judah bounded forward, rounded the desk, and got down on one knee beside Grant.

Grant's eyes were squeezed shut. He still clutched his stomach with tense fingers that now were red and slick with his own blood.

"You're gut-shot, Grant. You're dying. Tell me where she is!"

Grant's left eye flicked open. Then his right one.

"Mr. Grant!" someone shouted from downstairs. "The

fire, Mr. Grant. It's heading this way! You'd better make a run for it while there's still time!''

"You've lost her,'' Grant whispered to Judah.

Desperate, Judah wanted to hit the man for whom he felt an overwhelming loathing that was mixed with contempt. But he knew that such an action would not accomplish his purpose. It would probably only hasten Grant's obviously imminent death.

"She'll soon be dead,'' Grant said and groaned. His shoulders and head rose slightly and then flopped down, his eyes becoming vacant as they stared up at the ceiling they could no longer see.

Judah placed a finger against the side of Grant's neck. No pulse. Slowly, he stood up and holstered his Colt. He walked to the door and left the office, drained and furious with himself.

He should have shot to wound Grant, not to kill him, he told himself angrily. He ignored the pain in his left arm and paid no attention to the blood that was soaking his shirtsleeve and running down his arm as he made his way past the door that led to the empty room and the other one next to Grant's office which was locked. He went slowly down the stairs and stood for a moment in the empty casino, feeling defeated by Grant and by his own hasty actions.

A flickering at one of the windows drew his attention. He glanced through the window and saw the casino just beyond it beginning to burn. Numbly, he walked out of Sloane House and stood outside in the night, barely aware that almost all of the buildings to the north were on fire. He stood there without hearing the shouts of the men who were running frantically through the streets. He hardly noticed the men passing buckets full of water up one long human line and empty buckets back down a second similar line as they drew water from the bay in their feeble attempts to put out the spreading fire that was moving steadily southward.

The wind coming in from the bay sent flames leaping from one building to the next. In places, the dry grass was burning between isolated buildings, providing the deadly link that would doom them.

Judah turned and looked back at Sloane House.

Grant's lying up there dead, he thought. He'll soon be incinerated. And he died without telling me where Virginia is.

He started to turn and then stopped and stood rigidly where he was.

Grant's dead, he thought. But the bouncer—Judah searched his memory for the man's name. *Oscar!* Drake had referred to him as Oscar. And Drake had said that Grant had sent Oscar to Drake's tent to bring Virginia to him.

Judah began to run along the line of men who were feverishly passing buckets to one another, searching for Oscar because, he told himself, there was a chance that the bouncer might know Virginia's whereabouts.

Faces began to blur in the smoky night as he ran. He rubbed his eyes and ran swiftly on—down the length of one line and then up the other.

Suddenly, he saw a familiar face. Drake was running into a casino on the opposite side of the plaza.

Judah dashed across the plaza and into the casino, aware that it was on fire but determined to get to Drake.

He halted just inside the casino and looked around the empty room that was silent except for the sound of the crackling flames that were devouring the building's upper story.

He moved quickly through the room, darting between

tables, toward an open door facing him in the rear of the room. As he hurried toward it, the ceiling above him burst into flames.

He went through the door and into a small room that was obviously an office.

Drake was there, bending over a desk and using a hand axe to pry open the desk's locked drawers.

As Judah entered the room, Drake looked up. "I'm not the only one," he declared defensively. "There's looting going on all over town."

"Have you seen Oscar?"

Drake raised his axe and slammed it down against a drawer he had managed to partially open. As the drawer splintered, he said, "Grant's bouncer? No. I haven't seen him." He reached into the drawer he had broken open and pulled out a strongbox, letting out a shrill cry of delight as he did so.

"Where can I find him?" Judah asked, raising his voice so that it could be heard above the loud crackling of the flames overhead. "Where does he live?"

Drake didn't answer him as he continued to search through the drawers he had managed to pry open with his axe.

Judah was about to question him again when an ominous creaking sound joined the sounds that the flames were making. He looked up at the sagging ceiling. "Drake!" he shouted. "Get out!" He turned and ran. Just before he reached the door that led to the street, he looked back over his shoulder and saw the burning ceiling give way and come crashing down. He saw a screaming Drake go down as the blazing debris that had once been the ceiling struck and buried him only an instant after he had started to run for his life, the strongbox clutched tightly in both of his hands.

Judah raced from the building into the swirl of chaos

that was the street outside. He halted in the middle of it, scanning the faces of the men fleeing from the plaza. The bucket brigade had vanished. The fire was still moving relentlessly southward. Buildings blazed, sagged, and then collapsed in eruptions of bright sparks.

Sparks showered down upon him. He brushed them from his clothes.

"Mr. Grant!"

Judah spun around, making almost a complete circle. Where had the shout come from? He knew who had shouted because he had recognized Oscar's voice.

He spotted the bouncer standing outside Sloane House, which was beginning to burn.

Oscar cupped his hands around his mouth and shouted Grant's name a second time.

Judah sprinted toward the bouncer, ducking falling timbers as he headed through the thick smoke that filled the plaza.

When he reached him, he grabbed Oscar's shoulder and turned him around. "Grant's dead!" he yelled above the roar of the fire. "Up in his office."

"Dead?"

"What did you do with Virginia Bascomb?"

"How'd he die?"

"I killed him. Where's my wife?"

"That woman—she's your wife?" When Judah nodded, Oscar burst into wild laughter. "So you killed Grant, did you? Well then you've also killed your wife!"

Judah seized Oscar by the shirt and shook him until the man's maniacal laughter ceased. *"Where is she?"*

"Up there." Oscar pointed to the second floor of Sloane House. "In the storage room up on the second floor."

Judah released Oscar and ran toward the door of Sloane House.

"Won't do you any good!" Oscar yelled. "The storage room door's locked."

Judah turned quickly and without breaking stride, raced back to Oscar. "The key. Give me the key to the storage room!"

"Haven't got it. Grant's got it on him. And he's—" Oscar's laughter erupted again, "—up there you said." He pointed to the casino's second story. "Ask Grant for the key. Go ahead. Go on up there and ask him for it!"

Judah, with a brief glance at the inferno that the casino's roof had become, ran into the building and bounded up the stairs as a series of small explosions occurred. The coal oil lamps hanging from the ceiling continued to explode as burning beams fell from the second floor ceiling and struck them.

Judah raced down the hall to Grant's office, the intense heat causing sweat to coat his body.

Grant's desk was burning. The drapes on the windows were blazing. The carpet in front of the desk was a square sea of flame.

Judah raced across the burning room and around the desk. The papers lying on the floor beside Grant began to burn.

He dropped to his knees and frantically began to search through Grant's pockets. He found a change purse. A pencil.

He turned Grant over and went through his trouser pockets. He found the key in the second pocket into which he thrust his trembling hand. He leaped to his feet and quickly made his way back out into the hall, coughing as he inadvertently inhaled smoke.

Which door?

He cursed himself for not having asked Oscar for the exact location of the storeroom.

He remembered the door he had tried earlier. The one that had been locked. The one that was next to Grant's office.

He groped through the smoke toward it, thrust the key he was holding into its lock, and turned it.

The door opened. Smoke from the hall entered the square storage room with Judah, momentarily blinding him.

He waved his arms to try to clear the air and heard a dull sound.

And then he saw her.

Virginia, still bound and gagged, was easing her body along the floor toward him, her eyes filled with tears caused by smoke and terror.

He bent down, scooped her up, and ran out of the room. He raced down the hall as flames began to consume both of its walls.

He started down the stairs, trying to blink away the blinding smoke. Behind him, he heard a portion of the second story give way and go crashing down to the floor. Below him, flames leaped from the puddles of coal oil that had spilled from the exploding lamps.

He reached the bottom of the steps and headed for the door but, before he could get to it, flames shot up and engulfed it. He turned quickly and, coughing, headed toward the nearest window. With one booted foot, he kicked the glass from it and then kicked again several times to free the window frame of the jagged shards of glass that remained in it. He stepped through the window into the alley that ran between Sloane House and the burning casino next to it.

His chest heaving and his heart pounding wildly within him, he ran through the alley as sparks showered down upon him and Virginia. When he came out onto the dirt street, he put her down. He quickly untied her wrists and then her ankles. He stripped the gag from her mouth, Then, picking her up again, he staggered, barely able to breathe, toward the bay.

It took him agonizing minutes to reach it, and when he did, he found that others had also sought the bay as a refuge from the fire.

It was crowded with men standing hip-deep and even shoulder-deep in the water.

Judah strode into the water until it had reached his waist. Then he stopped and gently helped Virginia to stand up. When she began to sway, he wrapped his arms around her to steady her.

"Are you all right?" he asked her, kissing her cheeks, her neck, her lips.

She nodded. "But how—" She began to cough.

"Let's move deeper into the water." Judah began to lead her by the hand out into the bay as a powdery black ash borne by the wind drifted down around them.

"How did you—"

"I'll tell you later."

"Judah, Simon Grant, he—"

"He's dead, Virginia."

She noticed his bloody left arm for the first time. "You're hurt!"

"Grant shot me. Then I shot him—killed him."

A fierce expression swept over Virginia's face. "I intended to kill him myself. I told him I would kill him and I believe I would have, had I been given the chance to do so." She covered her face with her hands for a moment and then withdrew them and said, "Judah, I have to explain something to you. I know what you must have thought when you found I had left the valley. Vernon Drake forced me to leave with him. He—" She almost collapsed in a violent fit of coughing as acrid clouds of smoke and cinders drifted out over the bay.

"I know what he did—how he made you come here with him. He told me before he died."

"He's dead too?"

Judah told her what he had seen happen to Drake. "Virginia, I'm sorry for what I said to you back in the valley. I was wrong. I was a damned fool for not believing you when you told me about how Drake—"

Virginia interrupted him. "Is Joseph all right? Rebecca?"

"They're both fine. Rebecca did a fine job of taking care of Joseph after you left. Before I left to come out here to try to find you, I asked Olivia Ames to look after them while I was gone."

Virginia dropped her eyes. "Judah, I don't want to lose you. I want to be with you always." She looked up at him. "I'm willing to share you with Olivia. I'm willing to do anything I have to do to keep from losing you entirely."

"I'm not going to marry Olivia."

"Judah—" Virginia fell silent. She reached for his hands and gripped them tightly.

"You're the only woman I want," he told her softly.

They stood there then, watching the last of San Francisco's buildings die their slow red deaths.

Later, when only tendrils of smoke rose from the charred ground, they made their way out of the bay and onto the shore where they stood, their wet clothes clinging to their bodies, surveying the devastation that surrounded them.

"It's gone, all of it," Virginia said sadly. "It was a town. It might have become a city."

"It will become a city some day. Once the word about the gold that's been found out here spreads, people will come here by the thousands. Maybe by the millions. It's only been ten months since the first gold was found at

Sutter's Mill. I'll bet that by the end of 1849 even *before* the end of next year—there'll be a booming metropolis sprouting here on the shore and up there on the hills.''

"What will we do now, Judah?"

"Go home."

"How will we get there?"

"Walk if we have to."

"I feel as if I could fly home,'' Virginia declared happily. "And once we get back to the valley, we'll continue helping to build Zion.''

"The two of us—together you and I can do just about anything.''

"Judah." Virginia gently touched his face and said, "There is something else I have to tell you. Three of us will be going back to the valley.''

"Three of us?"

"I'm almost four months pregnant.''

A broad smile appeared on Judah's face. He seized Virginia and drew her close to him. "Why didn't you tell me before you left?"

"I didn't know then. I didn't know for certain until after I arrived here.''

Judah bent his head and, as their lips met, the end of the long and deadly night was being signaled by the first light of the new day that was beginning to dawn in the brightening sky above them.

EPILOGUE

IN the large house on South Temple Street, the doorbell rang.

Virginia cried out to the crowd of people eddying and flowing through the house. "It's him. It must be him at last." She hurried down the hall, pausing only long enough in front of the mirror near the door to pat her graying hair into place before opening the door.

"So sorry I'm late, Mrs. Bascomb," said the man standing outside. "Is everyone ready for me?"

"Yes, we are, all of us. If you'll just wait outside—we'll be right with you."

The man shouldered his box-like camera that rested on three long legs and started down the steps.

Leaving the door open, Virginia called out, "Come along everyone. The photographer's here and he's ready for us. Hurry!"

Middle-aged Joseph Bascomb brushed past his mother, followed by his twenty-three year old son, Moroni.

Next came Moroni's plump wife, Olga. In her fleshy arms she carried their year-old daughter, Virginia, whose eyes were as blue as her great-grandmother's, for whom she had been named.

"Where's Charles?" Virginia asked Olga, referring to Moroni's younger brother.

"The last time I saw him," Olga replied, "he was deep in conversation with Susan. They were talking about their missionary work in Saskatchewan—in the parlor."

"Charles!" Virginia cried. "Susan!"

The pair quickly appeared in the hall, Susan big with the first child she would bear in less than a month.

"The photographer's outside," Virginia informed them. "You two are always tardy," she declared, shaking her head in mock chagrin. "I do wonder how you two ever got to the Temple in time to be sealed!"

As Charles and Susan went toward the front door, Virginia's daughter, June, who had been born after Virginia's return to the valley from San Francisco, rushed down the hall with her own twenty-year old daughter, Rachel, at her side. "Mother," she said to Virginia, "I can't find Michael anywhere."

"There's your husband, now," Virginia said as she saw

Michael emerge from the dining room. "Hurry now, Michael."

As the others left the house, Virginia hurried down the hall and into the kitchen, where she found Joseph's wife, the ebony-eyed Catherine, with Rebecca. Catherine was peering into the oven at a cake she was baking while Rebecca vigorously stirred its icing in a large mixing bowl.

"Come along outside you two!"

"But I have to watch my cake," Catherine protested.

"It will wait," Virginia told her, beckoning. "The photographer won't."

Rebecca said, "This icing will surely thicken if I leave it."

Virginia brushed Rebecca's concern aside and ushered both women out of the kitchen. On their way down the hall, she asked Rebecca where her husband was.

"He's up on the roof. He said he was going to fix those loose shingles. The twins are up there with him."

"Do you think it's safe up there for your boys?"

Rebecca gave Virginia a reassuring smile. "You mustn't fret about Ralph and Parley. They're quite grown up now—they turned nineteen just last month, you know, and those two can climb like coons with the hounds baying right behind them. And John does so like to teach them how to be handy." She laughed. "Do you remember the time when Joseph was just a boy and his kitten became stranded in that swamp maple out back? You just climbed right up into that big old tree, got the kitten, and climbed right back down again without so much as batting an eye, as I recall."

"Ah, but I was young then, my dear, and the young have such an undeveloped sense of danger. I'm not young anymore—sixty-five sometimes seems ancient to me—and now I worry about things like your sons scrambling about on rooftops.''

As Rebecca and Catherine went laughing down the hall, Virginia followed them. Once outside, she stood on the porch watching the people assemble on the lawn waiting for the photographer to commemorate their long-awaited family reunion. She smiled to herself as she watched each person standing primly or with a studied nonchalance as they faced the camera.

She was about to descend the steps when she suddenly realized that Judah was missing. As Rebecca's husband, the Pawnee John Hawk-in-the-Sky rounded the corner of the house with the twins, a hammer in his hand, she fled back into the house.

''Judah!''

No answer.

And then a muffled oath.

Shaking her head, she began to climb the stairs to the second floor from which the oath had come. She found Judah in their bedroom trying to fasten his celluloid collar.

She hurried over to him. ''Here, let me do it, dear.'' When she had the collar fastened in place, she said, ''Now brush your hair. You're really quite disheveled.''

As Judah stooped so that he could see his reflection in the mirror attached to the top of the dresser, he muttered, ''They make furniture nowadays that's fit only for midgets to use.''

''Hush. And hurry.''

''Well, dammit, it's true. I'm a tall man. There are lots of tall men like me in the world. I wish someone would inform the furniture makers of that fact.''

Virginia peremptorily took his arm and led him from the room.

''Mother!'' Joseph called to her as she and Judah emerged

from the house. "You're to stand right here in the midst of us all with Father."

"Between Joseph and me." June beckoned to her parents and Virginia and Judah descended the steps and crossed the lawn.

As they took their designated places, Moroni whispered to his wife and Olga, her broad face beaming, placed the infant Virginia in her namesake's arms.

"The young men," said the photographer, "shall sit on the grass in front of their elders."

Moroni, Charles, and Rebecca's twins took their assigned places.

The photographer scurried forward, took the hammer from John Hawk-in-the-Sky's hand, and placed it on the ground well out of camera range.

A moment later, he ducked beneath his camera's black cloth.

Everyone went rigid.

"Relax!" he ordered them sternly. "And smile, please."

It took several more minutes for them to assume stances and expressions he finally deemed satisfactory. "Hold it please!"

There was a puff of smoke.

Some time later, as the warm April sun poured down on the assemblage, the session ended.

Virginia asked Judah what time it was and, when he had checked his Ingersoll watch and told her, she gasped.

"It's that photographer's fault!" she cried in mild exasperation. "He was so late in arriving. Now we have no time to lose or we shall miss the ceremony."

"Ceremonies like this one never begin on time," Judah commented.

"Well, I don't want to risk being late in any case. Think of all the years you've labored in the marble quarry to help build the Temple. Surely, you don't want to miss seeing the capstone set in place?"

"Wouldn't miss it for the world. Let's round up everybody and be on our way."

Five minutes later, everyone was walking quickly along South Temple Street.

Judah pushed the wicker baby carriage in which little Virginia was sleeping peacefully. Beside him, his wife walked briskly, her eager eyes on the towering Temple in the distance. Behind them came Joseph and June, followed by the others.

Bounding ahead of the procession and then racing back to the last of its members was Judah's hunting dog.

"Look at him," Judah said to Virginia. "That hound doesn't seem to know he's going to a ceremony. He thinks it's to be a celebration. And I guess it is at that."

As they neared the almost completed Temple, Virginia said, "I'm so glad I had a chance to contribute more than just my tithes to the building of the Temple."

"But if your father and you hadn't become reconciled at last and he hadn't left you his estate, you wouldn't have been able to," Judah reminded her.

"Then I think I would have joined you and all the other men in the marble quarry and I would have hewn out my own share of building blocks—with my bare hands if necessary."

"I do believe you would have done just that, old girl," Judah said, grinning and giving her an affectionate one-armed hug.

"It's so good to have all of us together again, if only briefly."

"It's great. But Moroni will soon have to head back to that ranch he's foreman of down in Texas. Our grandson has turned himself into a top-notch rancher, there's no doubt about that. He's become a man to 'ride the river with,' as we old-time cowboys used to say about a partner we could rely on.''

"Yes, thanks to all you taught him." Virginia sighed. "I do hate to think of Charles and Susan returning to Canada tomorrow. But their missionary work—" She glanced down at the carriage. "Moroni and Olga will be taking Virginia away from us next week when they return to New York."

"They've promised to come home for Christmas."

"But that's months away!"

"You know, it's a shame Brother Brigham couldn't have lived to see this." Judah gestured toward the gleaming white marble Temple, its upper section covered with a network of scaffolding. "He's been gone now for—how long has it been, honey? This old man's memory isn't as sharp as it once was."

"Brother Brigham passed away in seventy-seven."

They moved into the throng in Temple Square and took up a position near the completed Tabernacle that gave them a clear view of the wooden platform that looked so tiny up at the very top of the Temple.

Judah's dog crawled into the shade beneath the carriage, placed his head on his front paws, and closed his eyes.

"Judah, look!" Virginia pointed. "There's Olivia."

Judah shouted her name.

She was standing far in front of them and, after turning around, she tried to make her way back toward them through the thickly packed crowd but was unable to do so. She waved to them.

They waved back and Judah commented, "She's borne up well."

"As well as can be expected, I suppose. But she was devastated by the loss of her husband last year."

"Brother Tyler was a fine man," Judah said sincerely. "Well, she has her children. The five of them will help to see her through until time has had a chance to help her heal."

"I'm sure they will. But she thought the sun rose and set on Paul Tyler. I think a heart as loving as hers might not ever heal completely. I think she'll bear the scar of her loss until the day she dies."

A band began to play.

An official among the many standing on the seemingly sky-high platform raised his arm.

"You were wrong, Judah," Virginia said. "The ceremony—the *celebration*—is starting on time."

The crowd, which had been noisy until now, suddenly quieted. The band stopped playing. The sun streamed silently down. The upraised arm of the official slowly and dramatically descended.

As it did, the other officials on the platform carefully lowered the the Temple's capstone into place.

Heartfelt hosannas, spontaneously released from hundreds of throats, rang out and rose up into the clear spring sky.

A moment later the hosannas gave way to a song:

> Let the mountains shout for joy!
> Let the valley sing,
> Let the hills rejoice,
> Let them all break forth into song.
> And be glad before the Lord!
> For the wilderness hath blossomed—
> Blossomed like the rose.

Later, when the officials had climbed down from the platform and all the speeches were over, people began to drift out of Temple Square.

"Grandmother," Rachel said. "It's time to go home."

"You and the others go ahead, Rachel. Your grandfather and I will be along presently."

"My cake!" Catherine suddenly cried in alarm, looking stricken. "It will be burned to a crisp!"

"And the icing will have hardened beyond saving by now!" Rebecca lamented.

The two women hurried away as Judah's dog awoke, yawned, crawled out from beneath the carriage, and began to bark excitedly at nothing in particular.

Olga began to wheel the carriage containing her daughter, Moroni walking close beside her, Charles and Susan not far behind them.

The others followed.

"Judah, do you remember what you said about Moroni a little while ago?"

"What did I say?"

"You said that he has become a man to ride the river with. Well, I've been thinking and I'll tell you something, Judah Bascomb. All these years—*you've* been a good man to ride the river with."

"Honey, you've been an even better woman to ride it with."

Arm in arm and smiling, Virginia and Judah continued walking along South Temple Street together.